JU

SE

)

of
J

cr

V

V

F

EVERY STEP YOU TAKE

George Fletcher works all week in a City firm, and at weekends helps his mother look after his mentally handicapped brother Kevin. It's not an exciting life, until he encounters Alison. He becomes obsessed with her, but she doesn't know he exists. She does know Kevin. Polly leaves an unhappy home and moves into a room in George's mother's house. Alison becomes more friendly with Kevin, who is increasingly agitated, while George looks more and more ill. His childhood friend, Detective Inspector John Bright is worried about him. Especially when the body of a young girl is found in a nearby park...

EVERY STEP YOU TAKE

EVERY STEP YOU TAKE

by

Maureen O'Brien

Magna Large Print Books
Long Preston, North Yorkshire,
BD23 4ND, England.

British Library Cataloguing in Publication Data.

O'Brien, Maureen
    Every step you take.

    A catalogue record of this book is
    available from the British Library

    ISBN   0-7505-2508-8

First published in Great Britain in 2004 by Time Warner Books

Copyright © 2004 Maureen O'Brien

Cover illustration © Anthony Monaghan

The moral right of the author has been asserted

Published in Large Print 2006 by arrangement with
Time Warner Book Group UK

Magna Large Print is an imprint of Library Magna Books Ltd.

Printed and bound in Great Britain by
T.J. (International) Ltd., Cornwall, PL28 8RW

for Michael, again.

Acknowledgement

With thanks to Richard Goldberg for his invaluable help with the progress of an accountant.

Prologue

Summer Fifteen Years Ago

George was a happy man. He had passed his final exam and was coming home early to spend the afternoon with Marje. Rose petals showered him as he blundered up the path. He smiled as he let himself in, imagining her face when he told her the news. The hall was dim after the sun outside. The stairs were dark. 'Hello!' he called. 'Marje?'

No answer. His mother was out. Kevin was at his special school on Selhurst Road. George was glad they were not there. He wanted to have Marje to himself. He had come home early to surprise her.

He called again. Could Marje be still at work? No. Her shift at the supermarket finished at one. But she wasn't back yet. A desolate feeling, like hunger, made him feel hollow inside.

He trudged upstairs to their bedroom, tidy as only his mother could make it. George lifted Marje's pillow. Her frivolous gauzy nightie lay there, crushed. He lowered his face to it and breathed in its scent. He smoothed it with his hands. He replaced the pillow carefully on top of it.

He took off his suit and hung it up. He put his shirt in the laundry basket. He regarded himself in the full-length mirror on the wardrobe door. He was big: his head was big, his nose was big, his ears were big, he had big hands and feet and a big chest. And his bearing was odd, stiff, his feet in their grey socks useless as dead fish. He thought he looked pompous and weak.

Marje was as small as he was large. Five feet two, blonde hair just touching her shoulders, blue eyes, mouth as soft as the rose petals she smelt of. Her teeth were white, her hands, feet and breasts delicate, her gestures precise. She moved like an angel, without wings. He wondered why she had married him. It was not the first time he had wondered this. He recalled their first night together in this room, and all their nights since…

After the wedding his mother had taken Kevin to her sister's for a few nights. George and Marje waved them goodbye and then he shut the door. Her whisper fluttered against his ear. 'Carry me upstairs, George.'

She was as light as a flower. She wound her legs round his waist. Her silver shoes dropped from her feet and pattered down the stairs. In the room she let herself drop backwards on to the bed, keeping her legs locked round him. She breathed fast, eyes

14

closed, arms spread. George watched her, feeling a little alarmed. She opened her eyes. She smiled and lifted her arms towards him. He took her hands and held them. The little hands sat in his, warm, expectant, like day-old chicks. George knew the next step must be his but what was the step to be? His mother had given him no advice except, 'Don't you frighten her now, George.'

So he gave her hands back to her, placing them carefully by her sides on the bed. She took a sharp breath and her questioning gaze made George shyer still. He longed to express his ardour with smooth grace, like her, but was sure she would find him clumsy, or worse, ridiculous. Avoiding her eyes, he unwound her legs from his waist, placing her little soft feet side by side on the rug.

He started to remove his clothes, turning his back to her to hide his wildly tumescent state. Shyness made him clumsier, his clothes stuck to him. At last, in just his underpants, he sat on the bed, his big hands between his thighs. His mother had laid out his pyjamas on the bed. He hesitated. Should he put them on? He dared to steal a look at Marje. She was standing now, with her back to him, at the other side of the bed. She was pulling down the zip of her white satin dress. So instead he got into the bed and covered himself with the daisy-pattern duvet, dressed only in his underpants.

Then Marje turned to face him. She let the dress fall slowly off her shoulders. Her body rose inch by inch from the descending cloud of white. George, astounded, thought, *Standing by me at the altar she had nothing on under her long white dress!* Her small feet stepped out of the cloud. She looked at him. Her smile was uncertain: *Will you like me? Am I too bold?* But she walked proudly toward him just the same.

He lay still as she got into the bed and she lay still beside him. Minutes passed. George waited. He knew that Marje too was waiting, that she expected something of him, but he was frightened, excited, shy, fearful of causing her alarm, or shame. She was so small too and he was so big. At last, certain she would be crushed under his weight, he positioned himself awkwardly on top of her.

She wound her arms round his neck and her legs round his thighs. The soft warm flesh under him and around him gave him a storm of excitement so intense he had no idea what happened next, except that when he recovered he knew that it had not gone quite right. He had not even had time to remove his underpants and their stickiness now confounded him. He would have to get out of bed to clean himself up. How would he explain this to her? He had no words to explain, such words had always been forbidden, so he got up and went out to the

16

bathroom without saying anything at all.

When he came back and got into bed beside her Marje was crying. He told her he was sorry. She wiped her eyes and kissed him lightly on the cheek before turning on to her side, away from him. George thought, *She loves me; it will get better with time.* It had not got better by the third day, and George despaired.

Then his mother returned with Kevin and all at once laughter filled the house. Even his mother was heard to laugh, a short sharp sound like a dog's bark that George hadn't heard since he was a boy, before his father died and Kevin was born. Marje and Kevin chased each other up and down. They might both have been eleven years old. George cheered up. Hope revived.

But that evening Marje sat in the kitchen with his mother. They drank cups of tea and Marje chattered. At bedtime George stood bashfully at the kitchen door.

'You go on up, George.' Marje smiled. 'I won't be long.'

He stayed awake some time but didn't hear Marje come to bed. In the morning she woke him already dressed. She was cheerful. She said it was a lovely day.

On the Saturday she suggested they go into the country. They had lunch in a pub. Afterwards in a field she pulled him down on top of her. She held his head and pressed her mouth to his. She pushed her little tongue into his mouth. George was afraid someone might walk past in the lane and see. This inhibited him. It also excited him. It over-excited him.

Again Marje cried. Again George apologised. He was too ashamed to explain. His mother had never allowed him to use the words he needed for this. *Filth!* she would have said. Marje dried her tears and kissed his cheek. And though he was sticky and uncomfortable again they went for a walk in the long grass and she held on to his arm, smiling up at him. He felt forgiven and that Marje was making a silent promise to be patient with him. That this was only the beginning of a long journey together in the course of which both would learn all manner of things. Hope returned.

That night she came to bed when he did. They undressed quickly and got in between the crisp cool sheets. George for the first time didn't even feel shy. He moved his bulky body towards Marje. 'Oh, George,' she whispered, clasping her hands round his neck and pressing her small breasts to him.

Then his mother's bed springs creaked in the room next door. They heard her cough. She had come to bed early too. Marje whispered, 'It's all right, we'll be quiet, George,' but his urgent desire had died. Marje said, 'Never mind.' But he minded. This was the one occasion when he knew for certain it would have been all right.

Every Friday evening his mother took Kevin to her sister's. Every Friday George tried to make it right. But something always made it wrong. Even when George thought improvement had been made, managing at least to hold out until he was safely inside her, Marje seemed no happier. Indeed she seemed sadder. But she was kind. She was always kind.

Nonetheless her laughter faded from the house. And after a while, even on Fridays, she would wait up for his mother and stay in the kitchen with her when George went up to bed, kissing him lightly and saying, 'I won't be long.' If George touched her she wriggled gently, smilingly, out of his reach.

This state of affairs continued for many months, but still George swelled in all senses of the word with love for Marje and still he couldn't give up hope.

And at last one day quite suddenly Marje began to laugh again. She swung in circles with Kevin. She laughed into George's eyes. She gave him light caresses, and though she would accept none from him in return, George was gratified. He didn't understand but he was content to wait.

Even now, finding her not yet home to hear his news on this lovely summer's day, his disappointment wasn't terminal. Soon he'd be able to make things right between them. He thought, *My finals are over. I'll start to earn real money at last. We can move. When we've got our own place it'll be different. We love each other. Marje will want a baby...* George and Marje with three pretty blonde daughters stand outside a Regency building with a brass plate that says *George Fletcher, Chartered Accountant.* Marje looks up at him, radiant with pride...

George roused himself. He put on his Marks and Spencer's shorts and the sweatshirt Marje had bought for him. He stuffed his big feet into his sandals and, cheerful again, lumbered downstairs. He would cut the grass while he waited for Marje. Because of his exams he hadn't been able to cut it for weeks.

The garden faced north. George breathed in, enjoying the cool air on this hot afternoon. His chest expanded barrel-like. The shed was at the bottom of the garden. The lawn mower was in the shed. The garden was long, brighter at the far end, light filtering through trees. There were buttercups in the grass. Bees. It was quiet in the garden. George opened the shed door. It was not quiet in the shed.

He saw first that she was wet all over. Her face was wet, her hair was wet, even her feet were wet. How? Not rain, he thought, confused. It had been fine for days. Then

20

George understood that Marje was soaked in sweat. *Sweat? Marje? Cool little blonde little Marje?* The man was wet too. He had rolled off Marje and was lying on his front supported on his elbows. They were on the narrow mattresses from the reclining garden chairs, down there, naked among the flowerpots and the tangles of garden twine. The lawn mower loomed in the shadows behind them.

The man didn't look at George. But George recognised him. He was just someone they saw on Saturday morning in the pub. A nobody. A nothing. A chap you see in the local, a car salesman or something, a nothing, a nobody. *With Marje.*

Marje stared at George with wide open eyes but no one moved. She did not even try to cover herself. It was the sweat that paralysed George. He didn't understand how people could get so wet, doing it. How did they? Wet as fishes in their element. He knew his face must have an odd expression, frightening or comic or both. Because Marje began to laugh. She put her hand to her mouth, she closed her eyes, she shook. The man put his hand over hers, on her face. She gripped his hand and took the fleshy part between her teeth. The man too started to laugh. She turned her face to his. Their faces touched. They laughed, clinging to each other silently, shaking.

George, blinded, turned and lurched through the long grass back into the house, up all the stairs, to the attics where he knelt on all fours in the back room. He beat his fists and his feet on the floor, quietly in case his mother and Kevin had returned. And the only thing he could think about was the lawn mower. That he couldn't get the lawn mower out of the shed because the naked wet man and woman were in the way. 'I couldn't cut the grass!' he moaned, his face on the dusty boards. 'I couldn't cut the grass!' And he fretted about how to explain this to his mother when she asked.

George stayed on the attic floor all night, sometimes asleep, sometimes awake. Next morning when he went down to their room, there was no one there. The room was neat, the bed was made. But there was no flimsy underwear in the drawer, no nightie under her pillow, no small bright clothes in his wardrobe. Not even a note. After three days, with stiff lips he asked his mother, 'Where has she gone?'

'Don't know,' his mother said.

'When will she be back?'

'Didn't say.' She didn't look at him and he knew she was lying because Marje had told her to and she would never tell him even if she did know, so he didn't ask again.

He stopped going to the local pub and did not see the man. Or Marje. No one ever mentioned what had happened in the shed. It may have been that nobody else knew about that. And Marje's name was not spoken in the house. Kevin had a short memory. He liked people but didn't remember them well. He seemed dejected for a week or two but soon it was as though she had never been.

After two weeks, when he knew she wouldn't return, George went to the shed and dragged out the lawn mower. The grass was long, tangled, hard to cut with the rusty old machine, but George sweated and strained until he had cut every last inch of it. At the end of his exertion he was panting and as wet as Marje and the man had been. He flung the mower across the place where they had lain, into the shadows at the back of the shed. He shut the door. He had finished with her.

And after a month he could go to the shed without recalling her. The memory seemed to have been plucked from his mind by an invisible hand. It was a kind of miracle. He didn't even grieve. The house became depressing to George, however, and at the end of the year he moved out. He rented a bedsit in a dreary part of north Islington which would do for now.

He had entered into a training contract straight from school with Lavery and Brown, a small firm of accountants with an office in a backwater of the old City of London where he fitted like a hand in its glove. After passing his final examination (on the day he found Marje and the man in the shed) he could have afforded a better place to live but he gave much of his money to his mother so that she wouldn't miss his contribution to the house.

Seven years later Richard Brown retired and George became a partner. The name plate now read *Lavery and Fletcher, Chartered Accountants.* This was the only change to their little firm, though around them the City was changing out of recognition: Liverpool Street station transformed to a grand new shopping mall and headquarters building, and other architectural marvels rising like mushrooms overnight. Some of the old narrow cobbled alleys remained but the shabby Georgian buildings were going under the hammer one by one.

To celebrate his partnership George moved to a smarter flat closer to the office and played bowls on summer evenings in Finsbury Circus with other partners mostly younger and smarter than he. He visited his mother and Kevin every weekend, commuting by train, doing *The Times* crossword in his City suit.

But from the day of Marje's betrayal life had effectively stood still for George. The partnership, the flat, these were the only significant events in fifteen years. Until...

1

Spring Last Year

'A merger, George!'

'Yes.'

'Who with?'

'A bigger firm than this.' George spoke with gloom.

'But you don't want to be a bigger firm than this.'

'No. But Douglas thinks it's a good idea.'

'Douglas Lavery will loathe it worse than you!'

'Yes. I think so.'

'George, get him to stop it before it goes any further.'

'We've already had meetings.' The word meetings came out as a groan.

'Meetings! You haven't signed anything yet?'

'Not yet but it's inevitable now.'

'A verbal contract's not worth the paper it's written on. But seriously, George–'

'It's going to happen. We've got to do it or go under. Douglas is right!' George stood up. His face suffused purple, veins stood out, his hands banged the desk then shook.

Those big shaking hands alarmed Bill Warren. Big, solid, steady, immovable old George? The man was in a bad way. 'Listen, I'm sorry, old mate, I'm sorry.'

George's head hung low. 'Ginny Sposeto left me this morning.'

'Ginny?' No one knew better than Warren how George, in his shy way, valued his show-biz clients. 'I introduced her to you, in...'

'Nineteen ninety-three.'

'Ten years ago. Why's she left, George?'

'She's found a one-man band who works from home. He can do it cheaper. With the right technology, the spreadsheets and so on they've got now, you can do that these days. Everyone's cutting back. Computers. You can teach a monkey in three days to do all the ordinary stuff, the bookkeeping. No need for chartered accountants any more.'

This was the longest speech Warren had ever heard from George. Normally he paid out words as if they cost money. 'But other clients will come to take her place, old mate–'

George shook his heavy head. 'Not the same kind. Accounts like hers are too small to interest a firm like this new lot. And the bigger accounts have been getting too big for us as we are. We lost Amalgamated Electrical last month.'

Warren assumed his I'm-an-ignorant-actor expression. 'Who are Amalgamated Electrical?'

'They were one of our biggest accounts. They've been with Douglas twenty years. They've grown steadily. Now the son's taken over and they've expanded. Very sorry et cetera et cetera, but they've got too big for us. They're going public.'

'Well, get bigger with them.'

'We're not licensed to work for public companies.'

'Oh, I see, George. Squeezed at both ends.'

'Yes. That's it.' George sat again, his big face expressionless. But his hands still shook.

'Well, George, if you hate the idea so much, just say no.'

'Wish I could.'

'Why not? I know you're fond of old Douglas but–'

'Fond? He took me on from school. I began my training here when I was seventeen. For my – for my father's sake.' George looked as if he might cry.

'I know, I know. There's a debt of loyalty, but you've given years to the firm. You've been here since you left school. You're a partner. If you just say no–'

'I'm not an equal partner.'

'What, Doug can outvote you?'

'Sixty-forty.'

'Oh hell, George. I see.' Warren stood up. He was a big ugly man like George. But unlike George he had a lightness to him, he moved with grace. He looked at George, massive behind his old desk like a great Pasha about to be dethroned. Yellow sunlight bathed him and lit up the two lithographs on the wall behind him. George had bought them to celebrate his partnership years ago. Warren recalled him showing them off with touching pride.

The office was on the first floor. Warren looked out of the window at the dark green paintwork of the lawyers' on the opposite side of the narrow cobbled lane, a building just like this one, eighteenth-century, three storeys high, the name of the firm painted in gold on a window of each floor.

George joined him, leaning his great forehead against the lettering on his own window that said backwards *Lavery and Fletcher, Chartered Accountants*. His voice, constrained at the best of times, was strangled in the back of his throat. 'A developer has bought the building,' he said.

'This building?'

'Doug's family have practised here a hundred and eleven years.'

Warren took a breath and breathed it slowly out. 'Ohh. Well, that's it, mate. No more arguments.'

'We amalgamate next month.'

'Couldn't Whatsername Electrical have held out till then?'

'We couldn't tell them. Not before it was settled. Wouldn't have been honourable.'

Warren sighed. The old values died hard in people like George. 'I'm lucky, George. An actor seldom stays in one place long enough to develop that much affection for it.' They stood a while contemplating the narrow cobbled street below. 'Come on, mate. Let's go and have a jar. Get plastered. It's pretty well the answer to everything. Short term, anyway.'

'Can't do that, sorry, Bill.' George went back to his desk. He picked up two files and put them in his old leather briefcase. 'I've work to do tonight.'

'A drink would do you more good. I've never seen you ars'oled, George. In fact I've never seen you even moderately canned.'

'No. Suppose not.' Then George did a curious thing. He took down one of his lithographs and put it in the bottom drawer of his desk. Then he took down the other and did the same.

'You're not moving out tonight, are you, George?'

George did not reply. He shut the drawer and stood up. With no grace but much dignity, a heavy-bottomed boat with a high prow, he crossed the room and held the door open for Bill.

Thus it was that in the month of May, a few

years into the new millennium, George found himself cast adrift and rudderless, sucked into the belly of a whale. It was only a medium-sized whale as City whales go but it swallowed George and Douglas with no difficulty at all.

The whale was a growing firm of City accountants with a whole floor of smart new offices in the rushing hurl of Moorgate where gangs of workmen still dug up the road all day. Eight partners and twenty-five staff shared three secretaries and even stretched to a full-time receptionist who had silky black skin and dressed in black to match, from elegant head to delectable well-shod toe.

George's new office gave on to a deep well and looked across to a window like his and a desk like his and a partner of the same status as himself. No spring sunlight crept in here. He transferred his two lithographs from his briefcase to the bottom drawer of his new streamlined teak veneer desk. He could not bring himself to put them on the wall.

2

It was five o'clock on Friday afternoon. George stood up and pushed some papers into his briefcase, to work on at the weekend. On the way to pick up his umbrella from the stand, he stopped at the window to look at his view – the shiny window three feet away, the deep well – to the accompaniment of the incessant pneumatic drills. He sighed. Before he left he switched off the fluorescent light, leaving the mean little glass-walled room full of reflections in the shifting grey and silver light.

Coming out into the steel and glass lobby he stood shocked by the sunshine. He needed a moment to adjust. He tried to avoid the glare of the gleaming name plate: *Appleton, Canning, Chartered Accountants* with *Incorporating Lavery and Fletcher* in smaller letters below. But he found himself gloomily regarding it.

A sudden blow between the shoulder blades nearly knocked him off balance. George turned. Gary Appleton stood grinning at him on the bottom step of the marble staircase. 'Oh. Appleton,' George said.

'Cheer up, George, it may never happen!'

31

The boss's son, twenty-one years old, shiny as the apple of his name, smart as a whippet, Appleton honked his patronising laugh. 'Good weekend, George. Don't do anything I wouldn't do!' The glass doors slid open. He strode off ahead of George and sped across the street, dodging the crowds, the mechanical diggers, the traffic, the holes in the road. George plodded on down Moorgate.

Blindly he trudged into Finsbury Circus, over London Wall, down Copthall Avenue past the ancient Chartered Accountants' Hall, into Swan Alley where a gigantic hole in the earth now revealed the church and other buildings beyond. A minute later, with no idea how he had got there, he found himself standing in a narrow, deserted cobbled court outside a small empty building. The estate agent's board said *Valuable Office Development Site*. Each window with *Lavery and Fletcher, Chartered Accountants* was either broken or opaque with filth.

A man in dusty overalls with dusty hair came out. He looked at George a moment, expecting him to speak, perhaps. But George stood as though dreaming, wondering how his feet had brought him here without his knowledge or permission.

The man said, 'Can I help you?'

George's eyes slowly took him in. 'Er... Thank you. No.' And the mournful eyes moved back to his old office window, the jagged black hole in the middle of his name. *That's my life,* he thought, *broken in two, right down the middle, and nothing inside.* And into his head came Marje. A split second, like a glimpse from a fast-moving train, and she was gone. But George found himself clutching the breast pocket of his suit as though to hold his heart in place.

The man looked concerned. 'You all right, mate?'

George gave him a grimace that he hoped was a reassuring smile. 'Oh, yes. Thank you, I'm fine.' He turned and trudged back the way he had come.

Back on course, as on every Friday afternoon for fifteen years, he took the tube to London Bridge and got on his train. On the train he ate a sandwich, read *The Times* and started the crossword.

At Norwood Junction he folded his paper, put it in his briefcase, stood up and got out of the train. He came out of the station and trudged on down Station Road, leaving behind him the dark mouth of the tunnel that led to the other side of the tracks.

Station Road was short and broad, like a square in a small country town, with its newly painted clock tower at the junction with the High Street. He passed the Cherry Tree pub which he had never entered, the estate agent, the hardware shop with its

33

smart new frontage, brooms and garden implements hanging in swags outside. He walked the length of the small supermarket on his left, windows plastered with posters depicting incongruous giant green fruits and vegetables to whet the shopper's appetite.

But all the time, underneath these mechanical actions, he still felt that his life had cracked in two, like that pane of glass. And into the chasm fell image after image of Marje, each image sensual, visual, sudden as an accident. *Why,* he asked himself in pain, *when I haven't thought of her for years? Why now?*

He was almost level with the automatic doors of the supermarket. The doors slid open with a sigh. And George – and time – stood still.

A small blonde girl had come out of the doors. She wore the short pink-checked overall of a supermarket cashier and, hair brushing her shoulders, lovely legs flashing, she ran away from him, down towards the clock tower. He almost stretched out a hand to detain her. He almost cried out. *Don't run away from me, Marje!*

Under the clock a man stood. The girl greeted the man. She handed him a small package. He opened it. He smiled. He put his arms round her slim waist. He kissed her cheek. He was a short stocky man with thick greying hair, about George's age or even older. She reached up and put her arms around his neck.

Dark came down like a hand over George's eyes. The street sounds surrounding him disappeared. He heard Marje whisper, *Carry me upstairs, George.* And felt her soft arms wind themselves round his neck...

He forced himself to open his eyes again. He saw the blonde girl wave to the man. And now she started to run back towards George. *After all these years. She is running back to me.* But as the automatic supermarket doors parted for her, George saw that of course she was not Marje. Marje would be as old as he, or nearly: thirty-six or -seven. The supermarket girl was eighteen, perhaps not even that. *As young as Marje was when* ... young enough to be Marje's daughter. His, even. *And oh so like, so like.*

He stood for a time after the girl disappeared, getting his breath back, trying to clear his vision. He felt sweat trickle down from his armpits to his waist. He wanted to follow her into the supermarket and watch her there. He wanted... He had no idea how long he had been standing there. He forced himself to walk on. He reached the clock tower. The man the girl had given the present to had gone. The man she had embraced. George crossed the road into Oliver Gardens.

He turned the corner into Lisson Avenue. At number thirty-five the laurels were overgrown. They darkened the path. *I must prune them,* he thought. He opened the door. He called out. He always did though he knew there would be no reply. Kevin still did something they called occupational therapy in the afternoons at his old school on the main road. His mother went at this time to pick him up and do some shopping. In the supermarket probably. George went upstairs to change out of his City suit.

He stood in front of the mirror in his underpants and socks and looked at himself. He sat on the bed without taking his gaze away from his reflected face. His big hands were gripped between his thighs. Something weird was happening to him. Something over which he had no control. He felt like a wounded bird, shaken in the teeth of a big black dog, a sensation half terror, half joy.

He waited. He listened. His mother and Kevin were not due back till after seven. His watch said half past six. His breath was all contained within his big chest which felt as if it might burst. He had to get away from the mirror, out of the room. He went up the stairs that led to the top floor. No reason. Just for somewhere to go.

He imagined slipping up the stairs behind her, silently, creeping closer, then closer still until, unable to resist... *He lifts her easily, she's light, so small. His hand is over her mouth, silencing and caressing her at the same time. She is too afraid to struggle. Her wide eyes gaze into his. He carries her into the attic room...*

He opened the door of the back attic. Dust quivered in the light that shafted across the bare floor. He went in. He shut the door. He lay face down on the dusty boards: *bare boards, a bed with a striped mattress, a rope coiled under the bed. He throws her on to the bed. He ties her there. He gags her with his clean white handkerchief. He removes the gag to feed her titbits when he visits her. He brushes her lovely hair, he washes her lovely skin with a warm face cloth and soap smelling of rose petals. He is gentle, courteous, respectful. She starts to look forward to his visits, she starts to depend on him. And then one day... He comes into the room, sunshine just like now, she opens her arms to him, looks in his eyes and whispers shyly, 'Love me, George. Never let me go.'*

That was how the fantasies began.

At first they were not overwhelming or continuous. But many times the following week he lurched suddenly back to consciousness in yet another interminable business meeting, to discover that his mind had been following the girl-like-Marje, down another street, up another shadowy flight of stairs, into a dusty sunlit room...

He felt enriched by these imaginings. They

37

showed him how empty his life had been all these years, but they consoled him for that emptiness. They were a surprise to him, a sort of gift – the gift of a girl like Marje running ahead of him down all the streets and up all the stairs and into all the empty attics of his mind. Wanting to be caught. Wanting to be caught by George.

3

George stood up, leaned over his desk and shook hands with his last appointment of the week. The man, an old client, looked at him oddly but George didn't notice. All he knew was that, although it was Friday and already after five, he had a meeting to attend. About the number of computers they should order next month, no doubt, or whether they should employ a new cleaning firm for the lavatories – the sort of thing he and Doug had taken care of for years without the tedium of discussion. And the prolixity of some of his new colleagues would force him into taking a later train.

It was worse than he had feared. Coming out of the station he saw that the super-market was closing: a man in a suit was locking the main door. There could be no chance of seeing her today. In a state of utter desolation he plodded the length of the poster-covered windows. He even tried to peer in through the glass doors to see if any of the staff might be working late. A spotty youth, stocking the shelves, gawped at him. Shamed, he trudged on towards home.

He wasn't aware that the lilacs were fading, laburnum panicles turning to pale yellow dust, roses in bud in the gardens, that all around him summer had begun. He turned the corner into leafy Lisson Avenue. Hearing the noise of a gate clanging shut, he looked up.

Four or five houses ahead of him a small figure dashed out of the gate and flew towards him. This could not be true; she had materialised out of his head. But no, she was real, she was coming closer. Her feet barely touched the ground. Her hair and her shoulder bag swung. *She is running to me!* They were about to meet. She would stop, she would speak to him. He almost opened his arms to her. She smiled! And ran on past him.

He felt dizzy. He had to stop a moment, hold on to a fence. He yearned to turn and follow her, just to find out where she was running to. Whom she was running to. That man again, was it? *But I mustn't, I mustn't do that, I mustn't give any sign. At all costs I mustn't frighten her.*

He managed somehow to walk on. What was the number of the house she had come out of? He counted, he counted. It was this one. This one with the shabby front garden, the gate hanging on one hinge. Number twenty-nine. She had come out of number twenty-nine. Only three houses before number thirty-five, his mother's house. She couldn't possibly live here. Could she? How could he find out? Would his mother know?

John Bright, strolling along Lisson Avenue in the evening sun, had seen the bulky man stop, stare, hesitate, outside number twenty-nine. 'If I didn't know you, George, I'd say you were loitering with intent.'

'Ha?' George jumped and turned to look at him. In spite of his shock, or perhaps because of it, the big heavy face remained blank, the eyes dead.

'George?' Bright said. 'Don't you know me, mate?'

George's inexpressive face made a slow slide towards recognition: 'John?' He shifted his heavy briefcase and shook hands. 'Sorry. I was – just – distracted for a moment.'

'What you up to, George? Planning a burglary?'

'Ha. Yes. Something like that.' George tried and failed to convey amusement.

'Don't worry, you look too respectable to get arrested. Even by me.' Bright looked at the broken gate. 'This isn't your mother's house, is it?'

'No, she's still at...' George waved his newspaper vaguely.

'A-ha. Number thirty-five. Hasn't changed, has it? Still got those dark spotty bushes.'

'Yes. I meant to trim them last weekend but...' Again George's voice tailed off. It was clear his mind was somewhere else, and that he wished his body were free to follow it.

'You haven't moved back in with your ma, have you, George?'

'What? No, no. I have a flat in the City. Just come home for weekends. To help her with Kevin, you know. And the house.'

'How is your dear old ma these days?'

George ignored the humorous sideways squint. 'She's very well, thank you.' He looked up and down the street, then at Bright again as though surprised to find him still there. He seemed curiously reluctant to move from the gate of number twenty-nine. But at last his big feet began to slap along in the direction of his mother's house. Bright turned to stroll along with him and George recalled his manners. 'Er, have you come back to work at South Norwood police station, John?'

'Nah. Can't retrace your steps in this life, can you, George? I'm taking a bit of leave, that's all. Staying with my old ma for a bit.'

'When does your leave come to an end, John?'

'I dunno. Maybe never.'

George looked at him with sudden interest. His old school-friend sounded as disenchanted as he with his chosen profession. 'You're not thinking of making a change?'

'I dunno. Maybe. It's not out the question, put it like that.'

'But you're doing so well. We read about the big gangland case.'

'Don't believe everything you read in the papers, George.' Bright's face closed in the way George remembered from school, a shutter coming down. 'Talk about something else, mate, eh?'

'Oh. Yes. Er...' But George could think of nothing. They stood in uncompanionable silence outside his gate. George shifted the weight on his feet. He seemed to be having more trouble shifting the weight on his mind.

Bright smiled grimly. 'Well, you're looking prosperous anyway, George.'

George looked down at his well-cut suit, his expensive briefcase, shirt cuffs, burnished leather shoes as though seeing this evidence of his prosperity for the first time. 'Yes.' He sighed.

'Business good then?'

George nodded and sighed more heavily. 'A bit too good,' he said.

'Is that possible?'

'A merger. With a bigger firm.'

'A merger? What, you and old Whatsisname? Not your style, eh, George?'

'All for the best, I suppose.'

'You don't sound too convinced.'

'Well. You know. Meetings all the time. Administration...' George's words tailed off. Impossible to express the depth of his disaffection, his big face a mask of tragedy.

Bright thrust his hands in his pockets, jingled his change. He suddenly looked just as he had when they were schoolboys – tense mouth, eyes sharp as razors, eager for mischief. 'Come and have a drink, George.'

'Oh.' George seemed in the grip of some fearful conflict. 'Well ... Mother might wonder, you know... If she gets back and finds I'm not here.'

'A-ha.' Bright sighed and stuck out his hand. 'Never mind, George. Some other time, eh?'

'Er – yes. That would be – er – yes.'

'Maybe I'll call in one of these weekends. Work up the courage to brave your ma.' And Bright loped away, wide shoulders in his old leather jacket, wiry still, and light on his feet as a fox.

For a moment George almost called after him. He almost went for a drink with his old school-friend. It might have changed everything. Instead he turned in under the untrimmed laurels of number thirty-five.

He felt disturbed by the encounter. Saddened. Why hadn't he said yes to a drink?

Surprise, perhaps? Shyness? Fear that after all these years they might have nothing to say? Fear of being reminded of things lost, time past? No. It was that Bright had always either said the unspeakable, or implied what he didn't say. His stiletto-sharp eyes had always seen too much. And now George had a secret to keep. That was one reason he had said no. He knew it. And the other more pressing reason – he needed to get into the house to be alone to concentrate on a life more real than this. And time was running out.

He shouted Hello, but his mother too was late, still out collecting his brother. He yearned to go up to the attic and lie on the sun-stained floor. But he couldn't risk it. Could he? He looked at his watch. No. She would surely be back any minute now.

He changed into his weekend clothes, went down to the kitchen and tried to finish the crossword. But only the girl was in his head, smiling as she ran towards him. Coming out of number twenty-nine. *Running towards me. Smiling at me...*

Kevin bounced into the kitchen and leaped at him like an overgrown pup. His mother greeted him with her accustomed parsimony of speech. 'They kept them late at the school.' She plonked his dinner down on the table. He ate it without noticing. Afterwards she took Kevin off to her sister's as she always did on a Friday night. At last.

He climbed to the attic floor. He collapsed face down on the dusty boards. *She smiled at me. Why did she do that?* In thirty-eight years George had had no use for imagination. He had no experience to tell him what to do with its escapes. He had no control of it. It shook him in its teeth.

Lily Bright sat in her bay window and watched a small blonde girl go by. A large tabby cat sat on the window sill beside her and watched also. The girl moved like a winged thing, each step a short flight. Such an exotic perfection of colour, line and limb looked out of place among the dusty privet and dismal lilacs rusting on the bush.

Lily was still amused with the loveliness of the girl when her son turned in at the gate. She and the cat watched him come up the path. She was glad of her net curtains. They hid the sadness that came over her at the sight of him. *At least he can't see me,* she thought. Just then he looked straight at her and gave her a wink. She wheeled her chair away from the window with an exasperated Scottish sound and the cat jumped down from the window sill and skidded to the front door. John's key turned in the lock. 'Spying on me again?' he said.

'Got to keep an eye on you. Never know what you might get up to.'

45

'You should have been CID, Ma, not me.'

'I know it well, my boy.'

The cat had rolled over at the sight of him and was now clutching his hand in its front paws and madly scratching at his wrist with its back feet, claws retracted, while Bright scratched the soft white fur under its chin. He lifted the wrist, cat and all, and held the warm soft creature close while he bent and kissed the top of Lily's head.

'All right?' she said.

'You bet.'

'See that girl?' she said.

'Girl?'

'You must have passed her at the corner. Lovely little thing.'

'Oh. A-ha. Yes.' He looked out of the window, still holding the cat in his arms, absently stroking while the cat purred. He was abstracted, vacant, at a loss.

After watching him a while, she gathered her courage. 'It's time you got back to work, John,' she said.

'Not yet.'

'When then?'

'Never maybe.'

'A man needs his work,' she said.

'A-ha.' Subject closed. He wasn't listening.

'John.'

'Mm?'

Lily sighed. 'I wish I could do something.'

'You can't, Ma.' He shrugged. 'Ne'r mind,

46

eh? Make you some tea.' He went out to the kitchen with the cat hanging in his arms like an old handbag. 'You too, old mate, eh? She starving you as usual?'

Lily wheeled her chair to the french windows and opened them. It was another golden end to the day. The crimson rose no one knew the name of was about to open, a month early. And even the Albertine was in tight small bud.

He'd put a crimson rose bud on the tray.

'Oh, John, the things you think of.'

'Not bad for a hard bastard copper, right?'

'If you got back to work you'd maybe stop brooding like this.'

'Ma–'

'Okay, okay.' They looked at the garden. She sipped her tea. 'Jude was such a wonderful gardener–'

She didn't go on. At the mention of Jude's name he was out on the terrace like he'd been kicked. And down the garden. It was a long garden for a small terrace house. He stopped at about eighty feet and dropped to his haunches, head down. She watched him, wishing she had bitten her tongue. There wasn't a subject that was safe any more. Last spring when he and Jude were about to set off on holiday they had come to say goodbye and leave Jude's cat with her. He was so happy then, so full of love and hope. But she

47

and Jude were awkward together, she jealous as hell if the truth be known, Jude trying to please, flattering her about the garden, professional to amateur. Both of them trying to get to grips with the new situation. She'd never seen him happier than he was at that time. Maybe she'd never see him as happy again. She felt bad because she couldn't accept Jude as a future daughter-in-law, had seen her as a danger and a threat. Lily was a woman at fault and would understand if he blamed her now. Not that he did. His grief was pure and there was enough anger against Jude's killers growling inside him to keep his vengeance off her.

He suddenly jack-knifed up, gripped the bough of a chestnut in salmon-y bloom and hung there, reminding her: *He used to do that when he was ten years old.* He dropped to the grass and came back to the house, dead-heading faded tulips as he came. The cat, always eager to turn anything into a game, bounded ahead of him down the lawn, John broke into a run after him, caught him up at the french windows. The cat rolled over at his feet and John dropped to his knees to commence battle. 'You got the attitude. Right, George? Don't let the bastards get you down.' He looked up from his mad game with the cat. 'I bumped into another George this afternoon, Ma.'

'George Fletcher?' she said. A subject that

was safe. 'He doesn't still live round here?'

'Stays with his ma at weekends. And his brother.'

'Poor creature.'

'Nothing poor about Kevin. See the happy moron, he doesn't give a damn. I wish I were a moron–'

'–My God, perhaps I am,' she said with him. 'I wasn't referring to Kevin. I was referring to George.'

'Poor creature? George? George is a chartered accountant, Ma, with a posh flat in the City. He's a big prosperous dignified fellow now. With shiny shoes.'

'George Fletcher? A poor awkward badly tied parcel with big flat feet that he never knew how to walk with,' she said.

'Ah well, that too,' he said.

'Believe me,' she said, 'that George is a sad case. He's upset inside. Always was.'

'You're talking about my best mate, Ma!'

'That was a long time ago. And I never knew what you saw in him.'

'He was the biggest guy in the school. He protected me.'

'Oh aye? A likely tale. Since when did you ever need protection? It's my belief you felt sorry for the big lummock. It's you protected him, if the truth be known.'

'He made me laugh – he was easy to shock. And he helped me with the maths homework.'

'Aye, you were never a genius at the maths.'
Bright and his mother smiled at each other,
each with the same non-smiling smile.

She didn't know – and he would never tell
her – just how much he and George Fletcher
had had in common. Already at twelve
George was seen as weird. He was never exactly bullied; he was too big. But he had no
friends. He was a solemn lonely plodder with
nothing special about him except his extraordinary affinity with numbers. He worked
in class, did his homework, passed the exams
and never took anyone home. Bright was
smaller than the others and was never
bullied either, because he had an acerbic wit
that they feared, he made them laugh and he
could take care of himself in a scrap. But he
never took anyone home either. It wasn't
that he was ashamed of his fatherless state,
or his mother in her wheelchair – he valued
his ma then as he did now – but he didn't
want to give them an advantage. In his heart
he despised them and he wouldn't give them
a chance to take the piss.

He first asked George for help with the
maths because he genuinely wanted to crack
the barrier between himself and the
numbers. George came home with him,
liked being there better than his own house,
and would never grass him up. But they
weren't exactly mates.

Then one day Bright spotted the big

50

awkward lad in a corner of the playground, alone as usual but something about him looked bad and Bright went over to check him out. George was crying.

'What's up, Fletch?'

George covered his eyes with his big arm and couldn't speak but Bright hung about, didn't go away and at last George said, 'My dad's died.'

They were both thirteen and now both fatherless. George did take him home then. Bright shivered still, recalling the gloom of that house, the coffin in the dark parlour and the black termagant of a mother as tall as George and hugely pregnant. After that there was no going back. They were mates from then till George got married and then left home, and Bright got posted to Haringey HQ and they lost touch. And now Bright was as bereft and rudderless as George looked. 'Maybe I will look him up one of these weekends,' he said. 'Hey, George? Whadda you think?'

Having passed John Bright at the corner, the little blonde girl glided on, down past the Stanley Halls, across the High Street, under the railway bridge to the other side of the tracks.

Brockhurst Road was a narrow street. Small terrace houses. Red-brick, single-bay, no front gardens, no trees. Litter blew and gathered in heaps. Number sixteen, unlike its neighbours, still had stained glass panels round its front door. The door was stripped, imperfectly. Its brass door knob and letter box did not shine. The girl let herself in.

Inside, the doors and floors were also stripped, and the fireplaces and the kitchen cupboards, such as they were. There was a certain lack and oddity of door handles, and the wood had not been sealed so that it was stained with years of grubby fingermarks. She looked into the living room. Large cushions lay about the floor, dust in the corners. The general effect, however, in spite of the dust and the grubbiness, was light and airy.

She listened. There was no one home. She smiled to herself and ran lightly up the uncarpeted stairs.

Her room was at the back. She closed the door, stood for a moment, then undid a zip. Her little yellow cotton frock slid to the floor. She stepped out of it. She opened her cupboard and felt behind the clothes. She brought out a padded hanger on which a pale pink satin dress undulated and shimmered. She wriggled into the slithery second skin, gracefully lifted the narrow straps on to her shoulders and smoothed the satin over her hips. She stepped into a pair of high-heeled sandals a deeper pink than the dress, their soles clean and new. In front of the narrow mirror from Woolworth's she brushed her pale blonde hair into a side parting that waved over her right eye. She stroked translucent foundation over her face, then palest blusher over her cheekbones. She smoothed shiny red over her lips and silver, almost imperceptible, above her eyes. In the mirror she studied her appearance severely and critically altered the position of her head. She stretched and moved her arms, perfecting their posture. She heard the front door open and close. She listened. Footsteps down the passage to the kitchen, then back again to the hall. Footsteps up the stairs. She stayed very still. He was outside her door.

'Poll?' The hoarse voice was insistent. 'Polly, are you in there?'

The door handle started to turn. She swiftly lifted a chair and pushed it under the handle, wedging it.

'Polly!'

She saw him plain though the door was between them. Dark, bony, shabby, he hadn't shaved in days. He sat down on the top stair, she heard him. He put his head in his long bony hands – she knew his gestures. He made a sound between a growl and a groan. She returned to the mirror and checked her reflection. Taking herself by surprise she could have been her beloved Kylie Minogue, just for the briefest glimpse.

Over the weekend George cut the grass. He

watched the cricket on TV, he took Kevin for walks. He trimmed the laurels, an excuse to hang about at the front of the house. But he did not see the girl. And he did not pluck up the courage to ask his mother about her. On Monday morning he willed her to come out of number twenty-nine as he passed, but she did not. The supermarket had not yet opened when he took his dutiful train back to town.

4

All next week at work the girl was in his head. She lived there now, she settled in, she was making herself at home. On Thursday he had a wonderful idea: tomorrow there was to be no meeting, but he would take a later train on purpose. He would try to arrive just as the supermarket closed.

On Friday, he found it impossible to sit an extra hour in his office pretending to work. Instead he drank a coffee at London Bridge station. He heard his usual train announced and for the first Friday he could remember he let it go. He returned to the kiosk, bought another coffee and a sandwich and sat down again at the small metal table.

George was not used to this kind of

leisure. It began to excite him strangely. He thought, *I'm outside time. Nobody can get to me. Nobody knows where I am. I am between two lives.* He felt invisible and, for the first time ever, free. He could go where he liked, do what he liked. He could not be caught. *Caught? Why am I thinking of being caught? I'm not doing anything criminal.* He made his sandwich and his coffee last but dawdling was not in his nature and after an hour he could bear it no longer. He left his table, rushed to his platform and just managed to squeeze into the last compartment. On the train he tried to read *The Times* but failed. Daydreams gripped him. Her image came between him and the out of focus columns of print on the page.

He arrived at Norwood Junction. He stood in the sunny street. And an amazing idea occurred to him: *I can waste time here as easily as I can in town. I'm as free here as I am there. Just because I'm here that doesn't mean I have to go straight home!* It did not seem odd to him that this notion had never occurred to him before.

He hovered about uneasily, looking at the brooms and dust-bins at the chandler's, the bits and pieces outside the antique shop. He did not know precisely the time the girl would leave. In half an hour perhaps? When he feared he might become conspicuous for loitering he wandered across to the supermarket window.

He couldn't go in, afraid equally of seeing her and not seeing her, of bumping into neighbours or, worse, his mother and, worst, simply of looking out of place. So he strode purposefully off down by the side of the building. This quiet little street, still almost a country lane, led to the so-called recreation ground where he often took Kevin for a walk. This sadly named place consisted of nothing but a flat green triangle, the railway line along one side, a few swings and a slide in a corner, a bench or two along the path. George walked all round the perimeter in the glaring sun, and out again the way he had come in.

The supermarket had still not closed. He crossed again to the shops opposite and found a box of second-hand paperbacks outside the antique shop. *All in this box 50p.* Unknowing he pulled a Mills and Boon romance from the box and held it upside down, turning its pages earnestly, his eyes on the supermarket doors. And then the girl came out.

She was dressed not in her uniform this time, but a short blue cotton skirt and a jeans jacket. And she didn't run. George watched her back as she walked down to the clock tower. A man greeted her there. Not the same man as last time. This one was taller, thinner, younger, and when he stretched out his arms she moved out of the range of his embrace.

George watched them cross the road. The young man's hand was on the small of the girl's back, his face turned to her. He was speaking but she did not look at him.

'Can I help you, sir?' The antiques woman was smiling at him.

George jumped. He hesitated. 'Oh. No. Thank you, no. I was just...' He dropped *Say Yes, Samantha* back into the box and hurried off.

The antiques woman had delayed him. The girl had turned right along the High Street. But when he turned the corner he glimpsed her. She was still with the young man. They were standing a hundred yards away, outside the Wimpy Bar. They were going in. Another minute and he'd have been too late.

George had never been inside the Wimpy Bar. His mother did not approve of such places and nor did he. But he didn't hesitate. He squeezed among the pygmy plastic tables and sat as far as possible from the girl, which was not far, the place was small. The young man's eyes flicked over him absently. The girl didn't look at him at all. She looked down at the table and George realised with a shock that she was crying. With the tip of her small index finger she wiped the tears off the table as they fell.

George felt a rush of rage. He wanted to hit this man who had made his girl cry. *My Girl!* The words formed in his head. He dragged his eyes off her to look at the man, to examine this monster. And saw that he was just a boy, not much older than she. His face was thin, with high cheekbones. He was fair. And handsome, George bitterly supposed.

The boy was speaking now, hardly moving his mouth, deadly quiet, pleading or threatening, George couldn't tell which. The girl shook her head. Her tears continued to fall, into her coffee now. One of her little hands shielded her eyes. Behind it her other hand surreptitiously wiped the tears away.

Suddenly the boy got up. He strode to the door. He stopped. He came back. He delved into his jeans pocket, pulled out some pound coins and threw them at the table. The waiter called, 'Thank you, sir!' but the boy was already in the street.

The girl got up and came towards George. He thought for a paralysed moment she was coming to speak to him but she moved towards the Toilets sign and disappeared down the stairs.

George quickly asked for his bill but made the dregs of his coffee last till he heard her footsteps return. He'd left it too late. He had to go to the till in order to pay. She passed within an inch of him. Panicked, he dropped some coins. He bent to pick them up. When he got up she was out of sight. Outside he searched the High Street, frantic. There were too many people. She could be anywhere. She was gone.

Hollow with loss, he turned right to pursue his heavy way home. Opposite the clock tower he looked down towards the supermarket. Useless. It would be closed now, she wouldn't have gone back there. He turned right again, leaving the High Street behind, and he nearly cried out. She was there, twenty yards ahead of him. Sitting on a low wall with her head bent. Just as he saw her she stood up. She smoothed down her little skirt, hoisted the strap of her bag on to her shoulder and began to walk on. He tried to subdue his big flat feet into silence, though she seemed too preoccupied to notice there was anyone behind her. His breath came fast, wet in his throat.

Her head was bent. Her hands were in the pockets of her jacket. He could see her elbows pressed against her sides. He imagined the small fists bunched in the pockets, under her breasts. Her pale blonde hair and her shoulder bag no longer swung. Her slim legs seemed too fragile to bear the weight of her sorrow.

He was inching closer. He shortened the distance between them. But she didn't seem to be aware of him. It was important that she mustn't be aware of him. *Not yet.* Not yet? What did he mean? *Not yet?* He couldn't think about that. Not yet was the future. This was Now. And Now he was here. And so was she.

He slowed his pace again to fit with hers. He saw her footprints as clearly as if they were imprinted in sand. He walked in her footprints. When she turned into Lisson Avenue he was almost close enough to reach out, to touch with his fingertips that bent fragile neck. *Not yet.* He held himself in check. He held himself back. He stopped at the end of the street and knelt to tie an imaginary shoelace. A woman with a pushchair made an exasperated noise as she skirted him.

He never took his eyes off the girl. He willed her to turn into number twenty-nine. And she did. She obeyed his will. She was pushing open the gate. He began to move again. She was going up the path. And as he passed he saw that she was turning a key in the door. She did live there then. Three houses away from him. From his mother anyway. As he heard her door close he blundered against a drooping branch and was showered with rose petals.

For the first time in fifteen years George felt flooded with happiness. He carried his happiness inside him as the warm yellow yolk is carried inside an egg. He could barely breathe. The smell of roses filled the quiet street. George would never be able to separate the smell of roses from this new happiness. He was overpowered by both.

At number thirty-five he saw with surprise that he had cut the laurels back last weekend. His path was radiant with light. He would go straight up to the attic, lie in the dust, imagine, dream, follow, reach out. *Touch.* He let himself in.

'That you, George?'

His mother had never in years been at home when he arrived. But then he'd never been so late before, sat in a Wimpy Bar or followed *his girl* before. His heart thumped. He tried to rearrange his face before braving his mother. She had always read his every thought as if it were written there.

The kitchen was a dark north-facing room. In its shadows a heavy sharp-boned woman banged at a sheet of pastry with a rolling pin.

'Hello, Mother.'

'You're late,' she said.

He could think of nothing to say in explanation. He mumbled something about work, a meeting. He longed to go upstairs. He longed also to ask about the girl. He framed a question in his mind: *Are there some new people at number twenty-nine?* Impossible. His craving would show all over his big hot face.

His mother was speaking. 'He can't go with me to Freda's tonight. She's got people coming.'

'Oh?'

'Will you be in? Can't leave him on his own.' She jerked her head in the direction of the window

'Yes, Mother, I'll be in.'

George looked out at the garden. Kevin was carefully watering some bright little flowers with a small can. Next door's dog, a brown and white Jack Russell, sat on the wall above him. Kevin lifted his head and spoke to the dog. The dog's tail wagged. Kevin came with his oddly graceful lolloping walk to fill the can at the outside tap under the kitchen window. He saw George and smiled his radiant smile. George's yearning flooded him. Oh, for a minute in the attic. Even one minute there.

'Just change my clothes,' he muttered and went upstairs. Standing on the landing he opened his bedroom door and closed it loudly without going in. He listened. Then he crept up the next flight, trying to control his big floppy feet. He turned the knob of his attic door. The door was locked. The key was gone.

5

The man prowled back and forth through the bare bright room. His back teeth gripped the insides of his cheeks, but couldn't control the shaking of his mouth.

A key turned in the front door. He folded his arms, squeezing his hands between his upper arms and his ribs. He stood still. The door shut. Footsteps went lightly up the stairs. Up there cupboards and drawers opened and closed. The light footsteps moved from bedroom to bathroom. Water ran.

He put his face in his hands. His hands were long and bony and strong, like his face. He stood with his back against the wall, his head down and his fists covering his eyes. The music she always listened to, some female pop star singing about a red-blooded woman, drifting thinly down the stairs. Half an hour passed.

When she came into the room his hands shook only a little. He looked all right. 'Poll,' he said.

'Oh, it's you.' She took one look at him. 'Thought it was Mum.' And went.

'Poll?' He followed her down the hallway

to the kitchen. Small, her blonde hair brushing her shoulders, she rippled, like water. He found her movement incredible. Always had. Even when she was a little girl, before... He rubbed his eyes and went after her into the kitchen. He sat at the scrubbed pine table. She walked about making the tea as though he wasn't there. Every step an unconscious dance. Or was it unconscious? He'd never been sure. Did she do what she did to him knowingly? Deliberately? Cruelly? Would he ever know?

'Poll?' He sounded hoarse.

'What?'

He swallowed hard and tried to speak. 'Polly, please!'

She gave an exasperated sigh and he banged the table. Her eyes got scared. He stood up. She moved away and held on to the edge of the sink behind her. He thrust the chair away from him, almost threw it back against the wall. She didn't move, just stood watching him. Her hand was close to the bread knife on the draining board but she didn't pick it up. She waited for him to calm down. She did not have to wait long.

He groaned. His head flopped. Only his hands flat on the table stopped his whole body from lunging forward. He stayed like that, propped on his arms over the table like a sack of bones. 'I don't know what to do,' he said.

'Where's Mum?' She had a small, clear voice.

'Nnn.'

'I think it's her yoga day. She won't be long.'

'Nn.'

'I'm going out tonight.'

'No.'

'Mum will be in.'

'Don't leave me on my own, Poll.'

'You won't be on your own. I just said.'

'Polly, for Christ's sake.'

She didn't bother to answer him. She started on the pile of washing-up, scraped off the dried muesli from breakfast, the lentils from the night before.

'Where are you going?' the man said.

She didn't reply.

'Who with?' he said. He got up and came towards her. 'Polly, I can't take it any more.'

'Hello?' The voice from the hallway was small like Polly's but years of smoking had made it huskier. When she heard it Polly gave Jack a small smile with her face sideways to him. 'I told you,' she said. He sat down.

Chloe came in. She was no taller than Polly but her hair was darker and dead straight and wispy, her face bonier. She fluttered like a frail little bird. There was an upward stretch about her back and her little nose pointed upward too. She wore a flimsy

Indian cotton frock that seemed too big for her, like a child dressed up in her mother's clothes. Her legs were bare. She was forty but didn't often look it. 'Any tea, Poll?' She floated a kiss to her daughter.

Polly turned her face to catch it on the wing. 'Kettle's on,' she said.

'Polly put the kettle on.' Chloe said that every evening. Polly raised her eyebrows, blinked slowly and rolled her eyes. Chloe smiled at her. Then she looked at Jack and her face folded into different lines. She looked forty now. She sighed. He had made no reaction to her coming in. She didn't speak to him.

'Was it your yoga today?' Polly said.

'Yes.' Chloe closed her eyes and folded her hands into a prayer position, elbows out. She lifted one leg and bent it, pressing the sole of her foot against the other knee. She stood there like that till the kettle boiled. Then she laughed. 'It's marvellous,' she said. Then she said, 'Want some tea, Jack?' and her voice changed. It went flat and hard and bored. Jack made no sign of having heard. Chloe lowered her eyelids and looked sideways at Polly then poured her own tea.

She picked up a large shoulder bag made of canvas unprofessionally embroidered with the signs of the zodiac. She sat opposite Jack at the table with the bag on her lap. She took out a small, well-thumbed copy of *The*

Prophet by Khahlil Gibran, a bundle of grubby tissues, a tattered plastic make-up bag, a pair of backless slippers, an Indian cotton scarf, a hair brush. The objects littered the table.

She reached in again and found a tobacco tin and a small pouch. She opened the tin and took out the packet of green Rizla papers and a pinch of tobacco. From the pouch she took a half-inch brown cube. She spread the tobacco on to a paper. She broke a tiny lump off the cube and crumbled it into the tobacco. She rolled the mixture expertly, lit up and inhaled. 'Rrr,' she purred. A fragrant smell filled the room. 'Want some, Poll?'

Polly's back had stiffened but nobody would notice. 'No thanks, Mum.' Her little voice was cool and polite as always. She finished the washing-up. 'I'm going out,' she said.

'Oh, no!' Her mother sprang up. 'Oh, don't leave me alone, Poll.'

'I've got to.' Over the washing-up she had been working on her story. 'It's the school. There's a meeting. About the adult classes. I've got to go.'

'Oh, your morons.'

'Yes.'

'Can't you get out of it, Poll? I can't stand another evening–' Chloe looked at Jack. He hadn't moved. 'I'm scared,' she mouthed at Polly.

'Go round to Jennifer's.' Polly watched her mother think. A slow process.

'Yes... Yes, I might. But I don't like leaving him on his own.'

'So stay with him.'

'It's okay for you. I always get left with him.'

'He's your boyfriend, Mum, not mine.'

There was a moment of terrified stillness in the room.

Polly broke it. 'It's not as if he's even my father,' she said.

'Oh, Poll!' Chloe's eyes filled up. 'He'd like to be. He loves you. Don't you, Jack?'

Polly looked sideways at Jack. His face was hidden by his hand.

'He gave you his name!' Chloe said.

'Who asked him?' Polly's voice was cool as water. 'I don't want his name. I don't want anything of his.'

'Oh, Poll!'

Polly shrugged. 'I've got to go anyway.'

She left.

Chloe's shoulders drooped. She flopped down, relit the spliff, inhaled deeply, closed her eyes. Jack didn't move. They sat at the table with the contents of the bag piled between them. The fragrance trailed into all the corners of the room.

Polly floated down the grimy main road towards the railway bridge. She passed the tarted-up pub with the fake leaded windows and the tables outside. People in summer clothes spilled all over the terrace. They sounded like a flock of starlings roosting.

She entered the shadow of the bridge expressionless but when she emerged into the light again her cool little face held the faintest suggestion of excitement. She sped up to the corner, where the High Street began. She stopped hurrying, and breathed out slowly for the first time that day. She was where she wanted to be, now. On the other side of the tracks. The right side of the dividing line.

She turned left and glided along the High Street. She ignored the downmarket shop windows in disdain, but spent a long time outside the estate agent's. House prices had started to fall at the end of last year but she saw that they were beginning to pick up again. Especially the big Victorian semi-detacheds in Lisson Avenue. There was one priced at £750,000 that just over a year ago would have been £680,000 at the most. It was shabby, too, but you could do it up. She gazed earnestly at each house photograph, reading the estate agent's details, imagining the day when she would have such a sum at her disposal...

She also read the cards in the newsagent's window. She knew them by heart: *Relaxing massage, Home help wanted three days a week.*

There was a new one tonight: *Wedding dress, ivory satin, never worn.* Polly saw neither pathos nor even black humour in this sad message. She would despise any hopeful bride who failed to bring it off. *Room to let in non-smoking house, suit quiet business lady.* She wandered on, musing on this.

The Wimpy Bar was packed as usual, lit up though the evening was still light. People her age and younger sashayed among the tables with dyed black hair, white faces, black clothes with silver studs, carefully ripped at elbow and knee. 'School kids dressed up,' Polly sneered to herself. 'Goths are *so* not cool, don't they realise?' A boy and girl in the window clasped plump hands among the coffee cups and leaned across the table to kiss. Their lips were painted black. *Love* and *Hate* were printed across their knuckles in black felt-tip. Polly turned her head away.

More of them clustered round the clock tower eating from polystyrene boxes. She turned her perfect nose away from the sweaty smell of junk-fried onions. She passed the sixth-form college, despised the people from her class who had gone on there from school. 'Mugs,' she said to herself. Education was the slow lane. She had different ideas. She passed the tree-shaded alley that led into the rec, the Church of the Holy Innocents, next to the school for the mentally handicapped where she spent her dreary days. She turned in at the gate.

'I'm sorry, Mrs Bridges, but my step-father's not well and my mum needs me at home tonight. So I can't come to the meeting, I'm afraid.'

'You know, Polly, working with the mentally disadvantaged is not just an ordinary job. It needs dedication beyond the call of duty. We can't hope just to keep office hours. Even a teacher's help like you needs special qualities.'

'Oh, yes, I know. It's just that my mum can't really manage without me.'

'This has happened before, though, hasn't it? A job like this is hard to come by, you know. Any job is, these days. And as a trainee you have to watch your step. I'm telling you this for your own good.'

'He's often not well, my stepfather. He was in a mental hospital once. Not one like this. A place for mad people. He sometimes gets violent. He attacks my mum. I don't like leaving her alone with him.'

'Oh, I see.' The woman pulled her lips together like the neck of a drawstring purse. 'Well, in that case. I'll excuse you this once.'

Polly gave her a pathetic smile. 'I'm really sorry. I really am.'

She was out. She was free. She resisted the impulse to run down the drive. Walking sedately until she was out of sight of the school, she savoured, as she delayed, the delicious moment when she would enter the region of her dreams. But at last she came to the zebra crossing, her black and white rainbow that seemed to lift her over the main road to her personal pot of gold, to what she referred to with a bubble of excitement as 'the posh part'.

She strolled along a leafy avenue. She studied the large houses, their gleaming windows, their lace curtains, their venetian blinds, their dignified front gardens. She gathered them in for future contemplation. Blossom fell on her shining hair. She shook it off.

6

'Mother!' George hurtled down the top flight of stairs and stood panting on the landing.

She stood down in the hall in her summer mac, an incongruous turquoise cotton, about to open the front door. 'I'm late for Freda's,' she said. 'What do you want?'

George tried to say the words: *Why have you locked my attic room? Where is the key?* He couldn't. The notion of challenging his mother in such a way was, after all, unthinkable. 'Nothing,' he said. 'Never mind.'

'Must have been something,' she said. 'Sounded like a herd of elephants, crashing down the stairs.'

'No. Nothing. Don't worry. Give Freda and Walter my – regards.'

'Make sure Kevin's in bed by half-past ten.'

'I will.'

The moment the door shut behind her he floundered back up to the attic floor and pushed open the door of the room where Kevin played with his trains. The Hornby train set inherited from their father filled the floor. Crossing the intricate landscape of rails he managed to circumvent the tiny station platform but not the station master, who cracked, then crunched under his clumsy foot.

Kevin bent to retrieve the injured manikin, but George grabbed his arm and dragged him over the crisscrossing lines out on to the landing. *Don't rush, keep calm, don't panic him.* George rattled the handle of the locked attic door. 'Kevin. Did you lock this?'

Kevin smiled uncertainly.

'Kev. Did you lock the door? Kev! Did you hide the key? Where have you put the key, Kev? Tell me. Tell George.'

Kevin shook his head. George mimed pushing the key in the lock and turning it. 'Did – you – lock – it – Kev?'

Kevin shook his head many times, smiling,

puzzled and alarmed. Kevin always told the truth. He lacked the inventiveness for lies.

George gave up. He let go of his arm. 'All right, Kev. All right.'

His mother had locked the door then. A door that had never been locked. And taken away the key. *Why? Why now?* Kevin's attic ran the length of the house from front to back and had a narrow window that overlooked the back gardens. George went to the window, placing his feet with care. Kevin, trailing behind him, picked up the broken bits of station master and looked at them, cradled in the palm of his hand.

'I'll buy you another one, Kev.' George sighed. His eyes idly roamed the gardens, thick with still-of-evening, sweating, summer leaf. Then he saw her.

She seemed to glide on a diagonal shaft of sunlight down the garden of number twenty-nine. She was in a short pale blue frock that revealed the length of her fragile legs. She stood at the bottom of her garden next to the wall of number thirty-one. She looked all around like someone who thought she might be observed. Did she know he was there then? He pulled back to the side of the window where he could not be seen.

Suddenly she was perched on the wall, hair swinging. And then like an angel descending she dropped into the grass next door. She ran lightly behind a row of overgrown shrubs. Now she was at the next wall, looking this way, then that. She was up on to the wall of number thirty-three, flying again, graceful arms wide. She was coming here, to number thirty-five!

He hurled himself across the room, nearly knocking Kevin over, not caring how many station masters he crushed, how many stations, trains, lines, signal boxes, small wooden passengers. Then down both flights of stairs, across the hall, down the dark passage to the kitchen. He dragged open the back door. She was balanced on top of the wall. Their wall.

He stood in the doorway transfixed. Now she would turn her head and look at him. *Now*. It was as though they had silently arranged this, she and he. She must have known all along that he was following her. The day she smiled at him in the street. That wasn't a casual smile to a stranger as she passed. That was a special smile, meant for him, encouraging him. Just as he had seen it in his imaginings. Perhaps she engineered her comings and goings to coincide with him as he did with her.

At that moment she turned to look towards the doorway as though suddenly sensing he was there. Perhaps he had spoken aloud? Instinctively he pulled back into the shadow. What if he should be wrong? What if she were not here because of him? But no. She must have seen him. Her face became radiant with smiles. Just then Kevin squeezed past him out of the doorway and ran down the garden with his odd lurching grace. He stretched up his arms to her. George watched as, laughing, she descended from the wall into Kevin's arms.

The doorbell rang.

George's big face was greased with sweat, his eyes were dazed, almost as though he couldn't see, and he seemed to be short of breath. *Ma was right,* John Bright thought, *he doesn't look well.* 'George?'

George's eyesight seemed slowly restored. 'John?' he said uncertainly. He moved from foot to unhappy foot, like a beached elephant seal. He was clearly reluctant to invite him in.

'I keep telling you I haven't come to arrest you, George!'

The heavy face trembled into an expression of pain intended to be a smile. 'Oh, yes.' George shuffled backwards. 'Yes. I'm sorry. Of course.'

'Where's your ma?' Bright hunched his shoulders and whispered. He looked sideways out of the corner of his eyes, a pastiche of their schoolboy jokes.

Again George had either forgotten or was no longer amused by their schooldays humour. 'She goes to her sister's on Friday nights.'

'Still? Christ. Nothing changes in Norwood. The things we used to get up to on Friday nights, eh, George?'

George gave the painful smile again. They were still standing in the shadowy hall. Bright jingled the change in his pockets and looked up into the yellowish face. The whites of the eyes were viscous, like half-cooked egg-whites, and the lower lip was indented with marks made by George's teeth.

'Are you all right, George?'

'Yes. I'm fine.'

'You can do too much on the old exercise bike at our age, you know.'

'Oh.' George's face pulled together a bit. 'No, I don't go to the gym.'

'I thought all you City types worked out.'

'No. It's just been a – a long week. You know.'

Bright groaned. 'Tell me about it.'

George did not react to this remark, not interested in his old friend's problems or too absorbed in his own. Bright decided to get into the house. His curiosity, not easily aroused these days, was provoked. 'Come on, George, the Ma's out, invite me in. How's the old morning room these days? Mind if I...?' Bright opened the door and peeped round gingerly. 'Hell. Just the same. Know what I used to think? Mourning room. Room for mourning in.'

'Yes.'

'You too?'

'It was where...'

'A-ha. Your dad. Yeah.'

'Yes.'

'The coffin under the stag. Grr.'

'Yes.'

'The bloody stag's still there.'

'Yes. Bloody but unbowed.' George was recovering, it seemed.

'Least the coffin's not.'

'No. Ha.' George looked none too sure, and in the shadowy gloom behind the drawn curtains, Bright felt none too sure himself. He shivered. The room had a chill about it that had never seemed wholly natural. He stepped back into the hall. George carefully closed the door.

'What about the kitchen then – the dwelling of the troglodytes? Still painted dark brown? Like being down a mine.'

'No. Don't.' George's big hand floundered to stop him but Bright had gone, ingested by the shadows down the passage.

'Christ, George. Couldn't you afford to buy your ma a new kitchen?'

'You know Mother. I've offered of course but she didn't want–'

'No, she wouldn't.' Bright felt George arrive at the kitchen window next to him, looking out. He felt a strange tension in the man but the only person in the garden was Kevin, alone, gambolling happily with a large rubber ball, kicking it in the air, running to catch it, kicking it again. Each time the ball flew up, the little next-door dog flew up, yapping on the other side of the wall, and Kevin laughed. It was as though the little dog laughed too. *To see such fun,* Bright thought. Was Kevin the cause of George's unease then? 'How is he these days?' he said.

'The same.'

'Big for his age.'

'Twenty-four.'

'Going on six. He's grown up pretty, too.'

The tremble again of George's fleshy cheek but he didn't speak.

'Too pretty for his own good maybe?' Bright squinted round at George.

George swallowed. 'He's as innocent as– He might as well be a puppy dog himself for all he– Well...'

'No interest in the lady dogs then?' Bright said.

George reared back as from a nasty smell. 'I don't think he even–' he said, and stopped. Even as a kid he'd been prudish about the words. 'He doesn't – I'm sure he's never–'

'Not even humping their ankles yet, you mean?'

George let out a strangled sound, almost a laugh. Bright remembered that noise from their schooldays, up in front of the headmaster, Bright giving cheek generally in a form that defied punishment – in the army they'd call it dumb insolence – George towering at his side, as tall as the headmaster, not saying a word but choking with the excited laughter that Bright could always provoke in him.

'My mother keeps him on a tight rein,' George said.

'Leash.'

'What? Oh. Yes. Ha.'

'He doesn't get much opportunity then? With the lady dogs.'

'He goes to the special school most afternoons. Occupational therapy.'

'Not much humping there.'

'More basket work than – erm – humping, I think.'

Then the shed door opened and the girl came out.

She carried a seed tray filled with little green shoots. Kevin swayed towards her. She came a little way down the garden into a shaft of evening sun and knelt at Kevin's special flower bed. She gave Kevin the trowel and he began with immense concentration to dig little holes, while she separated the seedlings and handed them to him. He gently placed them in their holes and she showed him how to steady them in the earth without damaging their delicate stems.

Bright turned to George, his face stretched

with surprise. 'Very pretty little lady dog,' he said. 'Does your ma know about her? Or does she just come over on Friday nights when your ma goes to her sister's?'

'I– It's the first time I've – I've seen her. I didn't know about– I didn't know she knew Kevin. I don't know if Mother knows.'

'She'd make short shrift, wouldn't she, your ma?'

'I'm sure they're – just friends. After all, she wouldn't be interested in, in a – in Kevin. Would she?'

'Not thinking of trying a spot of humping yourself, are you, George?'

The haughty camel face creased with distaste. Bright had gone too far.

'I'm a vulgar bastard, George. You know me. Who is she then?'

'A – neighbour. I think,' he said stiffly.

They saw the girl lift her head, listening. She stood up and looked in the direction of number twenty-nine. She turned a tender face to Kevin, put out a hand and touched his spiky black hair. They smiled at each other. Then she was up on the wall, the little dog jumping and yapping. She turned to wave at Kevin. Then she flew off into next door's grass to the next wall, the dog dancing along with her, and then to the next and then she was gone.

The two men watched in silence. Light had left the garden with her. The room itself reverted to darkness and Bright felt George's desolation. It chimed with his own. He sighed. 'Listen, George, leave Kevin with my ma tonight. Let's go down the pub.'

'Well, I don't like to do that without telling Mother first.'

'Park him on Ma. He'll be better company than I am for her these days.'

'Well, I'm not sure...'

'Don't demur, George, it's girlish. Doesn't go with your great bulk.'

'Oh!'

Bright gave a short laugh and watched George's face force itself into a sad smile. 'Okay then? Right! Let's get Kevin in.' He went to the garden door, turned and grinned. He was unaware that his smile, like George's, was off-key. 'Just like old times,' he said.

At the corner Polly turned right. This was Lisson Avenue, her lodestar. At number twenty-nine she paused a moment to notice crossly that they hadn't cut the hedge or the grass, and they still haven't fixed the gate. They didn't deserve to have a nice house like this. She hoped it wasn't a sign that this street was going the way of the rest of the neighbourhood. As she stood there she saw a man come out of a house farther down, a man in a leather jacket, small, dark, wiry, light on his feet. He was not her type. But the house was the one with the very distinguished hedge, big thick shiny leaves with spots, and red berries in the winter time.

She looked up at the gleaming windows of the house and loosed her dream. One of her favourites: a man in the upstairs window of a house like this, in a street like this. Day after day he sees her pass, week after week. He is struck by her astonishing loveliness and her air of mystery. Where has she come from, the mystery-woman? Who can she be? He starts to wait for her to go by, unable to think of anything else, obsessed. Extremely rich but also shy, he cannot bring himself to speak to her. One day, however...

At this point Polly's fantasy varied. Sometimes she simply comes face to face with him in a doorway unspecified but elegant, somewhere up West, the Savoy or the Ritz, somewhere the grown-ups go, the famous and the seriously rich; sometimes she turns the corner of his street and there he is! He begs her to reveal her humble address, he sends her a formal invitation, a thick white card embossed with gold: *This is to request the pleasure...* She sees herself slender in her latest Kylie dress, her hand resting lightly in his, chandeliers twinkling...

And then, approaching number thirty-five, she saw, she was sure of it, a real man standing in the upstairs window watching her. This clatter of reality against her fantasy gave her such a fright that she walked on,

83

fast. As she passed the spotty-leaved hedge she felt rather than saw the small wiry man lurking up the path. She didn't turn to look.

George, changing upstairs to go out, saw the little blonde girl looking up at him. It was the girl from number twenty-nine! But something was different surely. She'd changed her clothes perhaps? But could she have done that so quickly? The moment he saw her she turned her face away and walked on, coming this way.

He hurtled out of the room yelling for Kevin, so intent on her that he was astonished to see down in the hall an oblong of sunlight from the open front door and John Bright and Kevin framed in laurels on the path, waiting for him. The girl passed through the light behind them. A fist gripped his windpipe and joy pinned him for a moment halfway down the stairs.

'Come on, George, get a move on.'

Big feet flapping, George went on down.

7

At the corner she half turned her head. What if it were he, her dream lover, following? She caught a glimpse of three strangely assorted silhouettes. None of them at a glance resembled the man of her dreams in his beautifully tailored clothes. She glided down towards the High Street, past the Stanley Halls, dismissing them.

She was perhaps fifty yards ahead, the girl from number twenty-nine. Her hair looked different, smoother, shinier, a greener shade of gold. It must be a trick of the evening light. And surely she had increased, if possible, in grace. The effect of the horizontal sunset light was to lift her off the ground so that she moved on air, a bird gliding, effortless, free.

'George, I know a pint of ale is an attractive proposition but it's not the holy bloody grail. Could you slow down a bit?'

'Oh. Yes.' He waited for Kevin and Bright to catch up. Kevin had not noticed her. But Kevin saw nothing that wasn't under his nose. Even now he was patting a cat on a wall, holding on to Bright's sleeve with his other hand. They didn't know the urgency. She mustn't get away. He had to be close to her. See where she went at least.

The girl turned the corner at the end of the street. The temptation to leave Kevin and Bright and race after her was almost irresistible. But they mustn't see how he felt. They mustn't know. He had to be patient. He had to plan. After all, there would be other chances surely. She lived only three doors away. Telling himself this did not diminish his sense of urgency, of panic almost. The sight of her had become a necessity to him.

When they reached the corner she was still in sight. Just. She stood down at the High Street waiting to cross. Where could she be going? What business could she have over there? Mean little grubby streets of red-brick back-to-backs, litter, dog-dirt and smells. She surely couldn't be going to the pub? A girl like her? An innocent child? She needed protection. She needed him.

'Where you going, George! You forgotten where my ma lives?'

George turned his big bewildered face. 'Paper!' he said.

'Eh?'

'*Standard*. I didn't get the *Evening Standard* tonight, I'll just–'

'Later, George. On the way to the pub. You trying to get out of saying hello to my ma?'

'Oh no, John, I didn't mean– No, of

course not.'

'Restrain your appetites, George.'

'Oh. Ha. Yes. You're right.'

She was crossing the High Street. He couldn't bear to watch her walk away from him. He actually closed his eyes. He was alone in the dark, all hope of comfort gone. They crossed the road to the corner of the cul-de-sac where Lily Bright lived. He stole a last look. The shadow of the railway bridge swallowed his Persephone, sucking her into the dark. He almost cried out, was aware in fact of uttering a strangled noise. He put a fist to his mouth and converted the noise to a cough.

At the High Street she half turned her head as though looking out for traffic. The three odd silhouettes had stopped, they were coming no further. Good. She could concentrate again on her dream man. Some nights he was more vivid than others. He was close tonight, yes, about thirty paces behind. She entered under the darkness of the bridge and smiled. Then she felt a little thrill of fear. They were real footsteps behind her now. Surely they were?

Polly could deal with anything. After all, she'd been dealing with Jack for most of her life. She despised victims. But she did walk a little faster under the railway bridge, no sense in asking for it, was there? She

87

emerged and saw there were enough people draped over the terrace of the pub to come to her aid if necessary. The Friday night crowd on the terrace was even louder now, all haloed in dazzling golden light. She wrinkled her little nose at the smell of booze and the raucous noise. The crumbling shop fronts opposite, the peeling lock-up doors, the mounds of litter also offended her.

At the corner of Brockhurst Road she glanced back at the bridge. A man was coming out from the dark arch. A real man, nothing like her fantasy. His long black shadow stopped as she glanced. That proved he was following her, though she couldn't risk a look long enough to see who he was. She was almost safe home anyway now. She didn't care.

Lily watched them turn in at the gate. George huge, his pompous body wrapped in a pompous suit, planting his feet as though they didn't belong to him. And Kevin, just under five foot six, dark hair, doggy brown eyes, juicy red mouth, lithe body, all flexible uncontrolled grace. A beauty he'd become, holding on to George's hand. She had an impossible desire to laugh at the sight of them. But John's face warned her. No.

'A long time since you came to see me, George Fletcher,' she said.

His discomfiture was immense, like himself. He coughed into his fist. 'Oh, I'm sorry, Mrs Bright. I'm very busy these days.'

She wheeled herself across to him. 'I'm only joking,' she said. 'How are you, George?'

He bent at the waist with great concern and took her hand. 'How are you, Mrs Bright?'

'Oh, call me Lily. After all you're almost grown up now. Either that or I've shrunk.'

'Oh, no.' George, drenched in embarrassment, not knowing how to react to this reference to her chair-bound status. 'Oh,' he said. 'Ha. No. You look well, er – Lily. Very well.'

There was something wrong with the man, certainly. John would find out what. 'You get off now, you boys,' she said. 'You don't want to be stuck here nattering to a boring old cow like me.' She stretched out a hand and pulled Kevin to her. 'We'll be just fine. Won't we, Kevin, my love? Now you sit here by Lily.'

Kevin took the hand like a gift and sat close to her, smiling into her face.

George stuttered thanks.

John said, 'Okay, George, that's enough.'

Lily laughed and Kevin laughed with her. Laughter was what Kevin loved best.

She was safe again now, out in the light. The black shadow was forgotten. Dismissed from her mind. Replaced there by her rich admirer who kept his distance, worshipping from afar. She dawdled a little on the step of number sixteen, tempted to throw him a smile over her shoulder before she went in. She turned her head. Jack was jerking like a great black crow towards her along the street. Pink with fury she banged the door behind her in his face.

Chloe lounged on a cushion in the big bright living room smoking a spliff. She watched Polly move about the room. So light. 'Thistledown,' she said. 'You should have been the dancer, Poll, not me.'

Polly never bothered to reply to her mother when she was smoking dope. What was the point? She listened to Jack outside fumbling with his key. She heard him come in.

Chloe heard nothing. 'I should have made sure you got proper lessons.' Her voice wafted with the smoke. 'But Jack seemed to take up all my time somehow. He was so demanding, Poll. Always saying he was an artist and all that, and needed my support.'

Polly listened to Jack breathing outside the room. She heard him decide not to come in. But he didn't go away.

'And there was never any money, him never being able to hang on to a job. They don't give money for singing lessons for your kids on the SS! God, I wish I'd got rid of him years ago, he's brought me nothing but misery. Even now, look at him. I suppose he's running around after some girl again. I've never seen him as bad as this, have you? Even when... It wouldn't surprise me if he cut his wrists. I don't know that I'd bother to save him if he did.' Chloe laughed.

Polly smiled. She felt rather than heard a movement outside the door. He'd gone. Down the passage to the kitchen. She flew out of the room and up the stairs.

'Wow,' Chloe said. 'That's beautiful. Look at that. D'you see how beautiful that is?' She was looking at the green eye of a peacock feather in a dusty vase. Chloe was, as usual this time of evening, stoned.

'Now, Kevin my lad, you pass that nice big picture book over here to me.'

Kevin lifted not the bird book she'd asked for but a book of garden plants.

'That's a weighty tome,' she said.

He grinned at her for all the world as if he understood. She held out her hands for it. But he refused to give it up. He kept it on his lap, leafing through it furiously. She tried to point something out to him. He stopped her hand in a surprisingly strong grip. He found what he was looking for, turned the book towards her and, spluttering one of his nonsense words, pointed at the picture he had hunted out for her. She looked at the picture. Then looked at him. Then looked at the picture again. Kevin nodded and laughed.

She searched his face. 'Yes, Kevin,' she said slowly. 'Lilies. Yes, they're lilies. Yes, Lily is my name.'

He was all smile. 'Ghlee-ghlee,' he said.

Lily was the word he had been trying to say. 'Lily! Yes, that's right!' She touched his glittering dark head. 'You're maybe not as daft as they think. Are you, Kevin my lad?'

The writhing smoke seemed held aloft by the continuous chik-a-chik-boom of the beat. 'Makes a change,' George said.

'Change? You can keep it, mate.'

George let out the strangled hoot that Bright remembered as his laugh. He seemed oddly excited now. The pub must hold some hidden delight for him. His big head kept turning, slow eyes swivelling.

'Looking for someone, George?'

'Eh? Oh. No. Haven't been in here before, that's all. Well, not for years.'

'A-ha. Full of plain-clothes coppers.'

'What?'

'Closest hostelry to HQ. Well, to the old HQ. They moved to the new station in Oliver Gardens in 1989 but police habits die hard. They're all still hanging out in here.'

'Oh, yes. Old haunts for you, John.'

'Haunts is right. Still, no one I know, far as I can see.'

'Noisy!' George raised his voice.

'Fancy the terrace? Only traffic noise to

contend with out there.'

George was like an ocean-going liner full-speeding ahead. He couldn't get out there fast enough. Then his eyes were going again, sidling over the people on the terrace, then up and down the street.

'Sure you weren't expecting to meet someone here, George?'

'No. No. It's just– You know. There might be someone you know.' George buried his face in his beer. He wondered where she was now. Not out here on the terrace anyway. Not inside the pub either. But where? With whom? *Don't let anyone be touching her.* He shut his eyes and swayed a little. *Touch…*

'All right, George?'

'Matter of fact, I'm thinking of moving back here.' George gasped. Head up, nostrils wide, he seemed to have given himself a shock. 'I want to – keep an eye on things here.'

'I bet you do.'

George knew Bright meant the girl. His mouth went into its expression of lemon-sucking distaste.

'Sorry, George. Forget I said that. Take no notice of me, mate, I'm off my stroke these days.' Bright changed his tone. 'What about your place in the City? What'll you do with that if you come back here?'

'I'll sell it. Flat near Finsbury Circus. It's worth a small fortune now.'

'Wouldn't that cramp your style a bit? Not having your own place?'

'Style?' George expressed blank disbelief at the coupling of himself with the notion of style. Bright grinned. 'You heard about Marje?' George said.

'Not lately. You mean she's surfaced again?' Perhaps this was the problem gnawing at George's entrails. It would explain a lot.

'Surfaced again?' This question foxed George completely. He pondered. Then he said, 'No! No, no! Not Marje. No! I meant – you know – at the time.'

'What, all those years ago? Well, I heard she'd – gone. No details, you know.'

'Yes. She went. A man who frequented this pub actually. I didn't know him well. Only by sight. She married him eventually. Well, I suppose it was him.' George spoke with sad dignity: 'There hasn't been much style to cramp since then.'

'Not in fifteen years, George?'

George buried his face in his pint glass.

'I see. Don't have much luck with women, do we, George?' As he spoke Bright felt a wounding stab of grief for Jude so sharp it took his breath away. He drained his scotch. 'Have another,' he said before George could question him on this subject too sore to speak of.

He needn't have worried. George slowly downed the last of his pint without replying and when Bright said, 'George?' he seemed to come back from somewhere far off. 'I've got to go now,' he said. 'Mother. Kevin. It's late.' He was already on his feet. There was nothing to do but follow him.

Off the terrace it was only midsummer dark: street lights, headlamps, the orange London sky. Then the black shade of the railway bridge. Where was she? He'd seen her go under the bridge to the other side of the tracks. Had she returned to her own side while they were in the pub? Was she back in Lisson Avenue now, preparing for bed, only three doors away from his mother's house? He had to get back, it was the only place he could watch for her.

'George, what do you think your ma's going to do to you? Give you a good hiding? Report you to the headmaster for bringing Kevin back three minutes late? Relax, mate, eh?'

George stopped in his tracks in the middle of the High Street zebra crossing. 'I'm going to take some time off work!' he said. 'See how it feels to be back here full time. A sort of experiment.'

'George? Meet George.'

The large man and the tabby cat stared at each other. The cat looked away first, ambling back to Kevin and clambering into his lap.

'Guess where George is going for his holidays, Ma. South Norwood.'

'Well, your mother will be pleased, George. To have you home for a bit.'

'Mother?' George blinked. 'Well, yes.'

Bright gave his mother a squinting glance which she encountered deadpan. 'Had a good time, Kev?' he said.

'We've had a grand time, haven't we, Kevin?'

'Ghlee-ghlee,' Kevin said.

'That's Lily,' said Lily, proud. 'He's saying my name.'

'No.' George shook his head with authority.

'Yes! I promise you.'

'Say Lily, Kevin,' said Bright.

'Ghlee-ghlee,' Kevin said and touched Lily's face.

Her eyes filled up. 'Oh, I'm a silly old cow,' she said.

George moved from foot to foot, unwilling to argue, unable to agree.

'George, will you sit down?' she said. 'You're making me nervous.'

'Er – actually, Mrs Bright – Lily – we have to go. Mother will be – worried, you know.'

'Ah well. You come back to see me soon, Kevin. We'll look at some more pictures. And have a proper talk.'

Kevin kissed her and then the cat. The human George, dignified, held out his hand.

Kevin took hold of it. The strange pair went out into the night.

'That's a dangerous wee man.'

'Kevin? How come?'

'He's young, he's strong, he's beautiful, he's full of love he doesn't know what to do with.'

'And he's frustrated as hell.'

'Aye.'

'As usual, Ma, you're right.'

'And he's not quite such a wee silly as they think he is.'

A jogger passed them like a shadow in the hot dark street. *I must buy some of those trainer things,* George thought. *You can move so silently in them.* Then, *What am I thinking of?* A woman was walking towards them. She passed under a street lamp and something jolted inside his chest. It was she, it was his girl. When the woman got closer she called out, 'Hello, Kevin,' and Kevin ran to her.

George's feet seemed to stick fast to the pavement as if it were mud. But when he caught up with Kevin he saw that the woman was not his girl. She was like his girl, she had blonde hair, she was small. But her body was a little thicker, and she looked stronger. She was like his girl but older, that was it. She was nodding to him. He must have been staring. 'Good evening,' she said.

He cleared his throat to speak but she had

walked on.

Jack went straight through the house to the kitchen. He wrenched open the back door and made for the woodpile in the corner of the tiny yard. He picked up the axe. He strode back through the house to the front door. He stopped. He leaned his forehead on the cool stained glass. The axe hung heavy in his hand. His breath came in dry sobs.

Upstairs Polly had wedged the chair against her door. She was dressed in her slit-side pale pink satin dress and high-heeled skinny-strap shoes, in front of the plastic-framed mirror. She writhed and sang, *sotto voce*, to her ex-lover: she was over him, she would make it through, and she hoped he'd never forget it. One arm gracefully floated. In the other hand she held a hair brush in place of a microphone. But she listened.

Chloe lay flat on her back on the cushions. Every detail of the ceiling was becoming sharp to her. She found herself pierced by the beauty and significance of her cracked ceiling as never before.

Jack prowled out again into the yard. He started to chop the wood. Savagely. Wood chips flew everywhere.

Polly watched from her window. She shuddered. Her mouth made a little twitch of distaste.

Jack threw the axe down. He waded to the

98

back door ankle deep in jagged bits of wood. In the kitchen he drank some scotch. He splashed water on his hands and face. He drank more scotch. His hands shook.

Polly heard the front door slam as Jack left the house. She said to her beautiful reflection, 'I wish he was dead,' and resumed her graceful pose.

'Taking him out and leaving him with God knows who! And there's beer on your breath. It's a wonder you didn't take him into the pub. You've got no sense of responsibility at all. Especially when you're with that John Bright.'

'He's a very distinguished member of the police force now, Mother. He's just had special condemnations–' George was not used to drinking two pints in an evening. He corrected himself: '–commendations. He is a detective inspector. In the CID.'

'People like him don't change.'

'Mother, I have some work to do.'

'Oh, you have work to do, have you? And I'll have my work cut out getting your brother back to normal again. He's over-excited. It'll take him days to calm down. It's all right for you. You come and you go. You don't know what it's like here day after day. And you don't care. Why should you? Go on then if you're going. Go and get on with your oh so important work.'

'Mother–'

'Oh, get on with you.'

He stood at the window of his room. Nobody passed in the street, until, quite late, he saw the woman who had said Good evening. The street lamp shone upon her. The resemblance to his girl was quite marked, he hadn't imagined it. She walked briskly past the house and went into number twenty-nine. Was she the girl's mother then? She must be. Had she been out looking for her? Was his girl lost? The woman hadn't seemed worried, but he knew from experience that feelings don't always show in the face. He stood in the dark behind the net curtains till 3 a.m. and still his girl didn't come back.

He got into bed with care. He didn't want his mother to wake. 'I was working on some accounts till late.' *What am I coming to? Preparing a story for my mother like a small boy.* He was too excited to sleep, kept sitting up and whispering to himself. He had to know where the girl had gone. He could not bear the not-knowing. Out of his sight she could be anywhere. Aware of the absurdity of his position, he yet felt a need to be where she was. But to achieve that he would have to follow her everywhere she went. *I need more time, weekends aren't enough. Between Monday and Friday anything could happen to her. It's right, what I said to John. I must take some time off work.*

George seldom took holidays and even in his heightened state he could see that, as John Bright had pointed out, South Norwood was an unlikely place for a vacation. But he was undeterred. *I'll take three weeks. I'll take four. But what about Mother?* He put his head in his hands. Mother was the problem. She had feelers like an octopus that could reach into the dark corners of your mind and seize your thoughts, pull them into the open and squeeze them till they shrieked. *Mother must not be around. But Mother always is around.* Then George had a marvellous idea.

8

'What would I want with a holiday?' His mother banged the pastry with the rolling pin. 'I wouldn't know what to do with myself.'

'You could go on a tour perhaps. I believe there are such things, where there are lots of activities and sights to see. They have guides, I think and–'

'A coach tour for old age pensioners! You won't get me on one of those.'

'Some sunshine would be nice perhaps?'

She looked at the window. Even over their north-facing garden the sky was an even

Mediterranean blue, as it had been for weeks. George creased his forehead. This had all seemed easier at three o'clock in the morning.

'Anyway, what about Kevin?' she said. She picked up the pastry with one hand, turned it over and slapped it down. 'He can't look after himself, can he?'

'Well, I've been thinking... I thought perhaps I could take some time off while you were away. That is, if... And look after Kevin myself.'

His mother looked incredulous. George felt his face redden as he said, 'It's a while since I spent time with him.'

'You can say that again.' She gave one of her snapped-off humourless laughs.

George though intimidated remained dogged: 'I'd like to spend some time with him. I'll take care of him all right.'

'Oh, yes? Like you did last night, you mean?'

'He was safe with Lily Bright.'

'Oh, *that's* what he's been on about all morning.' She continued her vigorous banging of the pastry. George had often wondered how it came out so tough, so leathery. Perhaps you weren't meant to bang it so hard?

'You could leave lists,' he said.

'They'd have to be as long as the Bible.'

'Well, you could give me instructions...?'

'No.' She made a last assault on the pastry.

'Holidays are a waste of time.' She pushed past him to get a dish from the cupboard. He moved his chair just after the cupboard door hit his head.

'Sorry,' he said. 'I'm in your way.'

She banged the cupboard door. 'Give me that knife,' she said. She thrust the pastry into the dish, pressing it hard all round. She cut the edge expertly, turning the dish on one hand.

'I like the way you do that,' George heard himself say.

She gave him an astounded look: 'What?'

'You do it – skilfully.'

She gave another short yap. 'So I should. I've had enough practice.' She piled chopped beef and kidneys into the pastry.

'Well, don't you think it's time you had a break?' George had never used such cunning in a conversation. Compared with his mother, tax inspectors were butter in the mouth. She was putting the top on the pie, signing it with her thumb print round the edge. She brushed her forehead with the back of a floury hand. It was one of her few graceful gestures. George was touched by the smear of flour on her forehead of which she was unaware. It gave her a vulnerable look. And that gave George the courage to persevere: 'Don't you think it would be nice to have a bit of a rest? I know how hard it is with Kevin and – and the house and – and me. You deserve–'

'Deserve! If we all got what we deserved in this life–'

'Yes but–'

'I don't know, George.' She slapped milk over the surface of the pie with an old stiffened pastry brush. 'Now stop bothering me while I get the lunch. It's time the grass was cut anyhow.'

George stood up. She was not a small woman but he towered over her. He had pushed the conversation as far as he could. He plodded outside to do the same with the old-fashioned lawn mower.

As he heaved it up and down the garden his brain scooted about in wild directions. George had always been a patient man. But George was no longer George, the matter was urgent and the new George couldn't wait, his plan somehow had to work. He pushed the rattling blunt machine, and he thought. And as he thought he kept an eye on the house three doors down.

He scanned its windows for signs of life. Nothing. Just the blank windows of the house where she lived. And he suddenly knew she had come back last night before himself and Kevin. She was there. He could feel her presence. She might even now be peeping out at him from behind a curtain. He stopped mowing, all his muscles softened with joy. And just then, a man came out of the back door of number twenty-nine.

George in his surprise couldn't move and was caught staring. The man, not much older than George but with thick greying hair, stopped and looked at him. 'Morning,' he called.

This was the man she had run to under the clock, the first time George had ever seen her! The man she had given the present to. The man she had kissed. The man around whose neck she had wound her lovely arms. Surely this was he.

'Oh. Yes. Good morning,' George said.

'You must be George,' said the man.

'Sorry? Er, yes. That's right.'

'Heard a lot about you.'

'O-oh?' George blushed.

'Your mum and my wife. Belong to the WI.'

'Oh. Yes. I see.'

'We babysit Kevin sometimes. My daughter and I. While they're out.'

So Kevin had been inside that house. With her. That was how they had got to know each other. His daughter... 'It's very – kind of you.'

'Not a bit. It's a pleasure. Nice lad, isn't he? No trouble at all.' The man grinned. He had a wide mouth, humorous dark blue eyes. He held aloft the bucket he had brought out of the house. 'Compost,' he said.

'I'm sorry?'

'Doing my bit for conservation. Ecology seems to have given up on me though. Never had a successful heap yet. Bloody thing never gets hot, the way it's meant to. Just turns to wet smelly gunge. I should give up on it, I suppose. I can't stand waste, though, that's the thing. Idiotic really.'

'Oh. Yes.' George, not at the best of times even a passable conversationalist, was now stupefied by shock and guilt.

'I'm Chris, by the way, Chris Hicks,' said the man.

'Ah. Yes. I'm – pleased to meet you.'

'Well, I'd better go and empty this.' The man waved the bucket and went on down the garden.

Weak with relief and hot with the desire not to be seen, George, for appearance's sake, took off the grass box and went down on his knees. *He's her father. This chap with the dashing manner. Her father. He's only my age. He knows Kevin, he knows my mother. So* must *she. Her name is – what was it? Hicks. I don't want her to have a name. Or a father. This father.* George got to his feet again, clutching the overflowing grass box to his chest.

The man was coming back, swinging the empty bucket. 'What a sky!' he said.

'Yes,' said George.

'Seems silly to go abroad when it's like this.'

'Just what my mother says!' George's

desperation gave him speech. 'I've been trying to persuade her to take a holiday, I've said I'll look after Kevin but she won't hear of it.'

'Pretty hard to shift, I imagine, your mum. If she's made her mind up.' The man crinkled at George.

George managed to smile back. 'Yes. I was thinking some kind of tour arrangement would be nice. She thinks they're for OAPs.'

'Not at all. We're going on one quite soon.'

'Are you?'

'Yes. Some of the more interesting bits of Spain. Sounds very good. I'll let you have the brochure if you like.'

'But you wouldn't want to go on holiday with– Well, holidays are to get away from the neighbours, isn't that the idea?'

'I hardly know your mum, but she and my wife get on all right. And there'll be thirty-odd people on the coach. She'd have other people to talk to.'

'Still...'

'I'll drop the brochure in anyhow.'

'Thanks. Good of you. She needs a break. I'd like to persuade her if I can.'

'P'raps my wife could have a word. She's a persuasive woman, Ros.' He crinkled his eyes again.

'That would be– Thank you– Most kind.'

'Not at all.' The man waved a hand– 'See you, George' – and was gone.

George found himself still hugging the grass box. He went down the garden to empty it.

In the cool corner next to the shed he got his breath. Why was life playing into his hands in this way? It was almost frightening. But it was exhilarating, like betting a thousand pounds on a horse at a hundred to one. Come to think of it, he had never done that, he didn't know how it felt, he was not a betting man. But it must feel something like this. Not knowing if you would win or lose. Letting go all caution, all the normal restraints. Cutting loose.

Coming back with the empty grass box he thought he saw a movement at the attic window. The back attic. His attic. The room of his dreams. In his mind the girl was always there, tied on the striped mattress, waiting for him. *Somehow she has come untied, she has got loose, she might escape!* But the room was locked, he remembered. Of course: his mother was in there. *She has found the girl. She knows my secret. That's why she locked the room.* He knew his thoughts were crazy. But he had really seen a movement up there. Someone was in that room.

He dropped the box and flapped indoors. He saw no sign of his mother downstairs or on the first floor. He climbed the top flight. The door of his attic was shut. Was his mother in there now? Kevin was in the other room playing with his trains. *Don't rush, don't panic, calm down.* 'Hello, Kev.'

'Gho Ghoghe.' Kevin smiled the big smile with which he always welcomed George.

'Trains going well?' While he chatted to Kevin he cautiously tried the handle but the door wouldn't budge. He knew he had seen a movement at the window; his mind couldn't have strayed so far as to imagine it. Perhaps the door wasn't locked as he had thought the other day; perhaps it was simply stuck? He rattled and pushed. It was locked, no question. 'Has Mother been up here, Kev?'

Kevin smiled. He waved a smart new engine at George.

'Yes, nice green train.' George opened the door of the third attic room. The junk room. He leaned in the doorway. All the furniture from the room his father had died in. His mother had changed everything in their bedroom after he had gone. An ornate walnut wardrobe and matching bed stood in the darkest corner. Candlewick spilled pinkly over commodes and mahogany chests of drawers. He squeezed through the lumpy landscape and dancing particles of dust to the small window that like his bedroom below looked on to the street.

Head and chest pounding, he saw the man he now knew as Chris Hicks come out of number twenty-nine followed by, he presumed, the wife. Yes, the woman he had seen last night under the lamp. What had he called her? Ros? They walked away, chatting. The wife carried two empty plastic carrier bags. Carrier bags. Of course. The supermarket. Did she work there on Saturdays, his girl? Their daughter. The supermarket opened at eight o'clock, he'd checked.

He looked at his watch. A quarter past nine. The Hickses turned the corner, laughing. If she worked today she would be there already. But what if she hadn't come home last night after all, was still somewhere on the other side of the tracks, in some grubby narrow house, setting off from there, frowzy and late, to go to work? The locked attic forgotten, he pounded down the stairs and out into the street.

9

He found himself almost running past the Stanley Halls, making for the High Street, which he crossed to the screeching of brakes. Now he was under the railway bridge, a train hurtling over his head. At the corner of Brockhurst Road, at last he stopped. He was breathing hard. *This is stupid. She could be anywhere. And it's daylight. Morning. Anyone could see me. I must go. I'll go to the supermarket. Why on earth didn't I just go straight there? Because I had some crazy idea that I'd find out where she spent the night!* He gave a laugh that was almost a sob and looked at his watch again. It was nearly half-past nine.

They were not early risers in Brockhurst Road. Saturday mornings were for sleeping in. A few houses down, a front door opened. What if she came out? What was he to do? Where on earth on this bleak bare street could anyone hide? An Indian man came out of the mean little house wearing a long dress-like garment in grey-checked cotton, with a suit jacket over it. He passed George. He said Good morning.

'Oh,' said George. 'Good morning. Yes.'

The man gave him a smile as innocent as Kevin's. Its purity made George feel dirty. *I've got to go,* he thought. *I've got to go home at once. Stop this foolishness.* He hovered. He turned. He started to follow the Indian man towards the main road. But at the corner he couldn't resist, and turned for one last look. She was there. His girl. She must have come out of one of the houses in this very road. She was floating along the grubby pavement away from him.

Was anyone watching him? He mustn't be seen following her. He meant her no harm, but it would look bad. He sneaked a glance

111

behind him. No, the Indian man had met a friend. They were deep in talk. And he was wasting time. She was almost at the end of the street. Escaping him. He flopped and flapped in his haste.

He longed to be closer; not to touch; just to feel – connected. But he kept his distance. Curiously happy, both elated and, just at being near to her, oddly at peace, George stalked his prey. He still had on the old plimsolls he had worn for cutting the grass. George the hunter, walking soft, skirting obstacles, silent, invisible, keeping the game in his sights.

They were approaching the station from a direction unfamiliar to George. The other side of the railway. Of course! The tunnel under the station leading to Station Road where the supermarket was. Nearer the station an Asian family came out of a house, then more people from a street on the left. They came between him and her. But George was glad. They were cover for him.

Strolling just ahead of him the Asian family talked softly. A pretty little girl clung to her father's hand, chattering. The mother carried a smaller child who gazed solemnly at George over her shoulder. In this guileless gaze George again felt soiled and wondered what he was doing on an innocent sunny Saturday morning following a girl he had never met, stalking her like prey. But over

112

the family's heads he could see her gliding along, and he couldn't stop.

She turned right, into the tunnel. It was dark in there and footsteps were loud. George's heavy flapping footsteps even in his plimsolls would surely frighten her, echoing in that long straight damp place that after the sunlight seemed total dark. The darkness alarmed the little Asian girl. 'Oh, my God!' she gasped. And her father said fondly, 'Hey, let's leave God out of this.'

They were coming up into the light. George glimpsed the shining blonde head which suddenly disappeared, blanked out by brightness. Cautiously he slowed and lingered on the ramp that brought the tunnel up to ground level in Station Road, the iron railings above his head. He meant to wait until she had settled into her place at the supermarket check-out, then he'd go in and buy something. Some milk. No. Some chocolates for his mother. George had come a long way in deception.

But he found he couldn't bear the delay. The moment she disappeared from his sight it was as though his connection with the world was severed, he started to grieve, he had to see her again. He came out into the light. She was not to be seen, she was gone. He stood at the top of the ramp, blinking in the sunny square. He'd delayed too long perhaps? She'd already gone into the shop?

There was a back entrance for the staff, wasn't there? Off the little street that led to the park. He crossed over to see. And there she was!

She shimmered along in the sun, not looking to right or left. There was a back door to the supermarket and a car park, yes. But she didn't go that way. She wasn't going to work? Where then? Where now? He kept well behind her. He seldom looked in her direction. On the contrary he became absorbed in gardens, plants, gnomic statuary, even babies in passing prams. She flicked in and out of his vision like a migraine speck. But he saw her go into the park.

She didn't take the path alongside the railway line, she took the right fork towards the Church of the Holy Innocents and Kevin's school. This path narrowed and darkened between two high walls. Large trees edged it but there was nowhere to hide and he mustn't lose sight of her now. His feet flopped hurriedly, almost mowing down a small boy on a skateboard who skirted George with rugby-winger skill. George hadn't even seen the boy. But suddenly his feet were rolling from under him. He flung out his arms. His hands grabbed empty air. He was on the ground, winded. As he fell he saw the girl turn left into the main road. Then his face was in gravel.

'Sorry, mister.' The small boy's face

loomed at George, frightened. He grabbed his skateboard, hovered a moment, then ran. George got to his knees. People stared. A woman came over to offer help. He waved her off, floundered to his feet, then broke into his awkward knock-kneed run.

He came out into the road. To his right the High Street was filling with Saturday shoppers. She hadn't gone that way. To his left the road became a fast traffic run between substantial houses and the school for the handicapped where Kevin still went most afternoons. She wasn't to be seen. He'd lost her! She'd gone!

George stood helpless. His hands shook, his knees felt weak, he touched his face where it was sore. The knees of his trousers were dirtied and scratched. He began to feel conspicuous. People might be watching from the windows of his brother's school. Or from the houses. The girl might be watching him: 'See that big ugly guy? He's been following me. Call the police, quick before he goes.' George moved off.

Bulging chest, head held back, streaks of dirt down one side of his face, he held his arms stiffly at his sides. He looked neither left nor right. Though he felt watched he stared straight ahead and made himself walk on, away from the High Street, past the school, following the curve of the road. He knew he ought to go home and clean himself up. But it was possible the girl was still somewhere ahead of him. He had to know.

Round the bend beyond the school the road became quieter. George studied each house for signs of his girl. He saw only suburban gardens exhibiting their owners' eccentricities. In one garden a longboat was tethered, stretching all the way from the house to the street, though there was no canal for miles. A stocky 1930s semi was embellished with Doric columns and, George counted, sixteen stone lions. But roses abounded. Even in the cool of morning before the heat had built up they drowned George in scent, and despite his battered state, in dreams.

The road had been steadily climbing as it curved, and he found the little recreation ground laid out below him. A narrow path descended between bushes. He found himself out of breath as he carefully negotiated the steep downward slope. He wasn't used to so much exercise. He felt curiously exhilarated. Perhaps his strange – hobby – would do him good? *All this – adventure – can't be bad for me.* George the lean keen hunter. He almost laughed.

Hanging on to the bushes with his sore hands to stop himself sliding, he noticed on the sloping grass next to the iron railings, a tiny copse, just a few firs, and an elder thick with flower and leaf. At the bottom of the slope stood a few swings and slides, a climbing frame. A train rushed by on the other side of the railings coming into the Junction. The noise was sudden, earsplitting but short. The little park returned to its sunny morning peace.

George was suddenly impressed with the barrenness of the place. An 'Open Space' it would be called in planning jargon and indeed that was all it was. Flat, green, bare. The fenced-off land bordering the railway was more attractive: lush, rich with hilly disorder, long wild grass. At least you could hide there. *Hide? Why am I thinking about hiding? I've done nothing wrong.* He started to sweat. He was doing wrong. He knew it.

In three minutes he was out between the gateposts, then turning into Station Road. Passing the supermarket, he gave it only a casual glance, she'd gone in the opposite direction, she wouldn't be there. Then he looked again. He peered into the shadowy interior.

Dressed in her overall, blonde hair covered by a white cap, she smiled at a woman in the checkout queue. Obscured though this woman was by reflections and special-offer posters, he'd know his mother anywhere. And Kevin leaned on his mother's trolley gazing at the girl.

Families coming out with loaded trolleys jostled George. He moved away, he knew not where. His face felt naked, an X-ray picture in which all his insides were exposed.

The girl had seen him, that was it. She had gone the long way round through the park to lead him a dance, to shake him off. She thought he was a joke. She and her friends laughing behind their hands. Marje had laughed. Marje and the man. They had laughed. The girl knew him, knew he had followed her. She was telling his mother. At this moment she was telling his mother. His breath came hard. Not from exertion; from fear and from shame.

'Hello, George.'

10

John Bright came over from the paper shop with the *Independent,* a loaf and a carton of milk. They met in the middle of the street. 'You all right, George?'

George was incapable of response. Why was John Bright always there to witness his most grotesque moments? *Damn him, is he spying on me?*

'You look a bit the worse for wear. We didn't have that much to drink last night, did we?'

George Fletcher, City accountant, grazed

knees, scraped face, panting, helpless. It was absurd, of course. He looked at his hands. The palms were red and swollen, little bits of soil and gravel gathered in specks of blood going black. 'Yes,' he said. 'Yes, I – I am a bit of a mess, I suppose.'

Bright examined his face. 'Been in a punch-up, George?'

'A bit of a fall actually. Kids. Damn skateboard thing. You know.' He let out an odd laugh. He felt mad, cracking; he saw cracks running all over the pink walnut coils of his brain. He wanted his bright empty attic room. It was locked against him. His mother had locked it. He wanted to lie down, close his eyes, breathe the dusty air. He needed to slow down his rushing heart. 'Better get back,' he said. 'Get myself cleaned up before–' He looked behind. His mother and Kevin had not yet emerged. 'Get myself cleaned up,' he said.

'A-ha.' Bright was looking at him in that way he had, his face a mask behind which anything could lurk – concern, amusement, suspicion, perhaps all three. George needed to get away. He moved off but Bright moved with him.

Across the road Bright said, 'Well. If you're going to spend some time at your ma's now, George, be nice to have another jar or two now and then.'

'I'm not!' George said. 'I'm not. I've

changed my mind. Too much work. Pressure. Of work. I can't.'

'That right? A-ha. Oh, well.' Again Bright's eyes sparked at him in that disturbing way. 'Okay, George.'

'I've got to go now, John.'

'See you round then, George. Go careful, mate.'

The large man lurched off up Oliver Gardens towards Lisson Avenue. Bright watched him, indeed curious, concerned and suspicious. For a moment he thought he might go after his old friend. But then he heard Jude say, *You suspect everybody, you see suspects everywhere*. He shrugged. He turned away, put the newspaper under his arm and slouched off down the High Street back towards his mother's house.

George looked in the bathroom mirror. He groaned. Had his mother seen him pass the supermarket with this shocked, naked, dirt-striped face? At this moment, was the girl handling his mother's purchases, giving her her change, talking about him? And then to bump into John Bright. Of all people. A policeman. A detective inspector for heaven's sake. A man who saw through him like glass.

'Mother,' he said to the mirror. 'Mother, I'm sorry. I made a mistake. I can't afford to take time off work after all. I shan't even have time to come home for weekends. For

120

a while. I have to spend all my weekends in town. Working. I'm going to be completely tied up. For the foreseeable future, I'm afraid. So I'm sorry but I'm afraid, well, there it is. You can't go on holiday after all.'

He prised the bits of grit out of his hands with a fingernail, then scrubbed them under the tap. He cleaned up his face. Under the dirt he was glad to see his cheek wasn't grazed. He'd have had a job explaining that to his mother. He didn't change out of his old trousers. After all, vigorous gardening could conceivably have got them into this mess.

There was no sound of his mother's return. He might have just a minute to see if by some miracle the attic key had been returned. Just one last time. His legs hurt as he floundered up the attic stairs. He tried the handle. No. He knelt on his sore knee and winced. He looked through the keyhole. Could see only the square of window and was blinded by light. He gave up. Sat on the top stair looking down the dimness of the well.

He'd sat here when he was thirteen and his father was dying. He'd sat here when he was fourteen and Kevin was born. He felt he'd been sitting here ever since. He'd never moved. Nothing had changed. Like he'd stopped growing up when his father died. A frightened lonely huge fourteen-year-old in grown-up's clothes. *A senior partner in a highly respected City firm. And look at me. It's got to stop. Got to. Before it's too late. No more. Mustn't come here until I've recovered from this craziness. Not even weekends. I'll spend my weekends in town.* Terror descended on George. His life in town was as barren as that little grass triangle he'd crossed and recrossed this morning in his hopeless pursuit. *Oh...* His head fell forward. His big forehead rested on his knees.

Sounds of entry at the back door. Startled, he got up. He crept ponderously down the stairs. He had to get to his own room before his mother appeared. He had just begun to turn the handle silently when he heard her voice: 'Is that you, George?'

A pause. She emerged from the kitchen passage below, still laden with bags.

'Yes, Mother.'

She peered up at him through the banisters. 'Where on earth have you been? I had to take Kevin to the supermarket with me.'

The supermarket. George felt faint.

'You know I can't stand him hanging around me while I'm at the shops.'

'I'm sorry, Mother, I went – I went out.'

'I know you went *out*.'

A spirit of defiance entered George, he knew not whence. He refused to elaborate. A lie breeds lies. *What you won't do with a tax inspector, don't do with Mother.* He managed to keep his mouth shut. He fleetingly wondered why he hadn't always thought of his mother as a tax inspector, how much easier life might have been for him if he had. He reached the bottom stair. Kevin hugged him.

'Let me take that.' George lifted two heavy bags before his mother could pursue the subject of where he had been. *After all, I am a free agent.* 'It was a nice morning,' he offered.

'Nice for some!'

He blundered around the kitchen trying to put away the shopping.

'Oh, leave that. You don't know where to put things. Let it alone.'

George scratched his forehead with a thumbnail. Kevin, behind her back, smiled. George smiled back out of the sides of his eyes. Kevin silently convulsed with laughter. George was overcome with a rush of tenderness for his brother.

'What's he laughing at?'

'Nothing, Mother, you know him. You can't tell what amuses him.'

Kevin crowed.

'Be quiet, Kevin.'

Kevin stopped laughing. That tone in his mother's voice was Kevin's night, the black cloth thrown over his cage.

George didn't like the sadness that filled his brother's eyes. 'Come on, Kev, let's go and look at your seeds,' he said.

'Ghee, Ghee, Ghee!' Kevin's moods changed fast.

'Sit down. I want to talk to you.' She who must be obeyed.

Both men sat down.

'Not you, Kevin. Go in the garden, go on.'

Kevin sadly went. George, too, didn't dare rebel. What was coming now?

'I've been thinking about this holiday business,' she said.

'Oh, Mother, yes, I–'

'I think I might go,' she said.

'But, Mother, you said– I thought you said–'

'I know what I said, but I met that Hicks woman from number twenty-nine at the supermarket. Her daughter works there. Alison.'

Alison. George's stomach muscles tightened like a fist. *Alison.*

'She's going on one of these tours. On a coach.'

'Who is?' Dared he say it? 'Alison?' he said.

'Ros Hicks is! No, not Alison, just her and her husband.'

'Oh.' *Just her and her husband. Leaving my girl here alone.*

'She says they're not too bad, these trips.'

That man is a fast worker He must have told his wife to mention it. Why should he bother? For me? We've never met before. If he only knew. None of them should go. He should be here to protect his daughter. From me. What have I done? What shall I do? What might I not do?

'She's given me a brochure thing. I think I might look into it.'

George didn't speak. He nodded. He looked at his hands, spread on the table to hide the pitted palms, the big fingers passive as sausages.

'Well, you did offer!' his mother said. 'You taking it back?'

'No. Oh, no. I'm– I was– No, of course. No, you must go if you– No, I'm very pleased. No.'

'Only don't you go changing your mind on me now that I've just got interested.'

'No, Mother, of course not. I won't.'

George stared hopelessly out into the half-mown garden. All the drama of his life seemed entangled with that damn lawn mower. Kevin wandered disconsolate in the dappled light. George sat on at the table. *Fate is stronger than I. What's a decision worth? You take an action. Everything follows from it, you can't take it back.* His mother didn't know, then, it seemed. The girl hadn't told. The girl hadn't seen him then? Hadn't tricked him? They didn't know about him, obviously they didn't, or his mother wouldn't be agreeing to go. George's secret was still his own. A terrible happiness began to flood his newly wicked heart. *How can I fight against fate?* But he had to fight it just the same. He plunged out into the garden and began again to heave the rattling old mower through the grass, Kevin larking by his side.

11

Early that evening Polly left her job at the school, crossed the park and came down the lane by the supermarket where Alison was still hard at work pushing plastic-wrapped chickens and limp sliced loaves along her little conveyor belt, even at this late hour still smiling at the customers. Polly didn't see Alison.

She did see Jack, however. He stood like a shadow in the sun in the doorway of the junk shop. Jack didn't see Polly; she turned swiftly down the tunnel entrance. In the tunnel she hurried. It was no place to linger. Even in this blazing heat it felt dripping and dank, only a narrow line of fluorescent lights overhead.

An hour later Alison came flying out of the supermarket. She saw Jack and Jack saw her. For an instant he thought she was Polly. He came out of his shadow and took a few steps

126

towards her across the street. She stopped in her flight, a little alarmed, she didn't know why. Then she ran on.

Jack realised his error and was left aimless in the middle of the street. He stood looking down at the cobbles in the sun. Perhaps Polly was working late. He might meet her on her way home. He shambled along the little side lane and into the park. He began to walk along the railings that bounded the railway, up to the little copse and back, the little copse and back, like a man tethered in a room. There was no sign of Polly but there was nothing else to do. A train rushed past him. He exulted at the noise, shuddering.

At five past eight George stopped pretending to work, stretched, and went to his bedroom window. Alison came running along Lisson Avenue. He groaned. He watched her disappear into number twenty-nine. Would she stay at home tonight? Or would she go again to the unknown place on the other side of the railway? He must not think like that any more. He had to fight his thoughts. He had to fight fate. He forced himself away from the window and went down to the kitchen. His mother wasn't there. He turned on the cold tap and filled a cup with water.

Kevin was in the garden again. He stood close to the wall laughing, gesturing, making his odd sounds. He often communed like this with next door's dog. George could not see the dog. But Kevin reached out his hands, laughing. And Alison appeared on the wall. She was laughing too. She jumped into Kevin's arms. Kevin hugged her. She released herself, touched his face, talked to him. Kevin looked blind with adoration. The two of them, he all dark, she all light, walked hand in hand towards the shed. She opened the door. They went inside together.

'What's the matter with you, George?'

George stared at his big helpless hands holding on to the edge of the sink. His mother opened the washing machine and stuffed it full. She stood up. 'Look as though you've seen a ghost,' she said.

I have. I have.

'I'm getting ready for my holiday!' Gaiety sat ill upon her. Her tone was forced. 'That's why I'm so behind.'

'Oh, yes?' George said.

'Are you all right? You're not going to get sick on me just when I've decided to go away, are you?'

'No. I'm fine.' *Are they still in the shed? What are they doing now? Has it happened before? Does Mother know?*

'I've been down and fixed it all up,' she said.

'What?'

She looked at him. 'George!'

'Oh, your holiday,' he said.

'Yes! It starts a fortnight today. Can you

128

get off work then? I know it's short notice but they had a cancellation on this trip. It's the same one the Hicks are on. Not that I'll be spending much time with them. He gets on my nerves, thinks he's God's gift. She's all right though.'

'I can take time when I like, Mother,' he heard himself say. His voice was faint like the wind in grass.

'Oh, yes, you're one of the bosses, aren't you? I always forget.'

George swallowed. 'Is the daughter–What's her name? Is she going with them on the trip?'

'Alison?'

'Alison.' *I've said her name. Again.*

'No! I told you this morning, she's got her job at the supermarket! Anyway she's grown up now. Seventeen. Girls don't go on holiday with their parents these days. More's the pity. Keep them out of mischief if they did.'

Mischief.

George left the room. He couldn't go to the attic, couldn't go down the garden and tear open the shed door, didn't know where to go or what to do. He found himself in Kevin's bedroom, which was above the kitchen on the first floor. It still had its nursery paper. Elephants in collars and ties and kangaroos in skirts cavorted round the walls. He stood at the window. The garden was empty. Not a leaf moved.

Then he saw the shed door open. The girl came out. She held the door open for Kevin who followed carrying a box of seedlings as carefully as if it were a crown on a cushion. The girl led the way to Kevin's little patch of garden. They both stooped down and began to transplant the seedlings. George's eyes filled with tears. He moved away from the window and sat on Kevin's bed. He heard his mother in the hall. She called, 'George?'

He did not answer. He crossed the hall, went into the bathroom and locked the door. He sat on the edge of the bath. He let the tears flow through his fingers silently, covering his face. His big body shook.

'George! Your food's on the table!'

He stood up, wiped his face and began to shave with a shaking hand. He considered the possibility of inventing an illness to stop his mother going. The approach of a real illness seemed not out of the question the way he felt now. *I can't stand any more of this. Next weekend I won't come here. I have to be strong.*

Sitting at the kitchen table George tried not to look as Alison kissed Kevin then jumped off the wall into the next garden. Kevin stood waving to her. Then he came with his odd attractive walk back into the house.

'Where have you been? The food will be ruined. How am I supposed to get on, waiting about for you?'

George and Kevin chewed their way silently through the bleak and heavy pie.

Jack returned in the dark. He had no idea where he had been, what he had been doing, or what time it was. It was half-past twelve.

Chloe was wide awake but far away, sitting in the lotus position on the living-room floor. Jack's return did not penetrate her perfect state.

Polly was asleep, dreaming of her escape.

George lay on his back all night with his eyes wide open, suffering.

So did Jack.

On Sunday George watched dully from his bedroom as Alison set out for church with her parents. Every bit of him felt tender, bruised and sore. He yearned to follow them but stayed riveted to the spot and was still at his window when they returned. After lunch he went straight back to his window and at two-thirty he watched them get into a dusty old black Saab and drive off. After dinner he watched the Saab come back and the three of them climb out. Going through the gate the girl's father laid an arm loosely round her shoulders. George envied the man, hated him. Rage shook him, he felt ill. This could not go on.

131

He usually stayed at his mother's till Monday morning. Tonight he took the last Sunday train back to town.

12

George sat behind his desk in his City suit. Bill Warren sat opposite, cool in an open-necked shirt and linen trousers. It was half-past five on Friday. It had been a long week. George closed a file, added it to the mound of files on a shelf and sighed. Bill stood up and stretched. 'Fancy a drink, George?'

George took time to respond. *The leafy streets. In two and a half hours Alison will leave the supermarket. Twenty paces behind her, ten paces, I could walk her home. If she comes over the garden wall I might – this time I might–*

'George?' Bill grinned and mimed the downing of a pint.

'All right,' George said. But he went on sitting there.

'Come on then, let's go.'

George looked at his expensive watch. 'I have to make a phone call first.' As he pressed the numbers George spread the big fingers of his other hand over his eyes and kept them there.

Bill Warren moved about the dreary little

room. 'See you haven't got your etchings up yet, George.'

'Hello, Mother. It's me. I'm afraid I won't be coming home this weekend.'

Bill Warren looked out of the window down the dark well and over at the window opposite and the glass room full of desks three feet away. 'Great view, George.'

'No, Mother. No, I'm not ill. I have a lot of work to complete before I take my fortnight off, that's all. You know how much more work there is these days. It's best if I stay in town.'

Bill Warren lifted a wrist and pointed at his even more expensive watch. It was time the evening's drinking began.

'I must go, Mother.' George was breathless. 'I have a client with me. I'll see you next Friday as usual. Goodbye.' He felt he had invented the client, which in a sense he had. It was the lie he would have told had Warren not been there. He had exerted more authority with his mother than ever in his life.

'Bit of a harridan, is she, George?'

'Well...' George was never disloyal. 'She has a tough life, you know.'

Warren laughed. He rubbed his hands. 'Right, George, let's go. Time for the serious business of the day.'

George was about to pack his briefcase, then realised there was no need. Feeling naked without it he preceded Warren to the door. For a moment his heart was almost light. *I have fought my obsession and won. Reason has prevailed.* He allowed himself the small triumph though he knew it was a cheat. There was something silkily delicious about denying himself sight of her until he could have her for a fortnight entirely to himself. The scene in the garden with Kevin, the two of them going into the shed, he had almost managed to forget. It came back fitfully, a magic lantern slide, from time to time, in flickering light.

'You can't go back there to live, George!'

It was late. In the dim light of the decrepit Arts Club Warren's face looked green.

'Not to live. Just to stay a few weeks.'

'You're going back to live there, George. I can see it in your eyes.'

'No.'

'Yes! Listen, I've been to South Norwood. It's all right as the suburbs go, it's got a nice little clock tower and the Stanley Halls, but it's not a place for you to live.'

'You know the Stanley Halls?'

'George, in the days when I was an actor–'

'What?'

'Yes. A struggling actor but an actor nevertheless.'

'You're an actor now, aren't you, Bill?'

'And I said nevertheless faultlessly and

134

faultlessly faultlessly which is pretty good for this time of night, but I am not an actor now, George, no. Now I am a face. Now there's the heavy in the pre-title sequence– Get Bill Warren, they say. Just the face we want. And it's *only* the face they want. I don't act any more. I just show my ugly face and say the lines in the right order and earn a lot of money. That's all. And you sort out my tax for me.'

'Oh, I see.'

'Yeah. Now in the days when I was an actor I didn't earn enough to pay tax. So I didn't know you and nobody knew me. I worked at a little theatre, the Croydon Warehouse, up the line from your mum. Fourpence a week, one dressing room for all, playing whacking great leads that I wasn't ready for, getting great reviews.' Warren stared into his drink for a while. 'Where was I?' he said.

George thought back. 'Stanley Halls?' he said.

'Very good, George! An orderly mind.'

An orderly mind. George looked into the writhing snake pit in his head. He winced.

'We used to rehearse in the Stanley Halls. That's how I know your area. Very nice, the Stanley Halls. Art nouveau. Lovely tiles, ceramic, blue and green. Metal flowers in stone vases all along the roof. Never seen anything like that.'

George showed his surprise.

'Didn't know I cared for the aesthetic beauties?' Warren said it with care and winked at George. 'The aesthetic pleasures of life, the lovely things. Did you? They think your feelings are as ugly as your face. That's what they think about blokes like us.'

The two men gazed into their drinks. *Mine are,* George thought.

'You should see my house, you know, George. All these years, four times a year, you do my VAT, we have a drink, you drop me off at my house when I'm pissed as a fart, you've never seen inside. Want to see my house, George? Come and see my house.'

'Bill! I haven't seen you for yonks! How are you, sweetheart?' A luscious, soft-skinned redhead enveloped Warren. She kissed him fulsomely on his cheeks and then his mouth.

'Hi, love,' he said. 'How's things?'

'Oh, you know, ticking over. You're doing great, Bill. You were smashing in that James Bond.'

'Spit 'n' a cough, that's all.'

'Yeah but still ... *what* a spit, *what* a cough!'

Warren and the Redhead laughed.

'Want a drink, hon?' he asked.

'No, got to get back to my crowd. God, I'm stoned. Great to see you, Bill. Keep in touch.' She floated away into the gloom with her husky drifting voice.

This happens to Warren wherever he goes. Men

clap him on the back, women drape themselves all over him. Would I be different if I had lovely women clinging all over me like Warren? Would I be going out of my mind like this?

'God knows who that was,' Warren said. 'Must have worked together somewhere. Can't think where. Maybe we slept together. God, hope not. Wouldn't like to have forgotten that. Nice girl. Let's go, George.' They walked carefully across the soggy carpet. 'Goodnight, Charlie.'

The amiable bruiser on the desk said, 'Night, Bill, mind how you go.'

Careful down the stairs and out into the night. Charing Cross Road was carnival with crowds. North and south they surged, happy, young, too late for the tube, too poor for a taxi. A couple of whales in a sea of porpoises, Warren and George joined the southerly tide. They crossed Leicester Square, still humming and buzzing, ablaze with lights, and on to Piccadilly Circus where the rent boys sauntered and leaned under the arrow of Eros, navigated the sea of swirling light into Piccadilly itself where Warren picked up a cab from the rank outside Fortnum's and without any awareness of how, they were soon bowling west along the Thames.

George had never been this drunk in his life. The lights in and the lights over the river, the reflected and the real, lurched towards each other with every movement of the cab. Trees, buildings, bridges, other cars, night buses swam in and out of his vision, weightless, his eyes failed to fix them in their place. For once, in Chelsea, it was Warren who helped George out of the cab.

'Just stand there, George, while I pay the man.' He propped George against the door of his house which was right on the pavement.

George could smell the river. The dirty brown smell felt good in his nostrils. He wanted to walk to the water and lie down by it. A breeze cooled his face. Objects came into focus. George had one of those brief moments of sobriety that can occur deep in drink. It was pleasant to watch lamps, window boxes, gateposts, reduce from double to single image. It was pleasant to have only that in his mind – the simple pleasure of not being as drunk as he had been a moment before. Warren propped him up with one hand while he opened his immaculate white front door.

The carpets were black. The walls were a cool pale grey. The sofas were white. Black vases held arum lilies like flowers of wax. Four large paintings took George's breath away – blocks of vibrating colour, with some areas of canvas not painted at all. George was paralysed.

Warren laughed. 'Sit down, George.'

He tried to sit respectably upright but the

sofa was soft, and low. He found himself sinking, splaying out. He felt his posture to be unseemly but he was too drunk to alter it. He tried to despise the pictures – *Modern stuff* – but found he couldn't. They reminded him of Kevin in some way. Why? They were strong, they were open, honest, simple. And beautiful. *That's why.* George wanted to weep again.

Warren appeared silently, carrying a tray. 'Want it black, George? Can't offer you a brandy. No drink in the house. Never booze at home. Don't know why. Never have. Superstition? Don't know. I'm a pub man, that's it.' Warren assumed a sepulchral voice: 'Don't want to become an alcoholic, George.' He laughed.

He was dressed in a black kimono and backless white slippers. His Samurai legs were bare. George felt disturbed. Was Bill Warren not what he seemed, then? All those stories about actors... But all these years – and all those women in the bars... George sat up stiffly. He cleared his throat. 'Yes. Black. Please. Thank you. Thanks.'

Warren laughed. 'Don't worry, George, I haven't brought you back here to have my way with you. Not my type, love.' He did the easy actors' imitation, and laughed again. 'Always preferred 'em female, myself. Still in a state of shock, George? Bit unexpected, isn't it, my house? You're even starting to

like my paintings, aren't you? They're growing on you. Don't deny it, mate. They are.'

George tried to adjust his face.

'You're easy to read, George. Sugar?'

George shook his head.

'Easy for an actor, that is. The actor is a
behavioural scientist, George. Observation.
Continuous. Compulsive. Can't stop it even
if you want to. Minute changes of expression
in the human face and body language. You're
a good study, George, because you're
masked, see?'

George took a mouthful of coffee. It was
blisteringly hot. He hoped his expression
didn't show his burning tongue. Or the
alarm in his mind. 'Masked?' he said.

'You wear a mask, George, because you're
afraid to show what you think, what you feel.
You don't want anyone to know what's going
on in your mind so you pretend there's nothing going on in there at all. Hardly a muscle
moves in your face, George, but everything
shows. Everything. You try to hide; you only
reveal. You want to be like me, mate. Open
book, that's me. Tell everyone everything, get
drunk, let it all hang out. Reveal all; conceal
all. See? You thought you knew me, didn't
you? Big ugly bruiser, friendly bloke, bit
crass, bit vulgar. Nice working class lad
who's had a bit of success. Well, that's the
surface, George. It's true but it's nothing. It's
my mask, George. Better than yours, eh? See

140

how surprised you are by all this? But nothing I found out about *you* would surprise
me.'

George said nothing. His eyes were fixed
on a black jar of waxy lilies. He didn't move.

Warren's puggish face became puzzled. 'I
don't normally bring people back here. I've
only brought women here before. And only
two of those. Why did I bring you here,
George?'

George gave a little cough. 'I don't know,
Bill.'

Warren's eyes searched his face.

Like hands searching inside my head. George
scratched his forehead with a thumbnail
and discovered for the first time that this
was his habitual gesture at extremes of
embarrassment.

'I know,' Warren said at last. 'There's
something wrong with you. That's it, there's
something very wrong. You're not the same,
George. You haven't been the same since
you moved to that horrible new office. But
it's more than that. There's something bad
going on inside. You're ill. Or you've had
bad news or... What? What's wrong with
you, mate?'

George put his spectacles on. He only wore
them for reading. They blurred the world
outside the paperwork. Warren watched him.
Time passed. They did not blur enough; he
would have to answer. At last his Adam's

apple moved. 'There's nothing wrong,' he said.

'You got troubles, George.'

'No. Really—'

'Yes!'

Silence fell. Like snow. It stuck. It didn't melt.

'More coffee, George?'

'Er ... yes. All right then. Please.' George felt deeply threatened. He knew he ought to leave. He wanted to leave. But he couldn't. He wasn't tempted to tell. The place in his head where he kept the girl was a strong fortress. But, and perhaps only because of the amount of alcohol he had drunk, George was almost able to believe that Bill Warren liked him. Cared, even, what became of him. This was a notion new to George. Warren's interest was making him feel almost part of the world. As though he might have a right to belong there. George had not been aware of his loneliness all these years. Not till now. So he sat on in the deep sofa and made no attempt to get up and go.

'It's something to do with this idea of going back to live at home,' Warren said at last.

George shook his head. He wished he'd never mentioned the idea.

'It's something to do with that, that's what's wrong. Not that, but something to do with that.' Warren's speech was slightly slurred, for the first time that night, as though the alcohol were only now beginning to take effect. It relieved George of some of his shyness, thinking that Warren was drunk.

'I grew up there,' George said, as though in excuse.

'All the more reason not to go back. Never go back, George. Never go back. It's against Nature. You got out? Stay out. You don't go back except to die.'

George heard echoes of John Bright who had used almost the same words.

'It'll damage you,' Warren said. 'You'll be trapped.'

'My mother–'

'Your mother my arse. Your mother's done without you all these years, hasn't she? How old is she?'

'I don't know, sixty something. Three or four.'

'*Sixty* something? I thought we were talking about a geriatric here. You got fifteen years before you have to start worrying about her. And anyway that's not your reason for going back.' He grinned again. 'Is it, George? Eh?' Warren waited.

Feeling as though he was falling, George spoke. 'I have a brother,' he said. The silence of a lifetime broke. George attempted to describe Kevin. 'He's twenty-four,' he said, 'but he's a child. He has a mental age of six.' And then he heard himself say, 'In the garden last weekend...'

'Yeah? In the garden last weekend?'

'Oh. Nothing.'

'Nothing? Something, George! Something! In the garden last weekend.'

'Well...' Incredulous, George heard himself go on. He drew the scene in detail. He cast himself as the protector, worried that his simpleton sibling might harm the girl. Or the girl harm Kevin. His paternal tone convinced even himself. 'You see, I've never considered it before. That Kevin is an adult now. Well, ph-physically. And that – well – people could get hurt.'

'I wouldn't worry about the girl, George. Pretty little blondes can generally take care of themselves.'

'Oh, no!'

'Oh, yes, George. Better than you think. Better than you or me.'

'No. Not this one. Actresses, maybe, but not–' He'd being going to say nice girls but in spite of his drunken state stopped himself in time.

Too late to fool Warren, however, who laughed, delighted. 'The way you say that! Centuries of received disgust. No, George, it's – Kevin, is his name? – it's Kevin you've got to worry about. Though innocence does protect the innocent, you know. Bit of dubious three a.m. wisdom, my God.'

What protects the guilty? Guilt? I'm not guilty

of anything. Yet. Oh no? You just talked about Kevin, to a stranger, to protect yourself. You're a betrayer, George.

'I'd no idea about your brother,' Warren said. 'I'm sorry, old mate.'

George overdrained his coffee cup and wiped the grains from round his mouth with his clean white handkerchief. He pushed his glasses up on to the bridge of his nose. Folded the handkerchief. Put it away.

Warren regarded him. He had not given up. 'That's not it either, though, is it?' he said. 'It's something else. It's not to do with your brother, this.' He leaned forward. His round blue eyes searched George's impassive face. 'Your brother's an old problem. This is something new.'

'No–'

'Yes! It's you who's in trouble, George. What is it? Come on, why not tell? Nothing much could shock me, could it now?'

George felt the strongest urge to pour out his secret like vomit on Warren's perfect carpet. He equally felt a desperate desire to escape, to lunge out into the street, away from here. He sat like a boulder, his hands clasped between his round-rock knees. The big strong hands of a big weak man. *I've used my brother. I've used Kevin. I've sacrificed him, to shield myself. The least I can do is make the sacrifice worthwhile. If I talk now the sacrifice of Kevin will have been a waste.*

'There's enough waste in the world,' he said.

'Eh?' Warren had not been able to follow him here.

And if I tell, I'll lose her. I shan't be able to go on. The guilty golden light flooded George's heart.

Warren waited for an answer. It didn't come. George sat with his eyes closed. Far away. Warren watched him. The two big ugly men sat in the elegant beautiful room, silent and drunk.

Warren wondered why he was fond of George, why George intrigued him.

George followed a small blonde girl through the secret suburban streets of his mind.

'Okay, George,' Warren said. 'Don't tell. Not if you don't want to. Why should you. We all tell too much these days. No sweat. Time for beddie-byes.'

George didn't hear. He was far away.

13

He woke in the morning still on the sofa, under a soft cashmere rug. At first he had no idea where he was. He looked at his watch. Eleven-thirty! He sat bolt upright. *I'm late!* His head was a peal of discordant bells. *Late for what?* His tongue was twice its normal size and glued to the roof of his mouth. His eyes hurt. And the eye sockets and the bones of his face. He couldn't breathe through his nose. He remembered where he was. *What did I say last night? What did I tell?* He checked his watch again, he couldn't believe he'd slept till now. In his whole life he could not recall ever having risen later than half-past eight. *I didn't tell.*

He remembered offering Kevin. The human sacrifice. The scene from the Bible, Jacob offering his son. It was always held up as a virtue, Jacob's sacrifice. But even as a boy at Sunday School it had made George feel sick. What right had a God to ask such a gift? What right had a father to comply? Remorse rose in him like bilge water. He needed to go to the bathroom.

Social embarrassment imprisoned him. The only house George had ever been a guest in for more than an evening was his Aunt Freda's in Wandsworth. He couldn't hear a sound in the house. Perhaps Warren wasn't up yet. He was afraid of breaking the rules.

Suddenly there was the unmistakable braying of upper class voices in the street. And laughter. Car doors slammed. People come to visit! They would walk in and find him here. George clutched the rug around him though he was fully clothed in his

147

crumpled City suit. A street door banged. The people had gone into the house next door. George let out his breath.

'Feeling a bit rough, George?' Warren's head appeared round the door. 'Bathroom top of the stairs, breakfast in the basement. Coffee's on.'

In the bathroom George found clean underwear laid out, and a shirt. The boxer shorts were silk. So were the socks. The shirt was Gieves & Hawkes, Savile Row. There was a knock on the door. George was fresh and flushed from the bath. He wrapped a towel quickly round himself. 'Yes? Come in!'

'Here you are, mate.' Warren leaned round the door and handed him a cup of coffee.

George was clutching the silk socks.

'Thought you might be glad of some clean things,' Warren said.

'Oh. Are they for me? Oh. Thank you. Yes.' Warren left.

George for the first time felt silk next to his skin. It was a sweet sensation which frightened him. He didn't know what to do with his own shirt and underpants. He held them in his arms for some time then folded them carefully and left them on a chair. Going down the stairs in his silk things he felt dressed in someone else's skin. He might get to like it. After all, he had never felt at home in his own. He then surprised himself by eating breakfast. Orange juice followed by eggs and bacon produced by Warren who whistled as he expertly cooked.

Around one they went out, strolled to the King's Road, bought the papers, went to the pub. George watched astonished as Warren downed several scotches without effect. He uneasily ordered a pint so as not to appear cissy. He surprised himself by enjoying that too.

They walked back along the embankment. Warren appeared to take it for granted that George would return to the house with him. They read the papers silently. Then Warren snored on the sofa with the *Independent* on his face while George slept more quietly behind the *Telegraph*.

In the evening Warren set off again for the West End clubs, and George went too. Warren did no more probing. He talked and laughed with acquaintances, the life and soul of everybody's party. George felt safe. Protected from himself. Almost normal. Acceptable. A member of the world. At 1 a.m., tired out, he got up to leave Warren in a dimly lit bar surrounded by drunken chums.

'Hey! Don't go, George.'

'I have to get some sleep, Bill.'

'Why? Sunday tomorrow.'

'Yes, but–'

'Oh. Okay. All right. Just hang on while I finish this. Two ticks.'

George suddenly suspected that in spite of his continuous social life Warren might be as lonely as himself. Taken aback by this notion, he hesitated a moment.

'What's the matter now, George?'

'Oh. Nothing. I don't know. Maybe I'll stay.'

'Good man!' Warren slapped him between the shoulder blades. 'Lenny! Another drink for George!'

Later in the night, after much drink, George thought, *I could live like this. I could spend all my weekends in town. I could have friends. I needn't go back home except every now and then. I could live well. Like Warren.*

But by the same time on Sunday night Warren's constant floating around, never still, never at rest, began to tell on George. He felt like a passenger on a boat on a choppy sea, that wobbling in the legs, that combination of claustrophobia – I can't get off – and agoraphobia – there's nothing but space all round – that marks out the man who is not a born sailor. George needed to be on dry land. His mother's house was his dry land, even though the sea was at high tide, the waves about to break down its walls. He was grateful to Warren but he left him late on Sunday, at another bar of another club with another laughing crowd.

'Goodnight, George!' His new friends who

wouldn't know him next time clapped him on the back. Just as they did to Warren.

But Warren put out an arm and pulled him back. 'George,' he said.

'Yes?'

'Don't do it.'

'What! Do what?'

'Whatever it is you're thinking about. Planning. Considering. Don't do it.' Warren gave him a push. 'Take care of yourself, mate.'

George would look back on this weekend, clubbing around with Warren, and see it as the turning point. The road he could have taken. The moment when escape was handed to him as a gift which he refused to accept. In the following weeks this weekend would come to seem a dream, an oasis, a lost world. But George knew he could do no different. He had no choice. There was no going back. He recalled the words John Bright had said the day he first bumped into him weeks ago: *You can't retrace your steps.*

14

Next Friday George was exemplary. He strode briskly past the supermarket without a glance to right or left, and in the evening he did not even wait at his window for a glimpse of the girl.

On Saturday morning he helped his mother up the steps into her coach. He suffered himself to shake hands with Hicks and wish him a pleasant holiday. He'd hoped – he feared – the girl would be there seeing off her parents but she was not. So intent was he on this – *Will she come at the last minute to wave?* – he hardly noticed his mother's departure.

He and Kevin returned to the house. George didn't make a detour round the supermarket; he was strengthened by last weekend. By his two strong weeks of abstinence.

At home he found notes for everything: how to lock up; how to treat the boiler; a menu for every day in the fortnight; what time to take Kevin to his classes; where to shop for which items; how to pay the milkman, the window cleaner; which day to put out the garbage with precise details on black plastic bags. They were instructions for a person who was a stranger to the house. They disturbed George, who had never felt that he had really left home, revealing to him that he and Kevin in their different ways were cuckoos in their mother's nest. He wondered if he had always unconsciously felt this – that he had no right to be there, always on trial, as it were, on sufferance, even though it was the only place he could call home.

He clumped round the house collecting the notes. Kevin caught on. He lolloped about finding the scraps of paper and bringing them to George. When it seemed there were no more to be found, George solemnly gave half of them to Kevin. He tore his share in small pieces. Kevin did the same, laughing in excitement. They dropped the pieces in the garbage bin.

George then opened the freezer and looked carefully for the meal marked with the day's date. He found it, thought for a moment of choosing one marked with a different date, didn't quite dare, and got it out to thaw. 'Good old George,' he said to Kevin. Kevin laughed.

After lunch, still strong, he didn't stand at his window to look for the girl, even though Kevin had gone up to play with his trains and he was alone.

In the afternoon he took Kevin shopping. At the clock tower Kevin dragged at his arm but George shook his head, firm, amazed at his own strength of will. Warren's voice was in his head: *Don't do it, George,* and George didn't do it. 'No, Kev,' he said. 'Not the supermarket today.'

Kevin was sad, and George's stomach, though full of lunch, trembled like that of a man who hadn't eaten for days.

In the evening they amused themselves in the garden. Kevin tended his little patch that was becoming recognisably full of lettuces and spinach. George mowed the interminable grass, then, thirsty, he put the mower away and went in to fetch a cool drink. He brought out a Coke for Kevin who was making noises and waving his arms but not at George. The girl, Alison, was in her garden, three houses down. She raised a little hand to wave to Kevin. Then she turned away and went back indoors. George caught only that glimpse: the turning head, the swinging hair, the little hand waving. He stood holding the can of Coke. He knew now it was for this he had spent these hours in the garden with Kevin. Just for this. All his strength of will had been a delusion, a chimera. The addict had got his fix. Just a little one, just enough to whet his appetite, and George was hooked again. He became aware that Kevin was gently patting his hand. 'Oh! Yes! Here you are, Kev. Coke.'

Kevin smiled his biggest smile. Had the

smile gained extra radiance from seeing the girl? *Are you addicted like me, Kev? What on earth do you feel?* No use asking Kevin. He couldn't say. George felt a maudlin kinship with his brother. *We're both in the same boat.*

However, he had not totally lost his will to fight. He went back inside the house determined to go on battling against his addiction. And he got unexpected help: he was kept unbelievably busy. He had thought his mother made work so that she could bang about all day expressing her temper. He discovered, 'cooking' for himself and Kevin, serving, washing up afterwards, cleaning, making beds, that the work she did was not invented. And nor was it easy. There were even moments, concentrating on not letting a pan boil over, on helping Kevin peel potatoes or chop carrots in his eccentric way, that the girl left his mind altogether. *If I can keep myself busy enough* ... he thought.

After supper, when Kevin went up to his train room in the attic, George refused to follow him, in mind or body. He stayed downstairs in the kitchen. He washed up, he wiped every crumb from the table, every drip off the stove. He even swept every speck of dust off the floor. But after that there was simply nothing more to do and, though he tried to stop himself, he went to his room and, feeling joy, guilt and self-contempt, he stood at the window until dark. The girl did not pass in the street. George's shame was absolute. And his disappointment felt like nausea, physical and acute.

On Sunday, however, he woke refreshed. He recalled the shame of the night before but decided not to dwell on his weakness. Instead he renewed his resolution to keep busy, fix his mind on other things. He helped Kevin to wash and dress. He made breakfast for both of them. He washed up, dried and put the things away. Then Kevin went up again to his train room and George could find nothing else to do. Work was the thing. He could always occupy himself with his work. But the accounts he had brought home with him were upstairs in his bedroom...

He told himself he would just go up to fetch his briefcase and bring the papers down here to work on, he would not go near the window, there was no need. He told himself this as he ran up the stairs. He crossed to the table in the corner of his bedroom where he did his work, he picked up his briefcase and crossed back to the door. But he did not immediately go out of the door. *Just for a second, that's all. Just a quick look. That can't do any harm.* He closed the door quietly and he went and stood at the window. It was nine o'clock in the morning. And at half-past nine he was still there.

A few people strolled down the street. The bells rang from a distant church. At ten to ten she came out. Dressed in a short little pale blue dress, shoulder bag swinging, she walked past the house. George was on the landing in a moment. 'Kevin, where are you? We're going out!'

Kevin came flying down the stairs. 'Owgh! Owgh!'

The odd pair swirled down the road, turned corners, crossed streets, keeping their distance behind the girl. George came to himself sufficiently, once, to check if Kevin had seen her. But Kevin, absorbed in each passing thing, did not give attention to distances. He liked dogs, cats, flowers, the smells of privet and roses. Things close enough to touch. George dragged him along, cruel in pursuit.

She was going into the Catholic church. George had never been in one in his life. He and Kevin followed the crowd inside. The place was hushed, footsteps echoed.

Kevin said loudly, 'Ghurgh, ghurgh!'

George seized him by the shoulder. People looked. But the girl had gone to the front. She didn't turn. 'Quiet, Kevin.' George's whisper was fierce.

Kevin nodded, vociferous, about to give voice again, eager to please.

'Sh.' George pushed him on to a bench at the back, sat him down and held on to him.

Every now and then when backs parted he could see the girl. *Alison.* Her fragile neck was bent, her forehead resting on clasped hands clenched in prayer.

So intense was George's concentration on her, he felt no embarrassment at not knowing the ways of the service, when to stand, kneel, sit, what responses to make. The priest faced the people every now and then and said, 'The Lord be with you,' and the nasal South London voices answered, 'And with you also.' George found this mode of address faintly unpleasant, embarrassing, but it barely touched him. His saint was at the front of the church, silk blonde hair falling over her face, her fragile neck bared by its falling. *What the sight of your bowed neck does to me.*

The priest at last disappeared through a door to the right of the altar. The people began to surge slowly back down the aisle. George lost sight of her. *If I stay here she'll see me. Us.*

He got to his feet, dragging Kevin with him. They joined the dense moving throng. Outside, for somewhere to hide, he took Kevin down a narrow strip of grass at the side of the church. Kevin became absorbed in a cascade of small pink roses, smelled them, touched their leaves. George, waiting, watched the people out of the corner of his eye. He sensed her presence before he saw her. She hadn't seen them. She didn't look their way.

With Kevin he had to keep a greater distance behind her than he would have alone. Kevin might see her, call out. She might stop and speak. George didn't want to speak to her. Not yet. He was not ready yet. He wanted to watch. Watch her? Or watch over her? The words of a song he didn't know he knew repeated themselves in his head. *Someone to watch over me.*

She didn't turn into Lisson Avenue, she went on down the hill. Passing the Stanley Halls, George thought of Bill Warren and remembered sadly last weekend. It didn't help. *Nothing can help me now.* His eyes and his heart were glued to her. *She must be heading for the other side of the railway. She must. I'll find out where she goes. I'll know at last. I'll know who she sees over there. I'll know the worst.*

But she did not cross the road and make for the railway bridge. She turned right into the High Street. About thirty yards along she went into a doorway. As he closed the distance, hauling Kevin away from shop windows, he saw it was the Wimpy Bar. Who could she be meeting there? That boy again? Surely she had finished with that boy. Surely George had witnessed the scene? His breath turned liquid in his throat. He couldn't follow her in there. The place was packed, but in the confined space there would be no way to stop Kevin seeing her. He pulled Kevin across the street and into the newsagent's opposite.

Pretending to peruse the magazines on the rack in the window he watched her. She sat in the window! She was alone at her formica-topped table! Perhaps she wasn't meeting anyone? The waiter brought her a cup. She put both her little hands round the cup and seemed glad of the warmth on her face as she brought it up to her mouth. It was a warm day like all this summer's days but she needed warmth from a coffee cup. *Oh, Alison, my dear little dove, I'll warm you with my hands.*

Kevin tugged at his arm. He was holding out a magazine for George to see. On the cover was a girl. She had silky blonde shoulder-length hair. She was smiling. Her enormous breasts were bare. She was half lying on a red velvet sofa, her legs open wide. Kevin glowed. 'Ghaighy, ghaighy,' he said.

A moment of perfect horror, then George grabbed the magazine from Kevin's hands. He saw that the rack he had been stationed at was stacked with such publications. *His girl,* blonde, young, lovely, innocent, posed for him in every inviting position known to man. It was grotesque. George felt sick.

Kevin was bewildered. He wanted his magazine back. George was scared. He knew

160

Kevin's rages. Big though he was he could do nothing with his brother once Kevin lost control. The shop could be wrecked, police called. 'It's okay, Kev, it's okay. Here, have this instead. Nice magazine.' He picked one with a train on the cover, a beautiful red and green train steaming through hilly countryside.

Even by this Kevin was not appeased. Under George's hand his flexible body began to arch and heave. His teeth clenched. He ground out noises, snarling, growling, spitting. George grabbed the magazine he had snatched from him and thrust it back into his hands. The noises died away. Kevin's face relaxed. He held it with reverence. 'Ghaighy, ghaighy,' he said softly, his eyes glowing.

'That's no lady, son,' a man in overalls said and George heard someone laugh.

Swelling with embarrassment he picked up the *Observer* and paid for both purchases, indicating Kevin's with a casual gesture and a cough. Without looking round he pulled Kevin with him out of the shop. He was too mortified even to look over at the Wimpy Bar to see if the girl was still there and whom, if anyone, she had met.

Kevin took his magazine to his train room in the attic where he solemnly propped it up on the mantelpiece. He positioned it with care like a priceless Leonardo drawing. Now

161

his Lady could see him wherever in the room he might be.

George downstairs tried to concentrate on the Sunday paper but, fist to his mouth, shaken, he could see only the girl in that lewd pose, and her uncanny resemblance to Alison. *Alison.* He had kept his mind pure around his girl. *Alison.* He had kept her holy there, wrapped in light. *Alison.* Those pictures, now here at home in his mother's house, the scene in the shop, Kevin's tantrum, that threat of lost control, had loosened everything, all George's restraints. He was falling through space. *But that isn't her. Those pictures. That is not my girl. To the pure all things are pure.*

To Kevin's innocent mind the girls on the magazines were pure. He knew that. But not to his guilty one. George craved help. He actually prayed. He heard the Catholic priest say, 'The Lord be with you.' He did not believe the Lord was with him. He trudged upstairs to his bedroom. He locked his door. He closed the curtains. He lay down on the bed.

At eight that evening, on vigil again at his bedroom window, George saw Alison pass by. He watched her go into her house. Her parents were on holiday. She was in there alone. His evil mind began: *You could knock on the door. You could simply walk in – she's so small, light as air – you could simply lift her in your arms and... No, no, no.* He strode out of the room on to the landing. 'Kevin! Out!'

'Owgh! Owgh!'

He almost dragged Kevin out of the door and down the street away from number twenty-nine. He had never before been so rough with him. He blamed him for the desecrated image of his girl that no matter how hard he fought it to keep it out, kept jumping back into his mind. He knew it wasn't fair to blame his simple brother but he could not help himself.

Now he found himself pulling the boy in the direction of the High Street. Not again? Why? Where was he going? He couldn't just walk about all night, not with Kevin in tow like this. But he kept going, fleeing from the top-shelf pictures in his mind. *Ah yes!* He saw the big pub beyond the railway bridge. The pub he'd gone to with John Bright. Kevin had never been in a pub before. Well, there was a first time for everything. George was finding that out. Why shouldn't Kevin? He tugged him along, under the bridge and across the road.

The pub was packed, people spilled in and out of it in constant movement, ants on an ant hill. A head taller than most of them, he shouldered through to the bar, holding fast to Kevin's hand. He found a space and squeezed Kevin into it, keeping him wedged in with his big body. Kevin eyes were big with excitement, his noises odder than usual. George barely noticed. He ordered a double scotch for himself, a Coke for Kevin, his once-in-a-blue-moon treat. He swallowed half the scotch in a gulp. Kevin made love to his Coke, both hands round the glass, nose bobbing against the ice. Like Alison in the Wimpy Bar with her coffee cup. *I'll knock on her door I'll say would you like to come round and – have a cup of tea? No. Coffee! Kevin would like to see you.* He shut his eyes. The picture that came to him was the girl on the magazine. And she was in the garden. In the garden with Kevin. *No.* He gestured to the barman. Another scotch. Kevin smiled lovingly at the man and held out his empty glass.

'Another Coke for the lad, sir? Bit of a handful, I should think. Your son?'

George's face stayed stone. *Son?* Had youth left him so far behind then that he could be taken for Kevin's father? He was trying to answer the man when he felt himself jostled from behind. He turned. A dark bony man was elbowing a way through the crowd to find a space at the bar. Jagged lines of electric air sizzled round this man – that's how they would depict him in the comics. People moved to give him space. He came to a stop eight feet from George round the corner of the bar.

He had a face like a crow, gaunt, big-nosed, single-minded. His eyes were red, he hadn't shaved. 'Scotch,' he croaked. He swallowed it in one, then thrust out the glass again. He drank like a suicide drinking hemlock, systematic, purposeful.

Though in appearance they could not be more different, George felt a powerful kinship with this man. He began to match him drink for drink. The man started to sway, not from drink, George could tell, but from some exhausted desperation of the mind. *He is me. He is me. He is the devil inside me.* George was becoming confused.

Kevin tugged at his arm. He was full of Coke and needed to be taken to the Gents. As they squeezed past, the man was going through his pockets, then, patting himself, bewildered. He couldn't believe he'd run out of money. He had to have another drink. *When I come back I'll offer him one. I'll talk to him.*

But coming out of the Gents, he saw the man turn away from the bar despondent and fight his way through the crowd. On impulse George heaved himself and Kevin out after him.

The air outside was still warm, petrol fumes hung in it. The man leaned his forehead against the pub terrace wall. Then he pushed off from the bricks with his long bony hands and staggered across the road. A car squealed to an emergency stop. The man didn't even turn his head. George and Kevin flopped down the steps and waited for the traffic.

The man turned left then right. This was the street where George had seen the girl. Brockhurst Road. *This is the street I followed her down, the street that leads to the railway tunnel.* Fascinated George watched. *God, don't let him have anything to do with Alison.*

After a struggle to get the key in the door the man hurled himself into a house. The door crashed back on its hinges, then slammed shut. In turmoil George stood swaying, Kevin holding him up. After some time he turned round and lurched in the vague direction of home. He was beyond noticing that it was Kevin who found the way. Kevin who gently prised the key from his fingers and opened the front door.

In the kitchen Kevin gazed at him, puzzled. Something was wrong with George. Kevin patted him. He made some coffee for him. He did it slowly, forgetting, then remembering again. He handed George the coffee. The kettle had not quite boiled. Undissolved coffee granules floated on the greyish surface. George started to laugh. Kevin was afraid.

George went out into the garden. Cool black air. It was like swimming. Swimming through cool black air. He remembered a river as a boy. He and John Bright with fishing lines. John Bright through the water like a minnow, small and thin and fast. Himself ashamed of his big pudgy body, lying in the shallows. He would like now to lie in cool black water. He lay down on his back in the grass and looked up at the houses revolving slowly against the sky. Some had lighted windows, some were dark. Kevin looked down at him, perplexed. Then he lay down beside him in the grass.

George sat up suddenly. 'It's bedtime, Kev,' he said. He stumbled ahead of Kevin up the stairs. Kevin came into the room with him and tried to help him into bed. 'No, no, Kev. You go to sleep, now. You go now. Go.'

Sad and puzzled, Kevin went off to his room. He got into bed fully clothed, like George. So this was what they did when Mother was away?

'Why the fuck don't you go off with the girl whoever she is if you're in this state about her? Think I'd care? I was past caring years ago.'

'You don't know what you're saying, woman.'

'Well, for heaven's sake forget her then. If she doesn't want to go on seeing you, that's that. Accept it, Jack! You'll end up in the loony bin again if you go on like this.'

Jack lurched off his chair. 'You think I don't know that, you cruel bitch? Think I don't know what I'm heading for? You stupefied doped-up hop head, you–'

'Oh, be quiet, both of you.' Polly's voice cut through their racket like a tiny ice-pick. Her mother looked like a caught bird, her face quivering and white. Jack towered over her like a scrawny black cat, shaking her in his claws. 'If you don't stop it, Jack,' Polly said in her cool little voice, 'I'll call the police. And you know what they'll do to you, don't you? And you know how you loved being locked up. Is that what you want?'

Jack threw Chloe away from him, sat again, folded his arms on the table and laid his head on his arms. Tears ran out of his eyes.

Chloe rubbed her face then her arms. 'He's out of his tree.'

'Are you all right, Mum?'

'I wish I had some dope.'

Polly's voice did not lose its cool: 'Sometimes I think you're as bad as he is, nearly. Actually,' she said, and went upstairs.

15

Stealthily he searched through the wardrobe. He found old black trousers and a dark green sweater with holes in the elbows. He got dressed. The only soft shoes were his gardening plimsolls streaked with green. He put them on. He crept to the door, looking at his feet. They looked too white. They wouldn't do. He went to the chest of drawers, found a pair of black socks and pulled them on over the plimsolls. Found also a pair of dark wool gloves, a present from his aunt who sent them every Christmas. He squeezed his big hands into them. All sound deadened by the socks, he padded silently across the landing. He listened outside Kevin's room: his brother's peaceful sleep-breathing, deep and slow.

He crept down the stairs, out of the back door. There was a narrow slice of moon and no cloud. He went right to the far corner of the garden and crouched by the wall. He raised his head cautiously, scanning for the next-door neighbours' dog. It had a tiresome Jack Russell yap that reminded him of his mother's laugh. The neighbours ignored their garden except as a convenience for their dog. The grass was long and shapes loomed of overgrown shrubs. George whispered, 'Dog? Hello? Dog?' There was no response. He thought he might be safe.

He clambered on to the wall, then dropped into the grass. He knelt there puffing, trying not to make a sound. No dog came sniffing through the dark. He ran doubled up to the next wall and again peeped cautiously over. This garden had some trellis running across it halfway down that would help to hide him from the house. He panted along behind the trellis and hauled himself on to the next wall. Over that wall, he dropped and scrambled through thick grass.

He started to feel thrilled. All the adventure stories he had read and never thought to live. The robbers, the chasers of robbers, the murderers making their escapes. He shut out what he knew he really was – a peeping tom creeping clumsily about in the dark. His knee was hurting from his fall. But he was there! He was in her garden. He was within the confines of her domain.

He became aware of an overpowering, unspeakable smell. He recalled her father Hicks saying something about a smell. Yes, the compost heap, that was it. He was crouching next to the Hickses' compost heap. But he didn't dare to move out of its shadow. Or out of the orbit of the smell. He put a hand over his face to muffle its effect.

He trembled and his breath came in gasps. 'Oh, God,' he whispered. And then a light went on upstairs. *Oh, God.*

It must be the bathroom window. It was frosted glass. Now and then a shadow wavered, nothing he could clearly make out. Water gushed suddenly through a down pipe and into a drain. The bathroom light went out. Darkness. Would she go to bed now? He had no idea where her room might be. It might be at the front. Then another light went on.

Who would believe his luck? She had the equivalent room to Kevin's, the small one at the back. He wondered if hers still had childish wallpaper, kangaroos and elephants. What did girls have on their bedroom walls? He didn't know. And then suddenly she was there! She was in the room.

First her shadow came to the window. Then she herself followed it. She stood there with her hands folded on the sill, simply looking at him. And he looked back. It was idiotic, he knew that, she couldn't possibly see him, she was looking out into the dark, as far as she knew into an empty garden. But for George it was perfect communion whether she knew it or not.

Then she put the palms of her two hands against the window, fingers locked, and rested her forehead on the backs of her hands so he couldn't see her eyes any more.

Then she leaned back from the window. Her hands moved from her eyes, the fingers slid apart. They swept back over her ears and behind her head where they lifted her hair up from her neck and held it in a soft bouquet, her body all stretched, her head back, the hair hanging over her hands like ripe blonde grass.

'Please, please,' George whispered, hardly knowing what he pleaded for.

The girl twirled round and let the hair go and, as if answering his plea, though shyly, with her back to him, pulled her T-shirt up and over her head. She undid the clasp of a white bra. The two little hands stroked the fragile white strings off her shoulders and pulled the thing off. She rubbed gently under her breasts. But she didn't turn back to the window. She moved away into the room.

'No!' George whispered. 'Please don't go.'

As if in answer she returned, though in a shapeless garment that hid her lovely flesh from him. She started to brush her hair. *She's doing it for me.* He knew she wasn't doing it for him, she couldn't be, but he pretended. He pretended they had an assignation in the dark. How he would love to brush her hair for her. To pull its silky threads towards his mouth, to– *Oh. Ohh.*

She turned away, pulling hairs from the brush. Then, as though remembering him, she turned back to the window. George held his breath. Had she really seen him then? Would she open the window, softly call out to him? What would he do if she did? But she pulled a curtain across and the other to meet it and George was shut out in the dark.

He put both his hands over his face. He started to feel the soreness in both his knees, to be overpowered again by the disgusting smell. Her light went out. He stood up and immediately fell down. His legs had gone to sleep, clenched in the same position for – how long? Ten minutes? An hour? He tried to extricate himself from the compost by wriggling on his backside. When he wriggled the slime released a foetid cloud of intenser smell. He was glad he had worn the gloves, and the old clothes which could be thrown away after this.

Released from the heap of rotting vegetation he sat on the ground and rubbed his legs with the smelly gloves. He staggered to his feet and toppled over again. He pulled himself along on his elbows to the wall, hauled himself up by his arms, lay along the top, then rolled off and crawled behind the trellis of number thirty-one. He crawled lopsided because one leg hadn't quite come back to him. Scrambling over the second wall he stumbled and fell into a terrifying noise. 'Yap, yap, yap!' It was his mother laughing. He was sure.

A white shape leapt at him and leapt again, almost to the height of his shoulder. The animal was gifted with astonishing vertical take-off. George turned and turned and turned again, not daring to utter. The thing was going for his face! *Oh, no!* The animal wasn't attacking him. Worse than that, it was delighted to see him. This was its game and George was on the team! Well, if it wanted a game it should have one.

He scrabbled in the undergrowth. The dog levitated around him. The rampant pins and needles sizzling inside his legs, he found a stick and flung it. The horrifying creature bounded off after it down towards its house. George made a limping run at the wall and hurled himself over it. He lay there heaving, clutching his leg.

Human voices now added themselves to the yapping of the dog. 'What's going on out there?'

He couldn't just lie there at the foot of his garden wall, they'd see him if they thought to look over. A door opened. Light flooded the next-door garden. He had to find refuge quick. The voices were raised. 'For Christ sake, Gyp! What's the racket about?'

George crawled painfully. His knees were on fire. There had surely never been so many stones in this garden? Where had they come from? Lying flat, he reached up and found the latch of the shed door. He wriggled on his stomach into the hot woody-smelling dark and pulled the door to after him.

The dog owners were coming down their garden now. A torch wavered. He could see it through the door crack. The woman said, 'Oh, don't be at it, Larry, there's no one there.'

'Shh!' the man whispered. 'Dogs don't imagine things, Sandra. There's an intruder about.'

'You've been watching too much *Crimewatch*, you're addicted. They shouldn't show people all that stuff. Specially late at night.'

'They could still be in the gardens. Can't you keep your voice down at least?'

'Oh, come on, they'll be gone by now anyway. Gyp will have frightened them off. Didn't you, Gyp? Oh, he's a good dog. Good dog, aren't you, Gyp?'

'Well, I don't know, I'm not so sure. I wonder if I shouldn't just pop over the wall and take a look. Mrs Fletcher's away, you know.'

'Are you going in for the Mr Neighbourhood Watch competition or what? The big posh son's there, isn't he? Keeping an eye on things.'

On the floor of the shed, George winced.

'Well, I'm going in. And so is Gyp, aren't you, Gyp? Come on, Larry, he's done his business now, haven't you, boy?'

The voices grumbled away up the garden.

A door closed.

George became aware of a smell even worse than that of the compost heap. Or perhaps it just seemed to be worse in the enclosed space of the shed. He could not escape it immediately; those people might come out again. He put a mitted hand up to cover his nose. It smelled of compost heap which was better by far than the new smell. He waited more than a minute to make sure all was quiet, then he crawled out.

Outside the smell was still with him. He wondered if he were suffering from a sensory distortion sometimes experienced by those in an unusual emotional state. But surely no one's imagination could invent a smell like this. And then in the sliver of moonlight he found the source.

Gyp had done his business all right. Gyp's business was plastered all over the black sock that covered George's left plimsoll. He sat in the grass in the lee of the shed and wearily peeled off the disgustingly weighted sock. Doubled up, one black foot, one white, he staggered to the dustbin where, trying to make no noise, he carefully lifted the lid and dropped the thing in. Still doubled up, he crept round to the back door and let himself into the house. Even after a hot bath the smell seemed to linger.

On Monday morning George slept late.

16

Jack hadn't slept at all. He heard Polly getting up, padding from bedroom to bathroom weightless as a kitten. He heard her go out. He lay on his front, his head pressed against the headboard, his hands gripping it so hard it shook the bed. But Chloe stayed fast asleep.

Polly tripped along Brockhurst Road, through the station tunnel, past the supermarket, where Alison smiled and served, into the park and out again on to the main road, and into the special school where she, without a smile, put on her overall, and started to lay out the painting materials on the tables.

In the afternoon George took Kevin to the school by way of the supermarket. He saw Alison. Her face was lifted sweetly to a customer. He thought of her in church yesterday morning praying so hard. He saw her naked as he had seen her last night. He felt sick with shame at what he had done last night, and at the postures his mind had invented for her.

Dropping Kevin at the school gate George did not see Polly and Polly did not see

George. He walked on past the school. Wanting to avoid the tree alley, scene of his humiliating encounter with the skateboard, he went the long way round into the recreation ground: past the elder copse, the play area, alongside the railings with the mist of rose bay willow herb all along the railway line. Utterly weary, he sat down on a bench. The sun moved overhead. Trains roared by. It was hot. His eyes closed. George slept.

Jack emerged from the black mouth of the tunnel into Station Road. He hesitated, blinded by the light, then turned down the side road into the recreation ground. He sank on to the bench next to the sleeping George. His head dropped. He crunched the bones of his face with his great strong hands. A faint strange unpleasant smell was coming off the big guy at the other end of the bench. Jack got up. He loped into the longer grass near the railings. He lay face down as though he'd been shot in the head. Both men slept in the park.

George woke. His neck was stiff, his mouth gluey. Where was he? He took some time to get his bearings. He looked in panic at his watch – how could he have slept so long? – and flapped off down the dreaded tree alley to fetch Kevin from the school. He had to go that way or be late for his brother.

The mothers milled about outside, talking, laughing. Their big grown-up children crowded down the drive, some in wheel-chairs, some on the arms of teachers and teachers' helps. Polly never came outside the school unless she had to. She didn't like to be seen with the merry unfortunates who greeted their mothers so joyfully, hugging and kissing.

George was embarrassed to be hugged, but no one seemed to mind or even to notice. Kevin took his hand. The innocents lurched past the Church of the Holy Innocents, but Kevin tugged on George's arm, dragging him into the tree alley again. The park was Kevin's big treat. His mother seldom indulged him. George could have refused. But this way they would have to pass two sides of the supermarket to get back to the High Street. And he needed to waste an hour or so. He couldn't resist.

Kevin went leaping away to the railings bounding the railway line. He almost tripped over Jack who lay there, still on his front, snoring. Kevin bent to look at the crow-like man. An expression of concern crossed his face. Then a train roared by and he darted off in excited pursuit.

George sat on his bench for a while, clearing the sleep from the corners of his brain. Then he tore Kevin away from his fascinating trains. 'Tomorrow, Kev.'

Outside the supermarket car park he sat Kevin on a low wall. A cat came stepping along the top of the wall to sit by Kevin. Kevin put out a hand and fondled the cat. Both made the same chirruping sound. The cat rolled on to its side, then its back.

George left Kevin with the cat and, crossing to the newsagent's, saw Alison in the supermarket still at her post. He bought a newspaper, opened it and watched her over it.

They kept Polly late at the school tidying away the play things. She ran through the park without seeing Jack in the long grass sleeping. She passed Kevin and the cat with a dismissive glance. She recognised him as one of the morons she helped to take care of each day, but her day's work was over. He was no business of hers now. Down the tunnel she went, under the tracks to the other side.

George folded his newspaper, crossed Station Road, passed the glass doors at the front of the supermarket close to Alison's checkout, then turned the corner and continued down the lane. He checked his watch. Only a quarter of an hour to closing time. He rejoined Kevin and the cat, which had now curled itself in Kevin's lap. Kevin cooed his intimate noises over the animal, his hand gentle on its fur. George turned the pages of the newspaper without absorbing a word of what he read. The sun was low but still hot.

At six Alison came out of the back door of the supermarket, deep in conversation with another girl. They crossed the car park and turned into the lane. George moved swiftly in front of Kevin, his back to the girls, hiding them from Kevin with the newspaper and himself. The girls walked off in the direction of the High Street without looking round.

'Come on, Kev.'

Kevin, reluctant, lifted the cat gently and put it back on the wall. He turned several times to wave at it.

'Kev, hurry up.'

At the clock there was no sign of Alison and her friend. They had already been swallowed in the sunlit crowds. After waiting so long, timing his pursuit so perfectly, he had lost her after all. 'Kevin, for heaven's sake!' George dragged him across the road, sore with disappointment and rage, trembling between the desire to shake Kevin like a rag and the duty to be kind. The frightening weak easy tears came to his eyes again. Kevin smiled uncertainly up at him. George said, 'It's okay, Kev. Never mind.'

Polly let herself in and listened for Jack. He wasn't in. She could always tell. The house

181

felt airy without him. Clean. She looked into the kitchen. The floor was sticky, the sink hilly with dirty crocks. Of Chloe there was no sign. Polly ignored the mess. She ran upstairs. For once she didn't change into her Kylie things. She ran a deep cool bath and soaked, washed her hair and dried it. She carefully ironed a pair of jeans and a pure white, low-cut lacy cotton top.

Jack slept on in the park.

Kevin sprawled on the floor of the living room, absorbed in his train picture book. George sat up straight in an armchair absorbed in terror and dreams. He held some papers on his knees, pretending to work.

The doorbell rang.

The two brothers raised their heads and sniffed the air. Silence. It rang again.

George answered the door.

17

The girl who stood there was small. Her blonde hair brushed her shoulders. She looked up at him with large blue eyes. She had been speaking for some time. George had not heard.

'I'm sorry?' he said. His voice sounded cracked and a long way off. 'I'm sorry, what did you say?'

'The room.' The girl's smooth forehead made a tiny frown. 'I've come about the room you advertised.'

'Room?'

'Yes.'

What is happening? 'I'm sorry?' he said again.

'You advertised a room.' She was trying to be patient. 'In the shop window. The newsagent's, you know.'

Is this a joke? Am I being set up here? What is going on?

She said, 'This is number thirty-five, isn't it?'

Of course this is number thirty-five, you know it is, you live at number twenty-nine! 'Yes,' he said. 'This is number thirty-five.'

'Well then.'

'I – don't understand...?'

'Studio, it said. Own cooking arrangements, share bathroom. Twenty-five pounds a week. Inc.'

'Ink?'

'I suppose it meant gas and things. Included. You know.'

'Oh...' He took a breath. 'Where did you see this – advertisement?'

'In the newsagent's. I said. On the High Street. Opposite the Wimpy Bar.'

The Wimpy Bar. I am being set up. She saw me watching her. The fracas with the magazines. Everybody knows.

'I saw it yesterday,' she said.

I bet you did.

'I came right away but there was no one in. Has it gone?'

'What?'

'The room. Has it gone?'

'I – don't know.' *She is even more beautiful than I thought.*

'I'm sure this is the address.' She consulted a small piece of torn paper with writing on it. 'Thirty-five Lisson Avenue. Room to let.' The little voice faltered. The eyes filled with disappointment. 'Isn't it true, then? Isn't there a room? Suitable for young lady, it said. Non-smoker preferred. I don't smoke. I hate smoking. Honestly.'

It's not a joke? But then? Why should she want a room here? She lives at number twenty-nine.

'Look–' George made an attempt to pull himself together. 'There seems to have been some mistake. I don't know anything about a room.'

'But why would somebody put up a card?'

'I don't know.' George felt lost in space somewhere between her eyes and his. A wild joy started to possess him. She was standing on his doorstep. *She is here.*

'Oh.' Her head drooped a little. He thought of all the poetic clichés – flowers too heavy for their stalks, branches bending under the weight of their blossom – but none was poetic enough. 'It's so hard to find a room. That I can afford, I mean. I'm a student, you see.'

Student? She works in the supermarket.

'I'd pay in advance. I've saved – I mean I've got a student loan and everything. And I'm very – clean and – and that. Couldn't I just look at the room?'

George's mind was spinning. *She wants to come into my house. She is forcing me to bring her into my house.* He saw the empty attic with the bed, the striped mattress, the ropes– *There is no room to let.* 'There's obviously been some mistake,' he said. 'My mother is away, you see.' *She knows my mother is away. Her parents are on the same coach.*

'Your mother?' she said.

What is this? 'Yes. My mother. She's away for a couple of weeks. I'm just here taking care of – things – while she's away.'

The girl's face opened up: 'It was your mother put the card in the shop then! She forgot to say!'

'No. I don't think so. We really don't have a room to let, a studio as you called it. I know we don't.'

And all the time he was thinking of the locked attic door. And he was thinking about Warren's warning: *Don't do it, George.* And he was thinking about how Warren

185

might handle this: *Well, come in, darling, have a look round, sit down, make yourself at home.*

The girl's eyes suddenly widened. In alarm? Fright? Her face took on a baffled expression. He wondered if she had read his thoughts. But no, she had stopped looking at George. She was looking somewhere behind him into the hall. George turned. Kevin was coming out of the front room. It was he who had diverted her attention causing this sudden fear. But why should the sight of Kevin frighten her? She knew him, didn't she? She played in the garden with him. Kevin came up behind him and stood at his shoulder.

'Oh,' she said, 'I–' She stopped. Kevin was smiling his wide smile at her. She didn't respond to his smile. She looked at George. For a moment she seemed completely at a loss. Then she said, addressing Kevin as though he were a stranger to her, 'Do *you* know anything about a room?' Her cool little voice took on authority. 'Did your mum tell you she had a room to let? Before she went away?'

Kevin looked at George in doubt.

'He can't understand, I'm afraid. He's–' *Why am I explaining to her?*

'A room,' she repeated in the same commanding tone. 'Your mother,' she said.

Kevin suddenly started to bounce. He lolloped away towards the kitchen. The girl smiled at George. Her smile hit him like a light going on. And all at once he saw: *It's not the same girl! It's not the girl from number twenty-nine! It's not Alison!* Confusion, loss, sadness, joy, relief, hope. George was whirled in a spiral. He was a spinning top. A humming spinning top.

The girl was talking to him: 'I'm sure it's not a mistake. There must be a room, mustn't there? She just forgot to tell you before she went. People do forget things when they're travelling. Journey-proud, my mum calls it. She's Yorkshire. When you can't sleep and that. The night before. You know. Oh!'

George, following her eyes, turned to look behind him. Kevin was laughing and holding up a key. He swung it from its string like a pendulum. 'Where did you find that, Kevin?' George's voice had hardly any sound in it.

'Gheegh, gheegh, gheegh!' Kevin sang.

George held out his hand with authority. Kevin, subdued, put the key into it. *This is the key to my attic.* His heart was pounding so hard it was making him deaf and blind. *What has my mother done?* 'Look,' he said, 'since my mother does appear to have advertised a room to let, I don't know but – I had better – look into the matter.'

There was a sparkle on the girl's face, sunlight on water. 'Oh yes!' She looked like a child.

Don't do it, George.

187

'You had better come in.' There, he had said it. The girl was walking into his house. 'Could you wait a moment. In here. If you wouldn't mind.' He showed her into the living room.

Kevin went in also, smiling at her. 'Ghoghee, Ghoghee,' he said.

But the girl ignored him. She looked only at George.

'Be quiet now, Kev,' George said. 'He's – all right,' he said to the girl. 'He wouldn't harm – anyone.'

She gave Kevin the merest glance. 'Oh, yes,' she said. 'That's okay.'

George bumped into the door jamb getting out of the room. He went upstairs. He stood on the first landing collecting himself. On this floor were only his room, his mother's, Kevin's. *The attic floor.* He slowly climbed the top flight, the key in his hand. His legs had a sort of tremble in them, just behind the knee. He was afraid to go straight to the door he knew it must be.

He looked into the front attic first. Still just the junk, from floor to ceiling. The bed his father died in, the scuffed Lloyd Loom chairs, the drooping candlewick bedspreads over the chests of drawers. Then into Kevin's train room. His train tracks on the floor, his shell and stone collection on the window sill. And in the place of honour on the mantelpiece his Goddess of the

Magazine sat propped. George panted across the room and snatched at her.

He squeezed her, face down, viciously into the middle of a pile of old train magazines, crushing the rest of the pile down hard on top of her. Almost trembling, at last he went back to the landing and tried the key in the back attic door. He held his breath. The key turned. He opened the door. He stared. He closed his eyes for a moment and opened them again.

The walls had been painted white. A grass-green carpet covered the bare boards. A divan bed was draped with a cotton spread in a deep gentian blue. Yellow cotton curtains hung at either side of the window. In the far alcove by the window were arranged a small sink, a microwave cooker and a small fridge. Pretty red mugs hung on hooks from a shelf above. A curtain hung across the near alcove to form a makeshift wardrobe.

A murderous rage shook him. He pressed his hands against his chest. *My mother has destroyed the room of my dreams. She did it in secret. She must have been doing it for weeks. Why didn't she want me to know? Why did she remove the key?* He was rushed, buffeted. His mind was an engine shed, thoughts grinding this way and that. Shifting, colliding, they clattered, they deafened him. But one thought separated itself and soared above the rest. *A girl is waiting downstairs for me. A girl more beautiful than my girl. A new my girl. A different my girl. A better my girl. A my girl who wants to live in my house.*

He went down slowly, needing time to compose himself. He stopped at the bottom of the stairs. He heard laughter from the living room. He stood silent in the doorway watching.

The girl was sitting on her haunches on the floor laughing up into Kevin's face. Kevin crouched in the armchair. He bounced up and down and laughed wildly. The girl's hand was touching Kevin's foot.

'Kevin!' George's voice came out louder than he had meant.

Both stopped laughing and turned. The girl took her hand from Kevin's foot. They looked at him round-eyed like children. George said without looking at the girl, 'If you'd care to look at the room.'

The girl stood up in one fluid movement. 'There *is* a room!'

'Yes.'

'Ohh!' And she came towards him. 'I knew there would be.'

Kevin hovered on his chair, hoping to be included but cowed by George's angry tone.

'Is he called Kevin?' the girl said.

'Yes. My brother, Kevin. Miss er...?'

'Adams. Kylie. Kylie Adams.' Her small voice was firm.

George cleared his throat. *Kylie. Kylie. Not Alison.*

'Can Kevin come?' she said.

'Come?'

'With us. To see the room.'

She doesn't want to be alone with me. She's afraid to be alone with me. What does she know? George didn't want to frighten her further. 'Yes,' he said. And to Kevin, 'Come on, Kev.'

Kevin flopsied behind them up the stairs.

George felt ashamed showing the room. *Bright shallow trashy – what was Mother thinking of?*

The girl gasped. 'Oh, it's beautiful!' She moved about, touching things.

The way she moves.

'Nice colours,' she said.

Both men watched her, absorbed.

She turned and parted her lips, revealing her little teeth, a kitten intense with a new scent. 'Oh, I'd like to live here,' she said. She came towards George.

He was on the point of opening his arms to enfold her. *What am I thinking of? This girl is not Marje. She is not even Alison. I must not touch this girl.*

Kevin, though, put out a hand and touched the girl's arm. She gave him her small smile. 'Nice, isn't it, Kevin?'

'Ghighe, ghighe,' said Kevin.

A volcanic eruption of jealousy surged

through George. He turned abruptly and started downstairs, leaving them.

The girl's cool little voice halted him. 'Where is the bathroom, by the way?'

'Oh. Yes.' He could barely speak for the hot lava in his throat. 'This way, please.'

She followed close on his heels down the stairs, almost as though she did not want to be left alone with Kevin. Perhaps he had been mistaken. She had simply been showing kindness to Kevin rather than preference. People did.

'I don't want to – you know – *go*,' she said. 'It's only that the ad said share bathroom, so...'

George's hot face flushed darkly. 'It's on this landing. I'm afraid we have only the one.'

'Can I see it then?'

He opened a door. It was a square cold room, shiny green paint, cracked linoleum from God knows when, as far back as he could remember. White tiles, cracked too, the bath enamel chipped. There was a heated towel rail, never switched on, and a hanging electric fire contraption high up draped with cobwebs and caked with dusty fluff. The mirror was pocked with black spots.

'Oh,' said the girl in a disappointed way.

George saw the bleakness of the room for the first time. His mother's obsessive house-pride had never extended here. This had never struck him before as odd. And in spite of his jealous rage of a moment ago he prayed: *Don't let it put her off.* 'I'm about to start decorating it,' he said. Decorating, as something he himself might do, was a concept that had never occurred to him in his life.

She looked at him without expression. 'Where's the loo?'

George scratched his forehead with his thumbnail, cleared his throat. 'Oh. Erm – the cr – WC – is separate.'

'That's a convenience.' She seemed to think she had made a joke.

The way she smiles. 'Yes,' George said. 'I suppose it is.' He indicated the door.

The girl opened it and Kevin pranced in and made as if to pull the chain. He liked flushing the lavatory, the swooshing of the water excited him.

'No, Kevin.' George was hot all over. Kevin stopped.

'It's the biggest loo I've ever seen. The room I mean, not – you know – the actual bog.' The girl smiled, unembarrassed by the use of these extraordinary words, never as far as George knew heard in this context in this house before.

'Ghogh, ghogh!' Kevin cried, delighted.

'That's enough, Kevin.' George led the way downstairs.

She followed him. 'It's a brilliant house,' she said. 'Have you always lived here?'

'Well, yes.'

'You're really lucky. I'd give anything for a house like this.'

'You are – from the North – are you?'

'The North?'

'Yes. Your mother. You said–'

'Oh! Yes! Yes, Leeds. A council house. Couldn't wait to get out.'

'Where are you – staying at present?'

'Oh. Erm. In Croydon. It's awful there. I'm sharing a – place with these two awful people. The space-invaders I call them. I can't stand them. It's terrible, sharing.'

George looked at Kevin, who gazed at her adoring, his arms round the newel post at the bottom of the stairs.

'Yes,' George said. 'It must be.'

They all stood there in the hall. Kevin looked at the girl. The girl looked at George. George looked at his feet. *Meeting her eyes is such unbearable joy, such unbearable fear.*

'Well...?' she said at last.

'Well...' George spoke slowly.

'I'd really like the room,' she said. 'Can I have it, please?'

Like a little girl asking for the last slice of cake. 'My mother will have to decide of course. As it was she who placed the advertisement.'

'Oh, yes. But I have to move soon. I can't stand it where I am any more. I'll make it all right with your mother, really I will. After all, she did put the card in the window, didn't she? She must have wanted someone. She can't blame you.'

She had an uncanny knack of divining meanings he did not want her to see. 'Oh, no, of course, no question of – well –blame. Naturally. But–'

'I'll pay in advance.'

Pay? George was affronted. He spoke stiffly. 'Monetary arrangements I will leave to my mother. They are nothing to do with me.'

'Oh. Yes. Right.'

There was a silence. She was waiting for him to speak.

Don't do it, George.

'When would you wish to move in?' he said. *There! I've said it. I have done it. It's done.*

'Oh!' Her face lit up. 'Would this weekend be all right?'

'Well, I–'

'Please let me move in this weekend. I haven't got much stuff. I'll be ever so quiet. I won't be a nuisance. You won't know I'm here.'

'But my mother–'

'If she gets back and doesn't want me here, fine. If she'd rather have someone else then I'll go, of course.'

Don't, George.

'Please.' Her voice was very small. And her mouth made a small trembling smile.

'All right then,' he said. A mixture of shame and relief made him weak at the knees. 'But it will be up to my mother when she returns, to—'

'Oh, yes!' Her face was alight. And Kevin had his all-over smile.

I've pleased the children anyway.

'I'm so grateful,' she said correctly. She put out her hand.

George in a dream took the small boneless thing. He held it. *Never since Marje have I held – have I felt–* He was looking at her eyes. She gave a little laugh. *She's laughing at me?* The hand pulled away a little. He let it go. It was like releasing a fledgling bird. His hand felt empty. Needy.

'I'll move in on Friday evening then. If that's all right.'

'Yes,' George heard himself say. 'That will be – fine.' Kevin took George's arm and leaned against him.

'He's affectionate, isn't he?' said the girl.

When she looked at Kevin, jealousy like a surgeon's knife opened George straight up the middle. *The shed. Marje in the shed with the man. Number twenty-nine girl in the shed with Kevin. BUT THIS IS A DIFFERENT GIRL.*

'They generally are,' she said.

'I'm sorry. What?'

'People who aren't all there. They're generally affectionate.' Her little smile included George: *You and I, we are all there, we're all right, we're the normal ones.* George's hurt was soothed. 'Well, so I've heard,' she said.

He smiled, gazing at her face. He had betrayed Kevin again. By his smile he was complicit.

'Well...' she said.

I'm supposed to do something now. The thing he could hardly bear to do. He opened the door.

She hopped on the step like a bird preparing for flight. She gave another little smile, shy this time, from behind her pale gold wing of hair. 'Well. I'll see you on Friday then!'

She has so many different smiles.

'Yes. Friday.'

'About six okay?'

Her small white teeth.

'Yes. Six is – convenient.'

'And thank you.'

Her cool sweet voice.

'No. No, not at all.'

Like a little bird.

She went. George closed the door. Terror and delight danced, pricking all over his skin. He leaned back against the door and shut his eyes. Kevin pranced about the hall.

18

Detective Inspector John Bright, strolling along Lisson Avenue on the way back to his mother's house, saw a small blonde girl with shiny shoulder-length hair come out from between the laurels and turn up the street ahead of him. He noticed the patch on the seat of her jeans, the liquid walk. Nice little arse, he thought. The response was mechanical, there was no heat in it.

The girl gave a sudden skip, reached up a graceful arm and pulled a branch down, heavy with bloom. She pressed her face into the roses. She stood very still. She let the branch go and leapt into a run. Bright watched till she turned the corner at the end of the street.

That was George's house she came out of, he thought. He remembered Kevin's little friend in the garden. So she was allowed in the house these days? He had an impulse to go up the path and knock on the door. But something about the girl, her youth perhaps, her carefree grace, caused a blank sadness to descend on him. He looked at the miserable front of George's house and walked on.

George, on his way upstairs, unexpectedly

shivered. His mother would have said, *Someone walked across your grave.*

Suddenly Bright wheeled round, retraced his steps, and darted up the path. The door opened before he had taken his hand off the bell. 'Hi, Kevin. Remember me?'

Kevin shook his head and went on shaking it, smiling his eager puppy dog smile.

'You don't remember me from the other night?'

'Who is it, Kevin?'

Bright watched the unwieldy feet descend the stairs. He'd always said George should have been the bobby, not he. He certainly had the feet for it. 'Hello, George.'

George loomed out of the shadows of the stairs. The whites of his eyes were more yellowish, his big lips looked strained and almost bruised. He had started to say something but when he saw John Bright he stopped and simply stared.

Bright groaned. 'Not you an' all? Am I becoming invisible or what?'

George's big features seemed to shift. 'John?' His voice had a wondering tone and his face a dazed look.

'Got it in one.' Bright grinned.

His face began to clear. 'Oh. Ha. No. Sorry. I was a bit– My mind was – preoccupied. Yes. Come in.'

'Not if your ma's in.'

'Actually, she's away.'

'Away! Your ma?'

Seven varieties of sheepishness ploughed through George's face one after another. He put a bunch of fingers to his mouth and coughed. 'She's gone on a coach tour of Spain.'

'You're kidding.' Bright whistled then gave a short laugh. 'I see. When the cat's away... So who are the mice playing with then, George? Kevin's pretty little playmate just flew out of here.'

'Well, actually, that's not–' George was having difficulty. He obviously now thought better of what he had been going to say and began again. 'Yes. Actually–' He rubbed the top of his head. 'That is, she's– Actually she's going to be staying here.'

'Staying here? While your ma's away? Christ, George.' Bright laughed again.

'No. No. It's not what you're– She – she answered an advertisement.' He scratched between his brows with a thumbnail and took a deep breath. 'My mother placed a card in the newsagent's window. Room to let. One of the – attic rooms. This girl came about the room. I suppose she might be – company – for her. For Mother, I mean. So I – so I – agreed.' At the end of his halting tale he said, 'So.' And cleared his throat.

'A-ha.' Bright gave him a sideways look, not quite a grin. 'Company for your ma. I see.'

George made an effort. Ignoring Bright's teasing he stepped back to let him in. 'It's good to see you, John,' he said in a different tone and led the way to the kitchen where he made himself busy with the coffee things. Kevin was in the garden now, alone, rolling a ball about with his foot. Bright saw vividly what his mother had seen the other night – Kevin was not just handsome, he was strikingly beautiful. The black hair, the liquid eyes, the full mouth. He looked seventeen though in his early twenties. For other – normal – young men of his age this was the brink of life. Bright stood at the window watching him.

Polly floated into the house in Brockhurst Road singing a quiet little song. She rolled up her sleeves and started on the washing up. She could hear Jack pacing back and forth upstairs.

Chloe came in from the living room. 'Hi, Poll! Have a good day?'

'Not bad.' Polly smiled to herself a neat little smile.

Chloe sat down and stretched out her legs. 'Hey,' she said, 'I'm going away next weekend!'

Polly's back went quite still for a moment. 'Are you?'

'Yeah! Glastonbury. Joan from the yoga's taking a minibus full. Someone dropped out at the last minute so I can go free. Ever so exciting, isn't it? We leave on Friday afternoon.'

'What about Jack?'

'Jack doesn't know whether I'm here or not most of the time. He doesn't know if it's August or breakfast. Nothing I can do. I ought to have him sectioned, that's what I think.'

Polly agreed though not aloud. There was a pause. Chloe hummed.

'How do you section people?' Polly said. 'Can anybody do it?'

'I don't know. I think it's quite hard actually. Unless the person gets in trouble with the police. Will you be all right on your own with him, Poll?'

'Oh, yes.' Polly gave another little smile that her mother couldn't see. 'I'll be fine.'

John Bright said goodnight to George cheerfully enough. But as he strolled down past the heavy midsummer gardens the familiar sadness descended again. He wondered what George did, alone in that house, just his brother for company. What was he doing now? And Kevin? He didn't know which was the sadder of the two. *Three sad buggers if it comes to that,* he thought, including himself.

George was lying face down on the grass-green carpet on the floor of the newly decorated attic room. The door was locked.

The key was in his hand. *Which girl did I see on the other side of the tracks? Which one did I follow into the park? Which girl have I been longing for all these weeks? It doesn't matter now. It's all fate. The girl at number twenty-nine – Alison – she was a mere precursor. A sign of what was to come. This girl is Kylie. Kylie, what a silly name. But lovely. Kylie. She is my second chance.* He pressed his face into the green carpet. *Don't let me make a mess of this.*

Alison was climbing over the garden wall of number thirty-five. Kevin was holding out his arms to welcome her.

Lily Bright looked sad when he came in. Everyone was bloody sad these days. Was it his own sadness throwing this pall over everything? 'What's the matter with you, Ma?'

'What's the matter with me is what's the matter with you.'

'What's the matter with me now is what's the matter with George.'

'George is fine! He's keeping watch on the pond. Just because he doesn't come running to greet you the minute you get in–'

'Not that George, Ma.'

'George Fletcher?'

'That's the one.'

'Ah, what *isn't* the matter with that poor thing?'

'I think maybe he's in love.'

'With someone as unsuitable as that Marje, no doubt?'

'In spades, Ma.'

'He's having his mid-life crisis, John.'

He almost laughed out loud. 'He's the same age as me!'

'He's having it early. He's kept himself bottled up all these years since Marje left him. But you can't keep your life bottled up for ever, John. It'll break out sooner or later. And when it does break out, it breaks out bad.'

'Who are we talking about here, Ma?'

'If the cap fits, John.'

'A-ha. Thought so. Never miss a chance, do you?'

She gave him a sly smile. He gave her his cross-eyed wink. It didn't cheer his face.

19

For the bathroom he took a leaf out of Warren's book. Walls pale grey, carpet white, black Venetian blind. He went to Habitat in Croydon and bought a big black jar and, so as not to be slavishly copy-cat, some black artificial tulips – or were they poppies? He wasn't sure. But they looked extravagant, large and sensuously open, their bright

orange stamens a contrast to their mono-
chrome setting. The cracked black and white
thirties tiles remained but took on a rakish
air. George, spattered with paint, felt proud
of his achievement. Kevin, round-eyed,
stroked the carpet lingeringly, bemused.

But decorating was harder than he'd
thought. It took him the whole week, working
from early in the morning till late at night.
During that week he saw the girl from number twenty-nine twice. On Tuesday evening
she came out of her house and walked past
his. She even looked up at his window. He
compared her with Kylie and wondered how
he could ever have got them confused. He
felt no desire whatever to follow her.

The next day he and Kevin actually met
her in the street. She even nodded at
George, and smiled shyly. Then she said,
'Hello, Kev,' in a husky small voice, nothing
like the cool raindrops of *his* girl's voice. A
few days ago this would have been exquisite,
undreamed of, tortured bliss. But now:
She's nothing compared with – Kylie. The
name was honey on his tongue. *She's just a
pretty girl. A friend for Kevin, that's all. How
could I have got into such a state about her?* He
nodded at her pleasantly and they walked
on. The pavement was his trampoline. He
felt almost graceful with happiness.

Kevin tugged his sleeve. He smiled up
sideways at George, spilling out noises,

incomprehensible but unmistakably fond. *Does Kevin love her then? What would that mean? Would he even know which girl was which? Come to that, would I have, once?* He asked himself again, *Did I ever follow Kylie in the street?* The thought made him hot with desire. *There's no need to follow her any longer. She has come to me. She's coming to live in my house. She has been sent to me.*

On Thursday evening, however, George glanced out of the kitchen window and saw Alison step from the wall into Kevin's arms. His heart did something strange, some actual physical lurch that made him unable to move for a moment. He watched them take hands and slowly make their way to the shed. She opened the door and Kevin followed her in. The door closed.

It was minutes before his power of locomotion came back to him. Quietly he opened the back door. His clumsy feet slurred through the grass. The shed had a small cobwebbed window at the back. George squeezed his bulk into the narrow space between the back of the shed and the wall. He put his face against the window and his hands on either side of his face. At first it was too dark to see, but gradually a picture appeared, framed by his hands.

The two young people knelt facing each other on a pile of sacks. They were naked.

Her hands softly touched Kevin's mouth, his eyes, his hair. She looked in amazement at him, as though her eyes could barely believe his beauty. Kevin had the same expression looking at her. His hands stroked her hair, her face, her neck, her shoulders. They hovered above her small breasts not daring to touch. She took his left hand and covered her breast with it. She closed her eyes. Kevin leaned his head against her breasts and closed his eyes too, in ecstasy it seemed. Their young bodies were fluid in the glaucous light, like reflections in water. Her arms encircled the boy. George couldn't move, even had he wanted to. He stayed where he was.

The girl lay down pulling the boy with her. They were no longer Kevin and Alison, they were any boy, any girl, every boy, every girl. They were Marje and the Man. George's head was splitting. *Kevin and Alison, boy and girl, Marje and the Man?*

He watched as the girl lay back. He watched as she gently guided his brother. He watched as she took hold of his – thing – the only word his mother had ever allowed him to use – and helped him put it into her. They recalled again himself and Marje that day in the long grass. He watched their exquisite long slow dance, the mutual long slow shudder, the sudden flailing as they both cried out, two fishes landed, entwined.

Then he watched as they lay limp, their two spent bodies shining. The sweat. George strangely felt no shame. He had watched as he might have watched two perfect animals in a glade. But he felt despair.

It was the shining sweat that caused his desolation. That fluid mutuality. The proof that two people could move as one. *How do they know how?* He had never known. He remembered how he used to clamber on top of Marje. He so big and she so small. He was so afraid of crushing her he used to prop himself up on his hands so that their bodies barely touched. Marje used to lie quite still with her eyes closed and her head turned to one side. George saw in one vision all Marje's behaviour with him and what it meant. *She must have hated me.*

He felt a bloom of horror opening inside him like the black flowers in the bathroom. Kevin. Pathetic, sweet, hopeless Kevin, unable to read, to count above three, unable to speak, Kevin could give lessons in this. Kevin had just given George the lesson of a lifetime. *Kevin.* George saw all at once that the only things that had ever made him feel all right in the world were based on being better than Kevin. The George who passed exams at school, George who became a chartered accountant, George the good son who supported his widowed mother. He saw now that these visions of himself were pathetic, based on a meaningless superiority. Any life form higher than a dog was superior to Kevin in these matters. But in the things that really counted, he saw now, Kevin was far above him. *Far. Far. Far.*

He didn't know if the act he had watched was happening for the first time or was one more time of many. He recognised in wonder that the girl must have instigated these extraordinary couplings. Kevin would never have– Or would he? George wondered about other girls. Kylie? *Kylie! NO!* The piercing jealousy of his brother shot through him, worse than before. *I won't let him get his hands on Kylie. I'll kill him first.* George's face was wet. His hands were clenched.

The two limp bodies began to move again. The girl pushed her wet hair off her face. She lifted her thin arms and put them round Kevin's neck. Their faces met. Then Kevin sat back on his heels. His liquid brown eyes looked wonderingly at her. His hands stroked lovingly every inch of her body. She lay watching him. He laid his head between her thighs. She reached down, clinging to his wet black hair. Her eyes closed, her face rapt in concentrated pleasure.

George could not believe she was allowing this. He had seen her at church the other day. Praying. As engrossed in prayer as she was in – this. Would Marje have allowed–? Had she ever allowed–? Did she allow that other man–?

Yes, yes, yes!

So why didn't she teach me?

She didn't know how? She was too young? She didn't like me enough?

I killed her joy. I killed Marje.

Marje is not dead.

I killed Marje.

George knew quite finally that all the lessons in the world couldn't teach him what Kevin knew. What the girl knew. As a fish knows water. As a swallow knows flight.

Does everyone know it except me?

George had seen movies. He'd thought those ecstatic couplings were some kind of stylisation, an artistic formula, poetic licence. But no! They simply showed what everybody knew. What everybody did. Everybody except him.

George was mad now with the loss of this thing he had never had. Had he had it even once and lost it he might die of the loss of it. They were clasped in each other's arms again now, Kevin and the girl, rolling over and over, laughing, drenched. Laughter and sweat. The two worst things. In the shed.

George drags open the door He grabs them, one in each huge hand. He lifts them off the pile of sacks. He swings them crashing against the walls of the shed, once, twice, ten times, twenty times, once for each time Marje did it with the Man, Alison with Kevin, Kylie with – how

*many men? He crashes them against the walls
till they are two rag dolls, bleeding, their faces
pulped, no features left, nothing, their hair
matted with blood, their blood spattered inside
the shed, everywhere. He throws them down on
the bloody sacks and crushes them with his big
ugly graceless feet until at last there is nothing
left except the saturated sacks. He has trampled
them back into the earth. They are gone.*

He opened his eyes. The girl was kneeling.
She was pulling a little garment on over her
head. Her face emerged smiling. She handed
Kevin his sweatshirt and helped him to put
it on. She kissed his body as she covered it,
as though bidding it goodbye inch by inch as
it disappeared from her sight. So tender.

I am sick.

Not caring even if they heard him, George
moved away from behind the shed. He was
surprised to see sunlight. *It's day then still.
What day? What day is it?*

Somehow he managed to get himself back
inside the house.

20

The next day, Friday, Polly packed her few belongings and composed a note for her mother to find when she was gone. Chloe was on her way to Glastonbury, bouncing along in an ancient minibus singing 'Amazing Grace' stoned out of her head. Jack was nowhere to be seen. Polly was glad of this. Though prepared for, she didn't desire a confrontation with Jack. She picked up one of the twenty or so cards advertising taxi firms that had fallen through the letter box and been left to gather dust behind the door. She dialled the number. She had never called a cab before. It gave her a feeling of importance. She was independent now.

She walked out of her room, and the house, without a backward glance, leaving the kitchen sink still piled with washing up. The note for her mother was propped against the sugar bowl on the kitchen table. It said, *Dear Mum, I have got a place of my own. I'm not leaving an address because I don't want anyone coming after me. I'm alright and I'll come and see you one day next week. Poll.* She got into the taxi feeling like Kylie Minogue.

'Thirty-five Lisson Avenue, please,' she

said, just the way she'd seen it in the movies. She sat back. It was a short journey but a sweet one to the other side of the tracks. Outside thirty-five Lisson Avenue the driver helped her with her bags. In her innocence Polly accepted such homage as an everyday occurrence. She paid him, adding a tip of precisely ten per cent. Since the cab had done little more than cross the High Street the fare wasn't great, but it was more than Polly expected and she had a momentary worry about whether she was going to be able to manage this flight to freedom as smoothly as she had always planned.

Then George opened the door and she walked up the path to him, leaving her bags at the gate. George went down the path to fetch her bags. He carried them easily to the top floor. She followed him, wrinkling her nose at the powerful smell of paint.

George looked different from the last time she'd seen him. His face seemed thinner, accentuating the size of his nose, his ears. He had had a solid dependable air which, while it didn't make him handsome, inspired confidence, respect. This had gone. He was just as large but he lacked solidity now. His eyes burned. He wavered. He put her suitcase and carrier bags down just inside her room. 'Here you are,' he said. He didn't look at her, he looked at a point on the wall behind her head.

'Thank you.'

'I – hope you'll be comfortable. Let me know if you – need anything. Lack anything. I'll be – downstairs.'

He hovered, but she said nothing else so he backed off. He trundled down the stairs, feet flapping. Polly/Kylie watched him, a faint puzzlement on her face. Something about him had suddenly reminded her of Jack. But that wasn't possible. Was it? They couldn't be more different. Could they? That was the reason she had decided this was the place for her: the prosperous dependability, the respectability of George. The only things the two men had in common were that they were men and roughly of an age. What was it that had puzzled her then? Was it something in his eyes? She gave a little shiver. She was being fanciful. *He's nothing like Jack.*

She closed her door, however. She locked it. She hugged the key in her hand. It was the first key all of her own that she had ever had. She placed it reverently on the mantelpiece.

She unzipped her bag and pulled out her performance clothes. She shook out and smoothed down the satin of the pale pink dress. Opposite the fireplace a full-length mirror hung. She could see her beauty whole, not parcelled out in bits as it had been in the cramped space at home. She changed swiftly and was enchanted by what she saw. To the music in her head she sang sotto voce from Kylie's 'Body Language' and danced the dance of her escape, from sordid Brockhurst Road, across the railway tracks to the leafy streets, the big respectable house, her own place, her own room, her own life. *This is my Kylie life.*

When the performance was finished she made a long slow curtsy to her image in the mirror. She took off her pink slinky strap shoes. She let the pale cool fragile confection fall to her bare feet. Polly/Kylie had never heard of Botticelli but he would have been as ravished by her beauty as she was herself. He might also have calculated as nicely the uses to which it could be put. Polly/Kylie liked it here. She wanted to stay.

The problem was Kevin. *The people here mustn't know I work at Kevin's school because then Mum might be able to trace me. And she'd never be able to keep a secret from Jack. Kevin can't tell them because they can't understand what he says. I can understand him better than his brother can and I can't make out much. I've really got a problem when his mum comes back. I'll have to make sure she doesn't see me when she brings him to school or picks him up. That shouldn't be too hard. I don't think she's ever seen me there. I never go outside the school with them. If she does recognise me I'll have to have an explanation ready, that's all.* Polly sat down on her bright blue divan to think.

215

George stood in the dark kitchen trying not to think. He wished he could control the shaking. Since yesterday he'd been like a man weeks at sea in a small boat, the movement of the ocean still in all his limbs. He thought he might have a fever – the state was flu-like. He had trouble remembering where he was.

Kevin was in the garden where George had banished him before Kylie's arrival. He was kicking a large red ball over the grass, running after it, throwing it up, catching it. He performed these actions with the same puppyish boneless grace as yesterday's – was it only yesterday's – activities in the shed. George found tears on his face again. Since yesterday he kept finding tears dripping from his eyes. He wiped them away with his hand. *Perhaps I should see a doctor.* The idea floated across his brain. But it left no trace.

'Excuse me.'

George jerked back and turned. Kylie was standing in the doorway. A picture in its frame.

'Sorry. But do you think I could borrow some bread or something? It's just it's too late for the shops and I suddenly realised I hadn't eaten anything.'

'Yes. Of course! Yes.'

'Thanks a lot. And some milk if you don't mind and–'

'Yes, yes. But look – sit down. Eat here.

With us. It's just – about time for dinner.'
George recalled that he and Kevin should
eat too. He went to the freezer, found the
container marked Friday and the date. He
knew the date because it was the day of
Kylie's arrival, therefore annealed into his
brain. The instructions said in his mother's
spiky script, *Heat in oven mark six, forty
minutes.*

Kylie joined him at the freezer. 'Wow!' she
said. 'A meal for every day? I never saw
anything like that!'

'Yes,' said George. 'It is remarkable, I
suppose.'

'It's really cool,' she said.

'Yes, my – mother. She – prepares – food,
in advance, for – myself and my brother.'

'Kevin, yes.'

'You remember his name!'

'Yes, I– Yes. Why not?'

He looked at her and the simple sight of
her stopped the shaking.

She broke the silence. 'What do you do
with it now?'

Something in her expression brought
George back to reality. *How long have I been
standing staring at her?* 'Oh,' he said, 'erm …
there are instructions.'

'Let me see.' She took the frozen parcel
from his hands and went to the stove. 'Have
you got a gas lighter thing?'

'Oh. Yes.' He handed it to her, careful not

to let their fingers meet. He still hadn't touched her hands, except that once.

She put the foil container in the oven. 'There'll only be enough for two, won't there?' she said.

'Oh, I'm not hungry.' George spoke the truth.

She put her head on one side to regard him. 'You don't look well actually.' There was no sympathy in her little voice, she simply stated a fact.

'No, I – I think I may be getting flu.' George could hear the great gaps between his words. Language was something he had learned once but appeared to have forgotten. Looking was something he had never learned and now couldn't get enough of.

Kylie wasn't at all put out by his odd staring silences. She glided about the dark kitchen finding things in cupboards and drawers. He stood and watched her set the table and put out the bread. Objects seemed to float into her hands and out of them. She didn't seem to need to talk. And he couldn't.

George's oddness didn't affect Polly at all. She was used to people odder even than he. She decided his silence was caused by shyness, probably at her beauty which he wouldn't be used to yet. She decided she had merely imagined his momentary resemblance to Jack. 'Where's Kevin now then?' she said.

'Oh. He's in the – garden.'

'Yeah?' She looked out. 'Oh, it's big, the garden. It's nice.'

'Yes, I suppose it is.' George's eyes rested on Kevin a while. As did Kylie's.

'They're like great big babies, aren't they?' she said.

George felt the inner shaking start again. 'He's twenty-four,' he said.

'I know. I mean I guessed. He looks younger but they do, don't they? I mean I think they do.'

'How old does he look – to you?'

'Oh ... 'bout seventeen, I suppose.'

'May I ask – how old – are you?'

'I'm eighteen.'

'Ah?' The sound was a sigh, a question, a relinquishment.

'I don't know how you can stand living with one of them,' she said. Again there was no heat in her tone. 'Still, I suppose if it's your brother,' she conceded. 'Has he always been like that?'

'Well, yes. Always.'

'I don't know why they don't kill them at birth.'

George found himself defending the strange attitude that had allowed Kevin to live. 'Well, we didn't know for certain until he was nearly two. We – we had got – attached to him by then.' George felt this to be a feeble excuse for their negligent behaviour in allowing Kevin to survive. At the same time he felt hysteria rising. These ruthless practical solutions from this exquisite child. Terrifyingly lacking in imagination. But how unutterably charming she was.

'Oh, yes, I see,' she said but her brow creased in a puzzled little frown. Then she shrugged, dismissing the question of Kevin's survival. 'Where do you keep the salt and pepper?' she said.

During the meal Kevin called her Ghoghee, kept telling George this was her name. She ignored him for some time then spoke to him with great firmness: 'My name is Kylie, Kevin. Ky-lie.'

Kevin's eyes were wide. He was perplexed.

'Say it,' she instructed.

'Ghighe – ghee?' he said.

'That's right. That's my name. Okay?'

Kevin stared at her in silence. He shifted his gaze to George and raised his eyebrows, questioning. But George was no help, he sat in a state of suspension between rapture and terror that resembled flu. Then, watching Kylie bring his mother's reheated rhubarb crumble to the table, he saw her touch Kevin's hand. Kevin gifted her with one of his most radiant smiles. George's terror flared. He had to hide his naked face. He dropped his napkin to the floor and bent under the table to retrieve it.

Her feet and Kevin's under the table were not touching; they were far apart. That comforted him. *But what have I come to? Grovelling under the table because I am jealous of my own brother who has a mental age of six!* At the same time he was shaken by an almost uncontrollable desire to run his hand up her lovely smooth pale brown leg from the ankle to… 'Hnnh!' He lowered his head, gasping for breath.

Her face appeared under the table. 'Are you all right, Mr Fletcher?'

'George,' he gasped. 'Call me George.'

'Are you all right?'

'Yes.' He stared at her face which hung upside down. She stared at him. Again he felt hysteria rise. *No wonder she's staring. I am a grown man crouching on all fours under the kitchen table!* He grabbed the dropped napkin and said, 'Actually I don't think I am very well.' This was true. 'A bit – faint, perhaps.'

'You should be in bed probably.'

'Yes, yes, perhaps.' He shut his eyes at the concatenation of these two ideas: Kylie and bed.

'I could bring you a hot drink up.'

'Hnh. What?'

'When we've finished eating, I mean. Get up now, Mr – George.'

I'm still on my hands and knees.

Her face disappeared. He wound himself

somehow back on to his chair. But the hysteria remained in his throat. It made his eyes water, not like his earlier crying, but almost as uncontrollable. He longed to go up and lie down and wait for her... But there was Kevin. What might they get up to if he were to go? He must not leave them alone together in the room. He held his napkin against his face to hide his trembling mouth.

Kevin slid off his chair. He came to George and kissed the side of his face. One of his soft wet tender kisses. But George could not respond. This filled him with a terrible unhappiness. But he remained quite still. He could not look at Kevin. Then he saw that Kevin was not getting back on his chair. He was leaving the kitchen! He was voluntarily leaving a room where Kylie was? He heard his brother go up the stairs. Joy flooded him. But then: *His trains are in the room next to hers. Such close propinquity. He and she side by side on the top floor ... I shall never be able to rest.*

'Where's he gone?' Kylie said.

'He has a train set in the attic. The room – next to yours.'

'Oh, yes. I saw it. There was a nasty picture there on a magazine on the mantelpiece. I tore it up.'

George's face filled, dark red. Mortification that she had been forced to look at such a thing. Anger at Kevin for retrieving his goddess and re-enthroning her. Greater anger at himself for not tearing the magazine up before. For allowing it into the house to begin with. *Weakness. I'm weak.* 'I'm so sorry. It's Kevin. I don't know where he... He doesn't know any better.'

'I don't like that kind of thing,' she said.

'No. Of course not!' George swallowed but no further speech came to him. *I am a weak man.*

'Anyway, at least I've got this.' Her little white teeth showed for a second. She took her key from her pocket and shook it at him. 'I'll lock my door.'

She is heavenly. Does she have any idea how she has put my mind at rest? 'I'll go to bed now,' George said.

'And I'll bring you a cup of tea.'

He decided not to put his pyjama jacket on. Marje had never liked him to wear it. He got quickly into bed and waited. He worried that the folded-down sheet exposed too much of his big barrel chest.

But when Kylie came in with his tea she barely glanced at him. Her gaze swept over the walls, the ceiling, the floor. 'It's a nice room,' she said. She appraised the solid mahogany furniture piece by piece. 'Nice things.'

Things seemed to interest her more than people. Strangely this came as a relief to

George. It simplified her for him. He too found people difficult; objects and numbers easier. Suddenly he smiled at her. George's smile didn't beautify him but it brought something innocent and youthful into his face.

Kylie didn't smile back. She put her small head with its aureole of gently waving hair on one side and regarded him. 'How old are you, George?' she said.

His heart sank. 'Thirty-eight.'

'Oh.' She considered this. 'That's not so old.' Her air of detachment lent weight to the statement.

George smiled again. 'Old enough to be your father.' He dared to say it.

'I don't have a father,' she said.

'Oh!' George was shocked. He was shocked because he was pleased.

'He went off just after I was born.'

'Oh dear, I'm so sorry.' He was about to say he knew how that felt, he having lost his father too, but she broke in– 'My mother's dead too.'

'No!' He was appalled. That fate should have dealt this defenceless young creature such blows.

'Yes. My grandmother brought me up.'

Again the guilty joy crept through. *She's mine. All mine.* 'In Leeds,' he said.

'What?' Her eyes went blank. 'Oh yes,' she nodded. 'In Leeds, that's right. You've got a good memory.'

He was grateful she didn't say For your age. 'You seem to have a slight – northern – accent.' He spoke shyly. *I'm having a conversation with her!*

'Oh, yes, I get that from my – from my gran.' She circled the room, lightly touching things. There was a silence. George wasn't conscious of the silence. His gaze was licking her, like flames. She stopped at last at the foot of the bed and looked at him. 'Yes,' she said. 'I like it here.'

George heard himself laugh. He heard himself say, 'I'm glad.'

'Is it all right then? If I take some food up with me?'

'Up? Up where?'

'To my room. My studio. Some tea and bread and things.'

You're not staying here, in my room, with me? 'Oh, yes. Yes. Of course you may,' he said. The words came out quite cool, polite. But when she left the room his whole body seemed to weep at her absence. *I need to have her near me. I need to look at her. That's not so old, she said. She meant it, she's a truthful girl – the things she said about Kevin.* He winced for a moment. But his need overcame his treachery to his brother. *I want her here. I need to have her here. Near me.*

Ten minutes later he heard her light little

footsteps come up the stairs. He held his breath. *She's coming back to me.* But the footsteps did not stop outside his door. They went on up. To the attic floor. Kevin was on the attic floor. He didn't want her up there with him. *No!* She had said she would lock her door, but what if that was simply to deceive him? What if she were not truthful after all?

He heard a door close but he couldn't tell which door. Which room had she gone into? Hers or his? Then silence. An unaccustomed silence. Kevin normally kept up an unintelligible running commentary on his own activities.

But not on the activities in the shed.

Not on those activities.

No.

He saw the same scene repeated in the attic room. It was going on now, Kylie replacing Alison. On the green carpet. On her blue divan. *She deceived me. All that concern and sweetness. She was softening me up. They planned this. They are up there together now.*

The terrifying tears bubbled up into his eyes again. Tears of anger, with himself as much as with Kevin, with himself as much as with her. Then he lifted his head. He heard footsteps, coming down again to this floor. He had been wrong about her. She was coming back. How stupid he was to think...

He wiped his eyes swiftly on the sheet. He arranged himself more upright in the bed. He composed his face. The door opened slowly. And Kevin's head appeared.

Kevin looked behind him fearfully then softly closed the door. He crept into the room on tiptoe. He stopped a few feet from the bed, reached into his jacket pocket and pulled out two thick wodges of paper. He looked at them with great sadness then held them out for George to see. In each hand he held a half of his girlie magazine, which had been crudely torn in two.

He gazed pleadingly at George but couldn't make George look at him. George's arms were straight by his sides, his fists were clenched. The expression of concern came back into Kevin's eyes. He sensed there was something wrong with George. He put the two wads of paper back into his pockets. He crept up to the bed and put a hand out to comfort him. George violently struck the hand away.

Kevin, mystified, backed off. He cradled his stricken hand as if it were some small creature he felt pity for. He sniffed. He turned away and wiped his face on his sleeve. George had never been unkind to him before. A sound came from Kevin's throat, not quite a sob, not quite a sigh. He wiped his face again with his sleeve. He went slowly to the door in the hope that George would call him back.

George did not call him back. Waves of nausea and feverish heat chased themselves over his body leaving cold sweat behind all over his skin. He was barely aware that Kevin had left the room.

21

Later that evening Jack lurched into the kitchen at Brockhurst Road. He had been sleeping. He was always sleeping these days, at odd times so that he never knew whether it was day or night. He noticed the envelope addressed to Chloe. He saw that it was Polly's handwriting. He picked it up. Opening it, he tore the envelope and the paper inside. Cursing, swaying, holding the two halves together, he read the words over and over. Because he could not believe what he was reading it took him some time to absorb its drift. When he did, he put the letter down where he had found it. He went to stand at the sink. He looked outside at the wrecked yard. When had he done that? Yesterday? The day before. He had a vague recollection of the axe swinging and biting, wood chips flying.

He went out there and brought in the axe.

Cheap plywood units chop easy, he thought. He was right. It took him less than an hour to chop up the kitchen. Then he left the house by the front door.

Polly/Kylie looked into George's room at nine that evening to see if he needed anything. George was sleeping. She fed Kevin biscuits and cocoa in the kitchen, much as his mother did, plate and mug banged down, no words. She sat at the table facing him but her eyes were fixed elsewhere. She was making plans.

Kevin went to George's room after his snack. George's eyes were wide open, but he would not look at Kevin. Nor did he speak. Kevin backed out of the room. He was frightened. Something terrible was happening to George.

He went up to his attic where he sat hunched over the two halves of his Goddess. He squeezed them between his hands, trying to fit them together. He hadn't the heart to play with his trains tonight.

Alison came home from the supermarket and didn't know what to do. She strayed in and out of the french windows keeping watch for Kevin. There was no sign of him. Then when it was almost dark and she'd given up hope she saw him.

He stood quite still in the grass, his lovely head drooped. Kevin seldom stood still. Something was wrong. She called, 'Kev!' His head slowly came up. But he didn't smile or wave. He looked as though he didn't know her. Uncertain, she whispered, 'Shall I come over, Kev?' He dropped his head again, half turned away. She climbed up on to her wall.

Polly stood at her attic window idly watching Kevin. He was quite good-looking really, at a distance. In this dusky light. *He'd be all right,* she thought. *If he wasn't one of those.* Then she saw Alison.

Polly felt her head split into two like a chopped apple. It was as though she was seeing herself jump off the wall into the garden. It was as though she were in two places at once. She was affronted. A girl with the audacity to look like her! Not as pretty as she, of course, and not as graceful obviously, but still, from a distance, unbelievably like.

The girl came close to Kevin and stood gazing up into his face, just as if he was a real man! Polly folded her arms with an expression of distaste, and watched. Kevin scuffed his shoe in the grass. The doppelganger touched his arm and her fingers slid down to his hand.

She was the girl from the supermarket! She had served Polly many a time. But she looked different out of uniform, with her hair down, without that stupid hat they made them wear. She looked better. That was why Polly hadn't recognised her at once.

The supermarket girl was pulling Kevin now gently towards the shed. She opened the shed door. He went inside with her, quite obedient. The door closed. Polly's eyebrows almost met over her perfect little nose.

Kevin sat sadly on the sacks. Alison wrapped her arms and legs around him from behind, and hugged him tight. In the sudden confidence of love she was sure his dejection was not to do with her. She wanted to attack the person who had saddened him. She hugged him tighter. He didn't respond. 'What is it, Kev? Who's hurt you?' Her hoarse little voice was hardly audible. She stroked his neck. His head drooped back on to her shoulder and rested there. She pressed her cheek against his. She rocked him.

George heard nothing as Polly passed his room. Stepping silently down the bottom flight of stairs, she let herself out by the kitchen door.

22

Saturday morning dawned. Another perfect day. Alison rose with it. She felt purified, smoothed. She had sent Kevin in to bed comforted. At seven-thirty a postcard fell on to the mat. It showed a monastery surrounded by scrubby hills against a background of impossibly blue sky. Her parents wished she was there. The card was a good omen, a sign of universal forgiveness and love. *And the greatest of these is love*. She loved Kevin so much she could save him from anything. He would never have to suffer again.

This was her week for the early shift. She seemed to swim to the supermarket through the pearly light. She showed the postcard to the girls at work. 'I bet you wish you were there,' Nina said.

'Oh, no! I *don't!*'

She had never known why she made them laugh.

She ate her lunch, a supermarket sandwich at staff discount, on the grass in the park near to the children's swings and slides. She liked to watch the children playing. She hoped she and Kevin would have children of their own one day.

Her parents would be back on Monday. She'd tell them then: *I want to marry Kevin and look after him. I love him and I want to make him happy.* She wasn't sure if people of limited intelligence like Kevin were allowed to make marriage vows but surely they could get round that. And because it was meant to be, and right in every way, her parents would see that it was best for her and give their consent. She was impatient to get on with the rest of her life.

George blinked. Sunlight zoomed round his room. Kylie, peeling the curtains back, was emblazoned by it. 'I brought you some breakfast,' she said.

George knew he couldn't eat. The bed was drenched with his sweat, a mallet the size of a house hit his head with a regular beat. He really did have flu then? How curious.

'Come on,' she said. 'Sit up.'

Her cool little hand held the back of his neck, lifting his head off the pillow. She put a clean pillow behind him. Cool cotton touched his back. He heaved himself upright. She held out his pyjama top and he put his arms into the sleeves. She fastened the buttons. She tucked it down under the sheet. *Oh...*

She put a hand on his forehead. 'I think your temperature's gone down a bit,' she said. 'Come along, you've got to eat.'

233

Delighted at being bossed by her he shook his head.

'Now, come on, George.' She dipped a spoon into golden egg yolk and lifted it to his mouth. He opened his lips. Nothing had ever tasted so good. He closed his eyes as the perfect egg slipped down his sore swollen throat.

Kevin peered in at the door to see how George was today.

'Go away, Kevin,' Polly said. 'I'll get your breakfast in a minute. Go downstairs.'

George's eyes were shut. He neither saw nor heard.

Kevin obeyed.

After breakfast George slept and later she ran a bath for him in the smart new bathroom. She had put some delicious-smelling stuff in the water. He lay in a cloudy cradle of bubbles which burst around him with soft little sighs, and when he went back to his room there were clean pyjamas and new sheets and he got between the crisp sheets and soon after Kylie arrived with lunch.

'I ought to get up,' George said feebly.

'Oh, no, you have to get properly well.'

'But what about Kevin?' he said.

'Oh, he's all right. Don't worry, I'll take care of him.'

Kevin kicked the ball against the wall. Then he stopped kicking and stood disconsolately in the grass. He looked for Alison but the gardens were empty of people. He lay down and the stalks of grass stuck into his face like needles.

For the first time in her life Alison didn't go to confession on Saturday evening. She ran home from work. She plunged into the shower and twisted and turned under the water like a fish. She dried her hair with her head hanging upside down. When she lifted her head she was flushed and her eyes were glittering. 'I am pretty!' she told her reflected self, also for the first time. She put little dabs of perfume in all her warm places including her ankles and behind her knees.

Standing on the garden wall she could see Kevin lying in the grass. Though he usually waited for her at this time, he didn't look up. But she was full of courage and didn't hesitate. She jumped off the wall and ran along the ends of the gardens. Gyp barked and leaped and Alison laughed. Kevin jumped up, hearing them. He ran towards Alison and she descended into his arms.

Polly watched from upstairs until Kevin and Alison were safe inside the shed. Then she went into George's room.

Jack sat on his bed. Around his feet on the floor were photographs of Polly. Some were holiday Polaroids, some were silly photo-booth snaps. Two were studio portraits in saccharine colour, posed in her silly best clothes. He started with those. He picked them up, put one on top of the other and tore them into shreds. He put the pieces on the bed beside him.

Then he went through the holiday snaps one by one, tearing them into tiny bits. There was one that had been taken at Brighton when she was ten. She had a pony tail and was holding an ice cream, just like any little girl at the beach. He tore it in two, right down the middle of her face.

He tore through them all till only one remained, it showed her and Jack together. They were in profile in the back yard, each grinning into the other's face. Chloe had taken it. It was the year before everything went wrong. The year before he fucked everything up. He looked at it for a while. Then he tore right down the space between him and Polly where you could see the bricks of the yard wall. Then he tore himself to bits. Then he tore her. And then he lifted all the scraps: eyes, teeth, fingers, noses, ears. He squeezed them in his hands. He put them in the hearth and put a flame to them. He watched them go black at the edges, curl, smoke, and crumble to fine grey dust in pale flickers of flame.

'Has Kevin got a girlfriend, George?'

She was sitting on his bed. He could feel her warmth against his thigh. He hardly dared breathe in case he blew her away like a scrap of dandelion fluff. He didn't hear what she said at first. Then it sank into the mud on the floor of his heart. He needed time. 'What?' he said.

'Well, does he – you know – do it?' She looked at him coolly.

'I don't quite know what to say–'

'Because I don't think he should. Do you?'

George shook his head. 'Well – er – it's rather a difficult question. I'm not sure that I–'

'What would your mum think about it?'

'Oh. My mother.' The very word made his heart sink like a stone.

'I mean, I just don't think they should. It's just not right. Well, it's not, is it, George?'

There was a buzzing in George's head. 'What makes you think that Kevin has a – a girlfriend?' he said.

She looked at him. Just for a moment. Then she said, 'Oh, nothing. I was just wondering, that's all.'

'Oh. I thought perhaps you had noticed–'

'No. But your mum wouldn't like it though, would she, George?'

Have you seen them together? What did you see? He couldn't ask her. He couldn't discuss with her what he had seen in the shed.

237

He had gone far in his betrayal of Kevin but not that far. And, worse, he had stayed to watch such a scene, he had not put a stop to it, he had taken no action, to protect Kevin, to protect the girl, Alison. And why? Simply because he was too embarrassed to speak of it! And, worse, because he was jealous, eaten up by, rotting with jealousy, of his poor retarded brother. So that he could not ask what he most wanted to know: *From what point of view are you asking these questions? Are you jealous of Kevin because you desire him yourself?* In fact he could say nothing at all.

'I think really they should be stopped from doing that sort of thing. Don't you? You know – with drugs or something.' She gave a little shudder. 'I don't know how anybody could. I couldn't, myself. I wouldn't have anything to do with a person who wasn't normal. I only like normal people, myself.'

George breathed out. Her rosy hands rested on the counterpane. So near to his own. He only had to move a finger to touch one of hers, but he mustn't, he knew that. Yet she seemed to be waiting for something. He mustn't let his imagination lead him astray. She liked normal people. He must appear normal above all things. He mustn't frighten her off.

'Would you like your meal now, George?'

'Oh. You mustn't. It's too much.'

She smiled. 'She makes a lot of pies, your

mother, doesn't she, George?'

He tried to look stern. It was his rule never to be disloyal to his mother as it was his rule never to be disloyal to Kevin. But she looked so disarmingly mischievous, she could never mean any harm. He smiled. 'Well, perhaps I could eat something,' he said. Then, to keep her, when she got to the door he said, 'Is Kevin all right, by the way?' He had a pang of conscience as he asked.

'Oh, yes,' her little voice floated back. 'Last time I saw him he was playing in the shed.'

Later his door opened a crack and the line of light from the landing hit him like a sword. He leaned up eagerly, off his pillow. Then he saw it was Kevin. He groaned and lay back. Kevin hovered, however, and George at last said, 'What is it, Kev?'

Kevin bounded over to the bed, spluttering his nonsense language. George didn't look at him but he did put out a hand and touch his arm. 'All right, Kev, all right.'

Kevin was grinning like a dog and tossing his head. There was something he was trying to tell, but George didn't want to know what it was. His face suddenly turned away on the pillow and his eyes were shut tight. 'All right!'

He had said the words quietly, but Kevin heard them as a shout. He knew that people could shout very quietly when they wanted to. 'Go to bed now, Kev. Go to bed.'

Then George seemed to regret his impatience. He calmed down and patted Kevin's arm. He said, 'Go on, Kev,' and turned his face away again. He didn't want to talk now, that was clear to Kevin who nodded several times. He touched the back of George's head, then crept out. He was wary of meeting Polly/Kylie. But he needn't have worried.

Polly was locked in her attic dressed in her performance things, singing and dancing her future plans. Her plans were not unconnected with George.

23

Sunday was another golden day. South Norwood thirsted in the heat. The gardens drooped and ached.

Alison, who'd been awake all night, too excited to sleep, suddenly closed her eyes at 5 a.m. She slept through the heat of the morning and every morning mass, right up to the one o'clock.

Polly took George his breakfast, placed a

hand on his brow, and suggested he get up. 'I'm going out,' she said. He didn't dare ask where. 'Want me to get a paper for you?' She danced out of the house to get the *Observer* and the *Telegraph*.

Though he still felt very odd George obediently got bathed and dressed. He regretted the shortness of his illness. He determined to be back in bed before long. Just a few more hours with her in his bedroom before his mother returned. Till tomorrow was all he had. *Today is our last day. Tomorrow Mother comes back.*

Kevin stood in the bay window of the living room and watched Polly/Kylie disappear beyond the laurel bush into the street. He heard George get up. He went up and waited on the stairs for George to come out of the bathroom.

George, shaving, became deeply alarmed. Now that his mother had got into his head he couldn't push her out again. *Kylie's questions: what if she were to say the things to Mother that she said to me? And what have I been thinking of, allowing Kevin to carry on like that? I am as irresponsible as Kevin. But I have no excuse.* He opened the bathroom door. 'Kevin!'

Kevin jumped. He heard the anger in George's voice. But he always obeyed when

George called out to him.

'Kevin!'

It didn't sound so angry the second time. Kevin went to the bathroom and put his head first, cautiously, round the door. 'Eggh? Ghoghe?' He put his head on one side and smiled charmingly.

The look on George's face in the mirror changed from indignation to a baffled helplessness. Kevin put his arms round George's big waist and nuzzled his Marks and Spencer paisley dressing gown.

'Get off!' George disentangled himself as though Kevin were an unruly dog. But when he saw the look on Kevin's face, he sighed and scratched through his hair. 'Look, Kev.' He sat his brother on the edge of the bath.

Kevin gazed up at him, waiting.

'Look. This girl. Alison.' There, he'd said it though he blushed remembering.

Kevin whispered a series of noises that might be his attempt at *Alison*. At the mention of her name a beatific devotion made his face boneless. He whispered frantic messages to George. Just like last night.

George, criminal, fearful, said, 'No, Kevin. No more Alison. Mother would say no. Mother be angry. Mother angry, Kevin. George angry too. George very angry with you. No more Alison, Kev. Understand?'

Kevin shrivelled visibly on the side of the

242

bath like something left out in the rain. His bewildered face moved from side to side. He shot George millimetre glances as he moved his head, as though he couldn't bear to look at him too much at one time. Small whimpers came out of him. George waited for a tantrum like the one in the newspaper shop. It didn't come. Kevin stood up. There wasn't a lot of space in the bathroom. He sidled round George, not touching him, and went backwards out of the door.

He went backwards down the stairs, and all the way out of the house into the cool garden. Only the shed was in sunlight at this time of day. It looked to Kevin a long way off. Gyp barked and jumped on to the wall. Kevin did not reply. He sat in the grass under the kitchen window, legs bent, face buried in his knees. Gyp jumped off the wall and ran at him. He stood on his back legs, trying to insert his nose between knees and face. He made the same whimpering noises that Kevin had made in the bathroom.

Kylie brought George his papers but she didn't stay with him. 'I'll be in my room if you need me,' she said.

Need her? He felt weak and sick when she wasn't there. He sat in the living room pretending to read the *Telegraph*. But his mind climbed the stairs to her room and opened the door. *She is lying on her bed, like the girl on Kevin's magazine. She lifts her arms to me. She says, 'George?' Inviting me.*

George buried his face in his hands. He soiled her with these images. He thought about going out, but when he stood up his legs wobbled and black spots dabbled about in his eyes. He had to get back to bed. It was the only place he felt safe.

Out in the hall he thought he'd better just make his way to the kitchen to check on Kevin. Yes, he was there, sitting in the grass with Gyp. George remembered the disgustingly weighted stinking sock. That was only a few nights ago. He recalled the grotesque experience like a memory from another world. A film even. He groaned. A *Carry On* film, no doubt.

Kevin looked dejected but not too tragic, George thought. As though sensing George's presence, he turned round and looked at the kitchen window. George waved at him. But Kevin didn't appear to see. George shrugged and floundered upstairs.

Alison woke to find it was afternoon. She panicked. *Kevin will wonder where I am!* She ran about cleaning and polishing to make things nice for her parents' return. Then she began to get herself ready to go out.

Polly came out of her room and found Kevin on the stairs sadly gazing at the two halves of his torn Goddess. She made an impatient noise. He wasn't still in a state about that, was he? She would put a stop to this. She said, 'Give me that.'

Kevin handed his Goddess to her, fearful but trusting. Polly went on down the stairs. Kevin followed her. She marched out through the back door. He lurched out after her.

She strode round the corner of the house to the dustbin, lifted the lid and thrust the Goddess in among the old tea bags and soggy remains of pie. 'There,' she said. 'I hope we've seen the last of that.' She banged the lid back on, brushed her hands against each other in case of contamination, and marched back indoors.

Kevin stood by the dustbin and wondered what was happening to his life. He hoped his mother hadn't gone for ever, leaving him here with Polly/Kylie and the fearfully changed George. He stayed by the dustbin. He didn't know where else to go.

Alison found him there later, crouched between the dustbin and the wall. He looked frightened when she appeared. He tried to run away from her. She thought this was because he was hurt that she was late. She caught him and held him. She told him she was sorry. She explained and explained. At last, by much coaxing, she tempted him into the shed. She had never seen him so sad. He was like a dog whose master has died, or at least gone away and left him. And she could see that he was frightened too.

She sat behind him like yesterday and murmured in his ear all the comforting things she could think of: 'Only till tomorrow, Kev. Tomorrow they'll all be back and we can tell them then. And after that everything will be all right.' She had a space in her mind when she said that, afraid that things might not be as simple as she hoped. 'But I'll be with you, Kev. I'll always take care of you as long as I live. I love you, Kev.'

He didn't respond to her nearness, her whispery little promises. He slumped against her, holding on tight to her hands as though scared that she would go and leave him too.

Polly, who had watched from the window of her room as Alison took Kevin into the shed, now came softly down the stairs. She crept silent past George's room, down to the hall, along the passage to the kitchen, and out of the back door into the garden. She did not approach the shed. She found herself a patch of evening sunlight, and stood in it, eyes almost closed, head back.

Alison at last unwound her legs from round Kevin. She tried to coax him to his feet but he refused to move. She gently loosed her hands and stood up. Her legs were stiff from sitting so long in one position. She looked out of the shed window and saw Polly standing in the patch of sun.

She felt dizzy and shut her eyes. When she opened them again the apparition would surely be gone? She hid to the side of the window and peeped out.

At first she was relieved to find it was a real girl standing there and not a disembodied part of herself that had somehow escaped and reshaped itself into this vision. 'No, she's not me,' she whispered. But the initial relief was immediately replaced by pain. *She's much more beautiful than me. She looks like an angel standing there*. Her heart felt squeezed as though in a big hard fist. She might never be able to breathe properly again. This must be how it felt to drown.

Kevin, at a small sound she wasn't aware of uttering, came to her side. He saw the girl too and when he saw her he backed away from the window.

Alison saw it all at once, the whole picture, as drowning people are said to do. 'It's her fault, isn't it? She's hurt you, Kev. She's much lovelier than me. You've fallen in love with her, haven't you? You love her now, not me any more. But she doesn't love you, does she? How could she, a girl like that? She'd despise people like you, Kev, and me too. She's a clever girl, and she's cruel, I can tell.

She's ruined everything.' She edged her face to the window again. The perfect cruel angel had gone. The patch of sunlight was as empty as if she had never been.

Alison looked at Kevin. He crouched in the corner with his knees bent and his head down, his arms hugging his knees. She waited minutes but he wouldn't look at her or reach out to her. With more sadness than she believed she had ever felt or could ever feel in her whole life she crept out of the shed.

Left to his own devices, Kevin, distressed, didn't know what to do. He didn't want to go into the house again, where Polly/Kylie was, who had destroyed his Goddess, who had upset Alison, who had created this new George who was angry with him. He wandered out into the street.

He strayed about, at first in a desolate state, later in a mixture of terror and elation simply at going out alone. A thing he was not allowed to do and had only ever done once before.

Late in the afternoon, Polly discovered his absence. She searched the house and the garden, including the shed. Her gaze scraped the backs of the houses. Which one did the girl live in? It must be close by, because she always came across the gardens. Then Polly spotted her pale face in an upstairs window three houses down. She counted down from number thirty-five. *Number twenty-nine.*

She slipped back indoors with a small smile. She had all the information she needed. She would use it at the right time. She wasn't going to have anyone butting into her newly formulated plans. Especially someone nearly as pretty as herself. At last Polly was going to have things her way for a change.

Alison trudged towards the church. She had believed that because she loved Kevin and he loved her, everything they did together was good. But now she saw that Kevin did not love her, that he could not distinguish between her and any blonde pretty girl, she saw that she had been wrong. She reached the door as people were leaving evening mass. She wanted to go in.

Alison had always been frightened of God. She had somehow never been able to believe in the forgiveness of sins. And she had sinned. In fact she was in a state of mortal sin. She had seduced Kevin. Everything was her fault. God was punishing her, and the innocent Kevin through her. And now she had even missed Sunday mass.

Dejected she turned away from the church door and wandered down in the vague direction of the High Street. She meandered listlessly from street to darkening street. Hardly noticing where she was, she passed the clock tower and from habit went up towards the supermarket. She felt forgotten by the world as though she didn't really exist. As though she had dreamed herself, or someone else had, and now the dream was over. Even the supermarket where she spent every day was closed. She was locked out of everything. That was when she saw Jack.

He was standing in a doorway opposite, dark, with burning dark eyes like the coals at the back of the fire. He was the devil, surely he was. If you can see the devil, if the devil can see you, you exist, but you exist in a world you don't want to inhabit. Terrified she ran.

Jack had walked all last night, and all day today. He'd slept on some grass somewhere. He recalled the noise of trains, inside or outside his head he didn't know. He didn't know anything for sure any more. His thoughts were tigers, his head was their cage. They prowled back and forth in it.

One side of his jacket was weighed down, he kept his hand in that pocket, gripping the handle of the axe. If the axe was still there then this was a real street, a real pavement, those were his feet, he was Jack, Polly had really left home, to get away from him. That was when he looked up from his shop doorway and saw her run.

He didn't know if she was really Polly, or really running, or an illusion crawling out of the labyrinth of his mind, but he ran after her, weighted down on one side by the axe.

Polly sat on the end of the bed filing her nails. She lifted a graceful hand and blew on it gently. She shifted and her thistledown weight bumped against his ankles. He held his feet stiff and then let them drop sideways so that they rested on her small hip. He looked to see if she minded. He could move them away, make it seem like an accident in no time at all if she did. But no, she didn't move away. Instead, unless he imagined it, she leaned a little, pressing against his feet. She didn't appear to notice. She concentrated on her little fingernail.

Everything she does, she does with perfect grace.

She blew on the last fingernail. Then she turned her hands this way and that, contemplating the small pink ovals, testing them for smoothness with the rosy ball of her thumb. 'George,' she said.

The way she said *George* made his toes curl with pleasure. 'Yes, Kylie?'

'Why aren't you married?' She looked at him.

George felt a tremor under his skin, as though all his features were moving around his face. 'Oh, well...' he said.

She sat up straighter and almost accused him. 'You're *not* married, are you, George?' As though he had practised a deception on her.

'No!' he said.

'Oh.' She relaxed. 'Well, why not then?' She looked sideways under her lids. 'Haven't you found the woman of your dreams yet, George?'

He had to close his eyes a moment. He took a deep breath. 'I had a wife. But. It was a long time ago. She. We parted. She didn't – stay with me. She left.'

'Oh.' Kylie had a thoughtful look.

'Marje,' George said. Kylie wasn't to know it was the first time in years he'd spoken her name aloud to another human being. Except once, he recalled. Quite recently. To John Bright.

'Are you divorced then, George?'

'She – after some years – when the easy divorces came in – we became divorced. Yes. I was informed by her lawyer and I didn't – contest it.'

'Mmm...' Kylie stretched out the sound. 'Haven't you ever thought of marrying again then?'

In George's wildest dreams... He shut his eyes again and shook his head briskly. He must not read too much into her words. She might mock him. 'No,' he said simply. It was the truth.

'Why not?'

'Well, I'm not sure.' He had no answer that he could give her. That he could give anyone.

'Well, I don't see why not. You're in the prime of life, as they say. You're well off, aren't you? What are you? A lawyer, is it?'

'Accountant.' George coughed. He couldn't get any sound into his voice. 'Chartered accountant,' he said more vehemently than he'd meant.

'Oh.' She nodded slowly. He thought she seemed disappointed that he wasn't a lawyer. He was desperate to explain that an accountant was quite a respectable thing to be, that glamour wasn't everything.

'Have you got your own – you know – firm or whatever?' she said.

'Yes! I'm a – well, I'm a – partner, you know. It's quite a – it's quite a large firm. It's in the – in the City, you know.' How could he expect her to have any grasp of such things? With every word he uttered he felt more inadequate.

But she was looking at him with considering eyes. 'Mmm,' she said. She started on the other hand.

George had come out in a sweat that was nothing to do with the flu.

She said, 'Do you like living with your mum?'

'Well–'

'And Kevin? You like living with Kevin?'

'Actually, I have a flat in town.'

'Do you?' Her eyes were wide. He saw that this was the most impressive fact he had yet disclosed to her. 'Oh, I'd love that.' She stood and stepped and twirled between the window and the bed. 'I'd love that more than anything. I'm going to have that one day.'

George felt God-like. 'I only stay here at weekends,' he said. 'Normally, that is. To help my mother with Kevin. And so on. Normally.' He stopped speaking. Normally seemed a long time ago. He scratched between his brows with a thumbnail. She was standing next to him, close to the bed, touching the bed with her thighs.

'Will you take me there one day, George? When you're better, I mean? Just so's I can see what it's like?'

Oh Kylie. Oh my angel. Oh the sweetness of dreams. He cleared his throat. 'Of course. Of course I will.' He dared to look at her.

She stared right into his eyes. Then she nodded. 'Okay,' she said. As though they had made a bargain.

He couldn't move his eyes away. At any moment his hand was going to reach out and touch her no matter how hard he tried to stop it. He saw his hand begin to move across the bedclothes–

'I've got to go and fetch Kevin in now,' she said.

Late Sunday night Chloe returned to find the chopped-up kitchen, no Polly, no note from Polly. And Jack sleeping deeply on Polly's bedroom floor.

Here, she discovered that Polly's things had gone: her tinkly bits of jewellery, her Walkman, her clothes, and, most significant of all, her Kylie Minogue things.

Chloe shook Jack but he wouldn't wake. He was sleeping as he hadn't slept for weeks. Like a dead man. She sat down on Polly's bed and howled.

24

On Sunday night the weather broke. The sky hurled hammers of rain that pulverised the roses and the petunias with petals soft as skin. The long heat had cracked. There was wildness in the air. When daylight came South Norwood was a swamp.

George had slept like a baby and woke late. He felt the change in the air and saw from the bathroom the drowning gardens. He shivered. Questions jostled in his head. Where was Kylie? How long before he had to meet his mother? Before *she* met his mother? *God.* How was he going to say the things he had to say?

He dressed fast. He must see Kylie before she went to college. His sausage fingers caught a lump of shirt in the zip of his fly as he heard the front door bang. He stubbed a toe on the dressing table, stumbling to the window. He grabbed for the curtain to steady himself. She was flying down the street in a little yellow cape with a hood.

She skirted a smallish man with his head down against the rain. George lost her. A clump of infuriating sodden lilacs separated her from him. He wanted to tear them out of the earth with his bare hands. She didn't come back into view. She was gone.

John Bright had stuffed the *Independent,* a loaf and a carton of milk inside his leather jacket to keep them dry. The rain was a nuisance as well as a relief from the long heat. He turned to look after the streak of yellow that had whisked around him. The flashing legs reminded him of the girl that had come out of George's place the other day. He had a faint niggle of worry about George, recalling his oddness the last time he'd called, and his mother's prognostications. He hesitated a moment. Well, why not? It would be somewhere out of the wet at least. He turned in at the gate. The laurels dropped heavy coins of water down his neck.

When George heard the bell he was still struggling with the trapped lump of shirt. *She's back! Forgotten something!* He trundled down the stairs, tugging at his zip. He tore the shirt getting his fly zipped up. He pulled the door open. He started to say Kylie but stopped when he saw John Bright and then couldn't say anything else. He knew that his face was an open map that he just couldn't get folded up. 'Ah,' he said at last. 'John.'

'You look worse every time I see you, George. Are you sick?'

'I've got – I've had – flu. I'm not too good actually.'

'Better let me in then, hadn't you, mate?'

George sat in an absent way at the table, while John Bright deftly dealt with the coffee things. He observed the water dripping from the trees, the gentle steam rising from the grass. Bright went to the window. 'Where's Kevin?' he said.

George turned a blank face to Bright and said, 'Was there a storm last night?'

'Certainly was. Seemed to go on most of the night. Thunder, lightning. Spectacular.'

'Oh, no.' George blundered to his feet. Falling over them, he made for the hall.

'What's up?' Bright followed him up the stairs.

'He can't stand storms.'

Kevin wasn't in his bedroom. The elephants and kangaroos looked down on an empty neatly made bed. Nor was he in the bathroom.

Bright ran light-footed up to the attic floor. Kevin wasn't in his train room, or in the junk room. He tried the back room. 'This door's locked.'

'Oh, yes, that's—'

'A-ha. The pretty little lodger.'

'He won't be in there.'

'Sure, George?'

But George was in no mood for teasing. 'Yes. I'm sure.'

'When's your ma due back?'

'This afternoon.'

'Christ.'

George looked like a gigantic candle that had started to melt. He flopped down on a stair. His head dropped into his hands. Bright said, 'Don't collapse, George, we've got to find Kevin.' He stepped neatly over the big feet, going down two steps at a time to the ground floor and out into the garden.

The grass was spongy. Dollops of rain still fell from the trees and the sky and found their way down the back of his neck. He wrenched at the door of the shed. Kevin was curled up on some sacks. Even in the dim light he looked in a bad way. Soaked. Shivering.

'Run him a hot bath, George.' Bright stripped wet clothes off Kevin while George ran the bath. They lowered him into the steaming water. Bright rubbed him hard with a rough flannel, then with a big towel. Kevin stared. He didn't make a sound, he showed no sign of knowing where he was. George brought pyjamas and Kevin's towelling robe. Kevin was so helpless they had to push his arms into the sleeves. 'Get him into bed, George.' Bright ran down the stairs again.

He came back with a hot water bottle and hot milk. Kevin put both his hands round the cup and breathed the milk. He drained it in one long draught and handed it with both hands back to Bright. Then he put both his arms round the hot water bottle, turned on his side with his knees almost up to his chin, and closed his eyes. He still shivered from time to time.

John Bright raised an eyebrow at George.

'I was in bed with flu!' George said. 'How could I know?'

'Take it easy, George.' Bright put a hand to Kevin's forehead. 'Wouldn't surprise me if he had it too.'

'I have to meet my mother this afternoon.'

'Christ, yes, you said. Anyone you can get to Kevin-sit?'

George's face rippled. He said, 'She probably won't be back and anyway...'

'Anyway?'

'My mother doesn't even know she's here.' George gave a sort of groan.

'Are we talking pretty little lodger here?'

George groaned again.

John Bright had a vivid picture of the petite blonde with the flashing legs. He wondered if George had been in bed with the flu only. His imagination balked at the incongruity of the idea. His slight squint became pronounced. It was the only change in his expression. 'What if I stay with Kevin?' he said.

Jack woke feeling fine. He was amazed to have had a night's sleep. He, too, felt the chill in the air and saw the earth lapping up the rain. He felt the rain had slicked down inside him and washed him clean. He was in Polly's room. That was odd. Chloe was breathing beside him with neat little snores like a cat. He covered her with a quilt. She still had her coat on, a strange affair made of large felt patches embroidered with zodiac signs. The one he was looking at was the scorpion. That was him.

The kitchen looked like a nuclear devastation. He was taken aback. He could vaguely recall breaking it up but not when or why. He set to work putting it to rights. On a trip to the yard to throw away some shattered plywood he saw the axe. It had been rained on and looked like it was beginning to rust. It made him shudder for some reason. Perhaps because he'd used it to devastate the kitchen. He put it into one of the supermarket carriers he was using for the bits.

When Chloe appeared in the doorway puffy-eyed, feeling her way, he was emptying the last shovel of detritus into a big black garbage bag. He tied the neck and put it with the others outside the back door. She stood like a little mole that had just put its nose above ground. He couldn't help smiling at her. She was so sweet. For some reason she looked a little frightened when he smiled. He couldn't understand why.

'What happened in here, Jack?' Her voice was a faint trail of sound.

'I know. I'm sorry, Chlo. I don't remember much about it. You know what it's like when I'm on a binge. I'll fix it though. I'll find some blockboard in a skip to mend the doors. I'll make it better than it was before.'

Her eyes filled with tears. 'Where's Polly, Jack?'

'Polly?' he said.

'Didn't she even leave me a note?'

'A note?'

Chloe's voice rose to a wail: 'Polly's gone!'

There was a skip down the street. He took the garbage bags down there and exchanged them for two nice pine doors some idiot had thrown away. He spent the rest of the day sawing up the pine doors to fit the kitchen units. He whistled as he worked and sometimes even sang. Snatches of Beatles ballads. *A man from the motor trade* kept repeating in his mind, he didn't know why, couldn't even remember which song it was from.

Chloe sat on a cushion trying to meditate. It was no good. She took out her tobacco tin and spliff gear but put it back again. She went to the kitchen and said, 'What shall I do, Jack?'

'Give it time, Chlo. She'll be all right. You know Poll. She can take care of herself.'

'Are you sure she didn't leave me a note?'

He lifted his shoulders and showed her the palms of his hands. He looked really concerned for her. 'With all this mess...' he said, 'it could have just got lost.'

'Yes.'

'I know she'll be all right, Chlo.'

'She'd hate for me to make a fuss, I know.' Chloe wandered down the passage a little way. Then she came back. 'But if she doesn't let me know by tonight...' She wandered again and came back again. 'I'll give her till tomorrow night,' she said. 'Then I'll have to call the cops.' The cops to Chloe were pigs who beat up peaceful demonstrators and raided nice, peaceful, good people for drugs. They were the other side.

'You could call the school,' he said.

'They broke up on Saturday. It's the vacation.' She turned round again. 'This is all your fault, Jack.'

Then she dragged herself back to her cushion and rolled a spliff. She sat there without lighting it, staring at nothing. She felt as though her insides had been all scraped out, even the inside of her head.

The rain went on all day. And during the day people put their old carpets, armchairs, gas fires, tree prunings into the skip. By evening Jack's bags had become the bottom stratum of its geological composition. No one would ever know they were there.

25

'Mother! Here. Let me take that.' He paid off the taxi and tried to stop his mother getting to the front door first. But she was marching ahead up the path. 'Laurels need cutting back,' she said, though he had trimmed them only recently.

The door opened before she had time to turn her key. 'Hello, Mrs Fletcher. Welcome home.'

She was not amused. 'It's John Bright,' he said. 'Friend of George's from school.'

'I know who you are. George said you

were back.'

'I used to call for George two or three times a week.'

'I haven't forgotten.'

'Yeah, well.' Bright bounced on the balls of his feet, rattled the change in his pocket. Didn't want to leave George alone with his problem but felt ten years old. Cowed. His legendary charm was no good here. She wasn't keen on males. She certainly wasn't keen on him. Never had been. She hung up her strange bright turquoise mac and marched off in the direction of the kitchen.

'Think I'd better go then now, George.'

She'd brought back memories. George's dad perpetually dying. Dying of George's mum, he'd thought. She hadn't softened with age. Poor old George.

Poor old George was barely aware of Bright leaving, of closing the door behind him.

'Oh, give me a cup of tea.' She sat down in the gloomy kitchen and eased off her shoes. She looked pale in the greenish light.

George ran water into the kettle. 'How was the trip?'

'Terrible.'

'Terrible? Oh dear.'

'The heat. Like a furnace. Don't know how they stand it.'

'The Spaniards?'

'Mind you, they wouldn't know any better. Terrible people.'

'Are they?'

'Those Spaniards. They're uncouth. They have beggars there. Everywhere you look.'

'Oh.' George forbore to mention the doorways full of homeless who importuned him every day in the prosperous City of London.

'And the food! Oil. Oil over everything. Swimming in oil. And the garlic! God! Makes me sick just to think of it. Where's Kevin?'

'I'm sorry you didn't have a good holiday.'

'It was all right, I suppose. Made a change.'

'Kevin's got flu.' George had worked out that much of his story.

'What?'

'He's in bed.'

She was pounding up the stairs, with George in clumsy pursuit. 'I knew it. I knew there was a reason you didn't bring him to meet me. I knew something like this would happen the minute I went away. I knew.' She opened Kevin's door.

He lay in the same position hugging the cold hot water bottle. She slapped a bony hand on his forehead. 'Fever,' she said. Kevin didn't stir. She marched back to the door glaring at George.

'I've been ill myself,' George pleaded, following her across the landing to her room.

'I said you were sickening for something before I went. Didn't I say? Have you called a doctor yet?'

'It doesn't last long, it was only a couple of days with me.'

'You don't know what you're talking about.' She took her slippers from the wardrobe and patted her hair in the mirror. She scraped a line in the dust on her dressing table with a finger. She looked at it with satisfaction – another proof that her absence had brought about general decline.

George took courage. He loomed into her room and closed the door. 'Mother. Why didn't you tell me you had advertised a room to let?' There. He'd done it.

She looked blank. Then she pulled her chin back into her neck. 'Oh,' she said. 'Oh, that.' She turned away to pat her hair again. 'What about it then?'

'Well, Mother, a girl came to the door. She wanted the room.'

'You didn't let it, I hope.' His mother's eyes were dangerous.

'Well…'

'George.'

'Mother, I told her I couldn't without your permission but she was– I think she'd been looking for some time. She's a student.'

'A student!'

'She offered to pay in advance.'

'You took the money at least. That's something, I suppose.'

'Well, no, I–' George felt sicker than when his flu had raged.

'George!' She banged the dressing table. It must have hurt her hand though she didn't let it show.

'Mother.' George mustered some dignity. Money after all was his profession. 'Mother, if you take money it commits you to an arrangement. I made it clear there was no arrangement until you – unless you – gave it the go-ahead. She was quite agreeable to that.'

'And when did you agree between you she will be moving in?'

'Oh, she's already–' George stopped when he saw his mother's face.

'I don't believe it.' She charged past George on to the landing. 'Where is this girl?' She galloped up the stairs.

'She's not up there.' He fumbled up after her unheard.

She rattled the door handle, rushed down the stairs again past him, into her bedroom and out again and up to the top floor again where she jammed the key into the lock. She threw the door open with a crash. Even in the rain the pretty colourful room appeared full of light. The bed was neatly made. The miniature kitchen sparkled. The clothes were hidden behind the yellow alcove curtain. Only a beautiful pale pink satin dress hung outside it. And a pair of bright pink narrow-strap high-heeled shoes stood prettily below. George came over quite faint. He could smell her perfume like a wraith of her spirit. *My Kylie. My own.*

Mrs Fletcher stopped in her tracks. There was silence a moment. Then she pointed to the pretty things. 'Student? What's that then?'

'She's a– She studies performance art. Singing and – so on.'

'Where?'

'Oh, I – I didn't think to ask.'

'Why on earth would she want to live round here?'

He asked himself this for the first time. 'She liked the room,' he said.

'Hnf!'

This was a sound George knew well, a sort of backward sniff. It could mean things were very slightly looking up.

'You have put me in a very difficult position, George.'

He had put *her?*

She went charging down the stairs. 'I want to see this girl as soon as she comes in. It is by no means certain she will continue in residence here. Unless I...' Her voice tailed off.

When George arrived behind her she was staring at the vision of Kylie in the hall. The girl had taken off her hood and was shaking out her lovely blonde hair. Her face was lifted charmingly to Mrs Fletcher with a tentative smile.

George's longing made his legs weak. No one spoke. He became aware that his mother was paralysed by Kylie's resemblance to Marje. He himself had forgotten it. He had forgotten Marje!

'Mrs Fletcher?' Kylie said. Her expression changed. 'I'm sorry. I know I shouldn't be here. I know I should have waited till you got back. It's not George's fault, honestly. I made him take me in. It was just that the room was so – nice, so pretty. I've never seen anything so lovely. And – well, anyway – I'm sorry George wouldn't take any money. If you turn me out of course I'll pay for the time I've been here and a week in advance for cleaning up after me and – and everything.' Her apologies faded away.

Without speaking Mrs Fletcher continued down the stairs. She held on to the door handle of the so-called morning room. George's father had lain in there in his coffin before being taken to the cemetery. And when they returned from the burial the funeral baked meats had taken his father's place. It was a room he avoided entering as a rule.

'Are you a person who makes noise?' his mother asked.

'Oh, no. I'm as quiet as a mouse.'

'Surely you have to practise your – singing, don't you?'

'Well, I was going to ask you about that. I

269

was hoping there might be, you know, certain hours when you wouldn't mind. When you were out or something. But it doesn't matter. I can stay on and practise at the college. Lots of the students do that. Certain evenings of the week.'

'Where is this college?'

'Er, Croydon, actually. But I'm hoping to go to a better one after my next exam.'

'We shall see. I have not yet agreed to your being here at all. Come inside, please.' She opened the door.

George expected as always to see a coffin on the big mahogany table and black crepe paper scrunched in the grate. Kylie looked up at the dead stag over the fireplace. Its neck was opened up and red bits and pieces spilled out. Kylie recoiled a little and turned a pleading face to George.

'Mother–' George said.

'Go and make me some tea, George. Miss...?'

'Er – Adams,' Kylie said. 'Kylie Adams. That's my name.'

'Kylie? What sort of name is that?'

'My mum called me that after Kylie Minogue. She was in *Neighbours* then, she wasn't even a singer or anything but she was my mum's favourite. She's my favourite as well. The other girls think she's *so* not cool, nearly old enough to be my mum and that, but I love her. I look a bit like her. Well, so people say, anyway.'

Mrs Fletcher made another of her sniffing grunts, 'Hnf,' then turned to George. 'Miss Adams and I are going to have a talk.' The heavy door closed in George's face.

He had a strong inclination to curl up on the floor outside, Kylie's watchdog, but he dragged himself to the kitchen. He made the tea but didn't dare to interrupt with it. He took some up to Kevin who sat up in bed still hugging the hot water bottle. 'Mother's back, Kev.'

Kevin made no sound. He seemed nervous, listening. His eyes sent rays of trust towards George. George saw that his brother's beauty had gathered darkly in the past few days, it swarmed about his head like a cloud of bees. It scared George. He loosened Kevin's hands from the cold rubber and closed them round the warm cup. 'Drink your tea, Kev,' he said.

His mother and Kylie were in the kitchen when he went down.

'Miss Adams has answered my questions satisfactorily. I have decided to allow her to stay for a trial period of one month. If the arrangement does not suit it will be terminated one month from now.'

George hoped his mother's new status as a landlady wasn't going to cause a permanent change in her use of language. He wanted to sing. He hardly dared look at Kylie, but

271

when his mother turned away he snatched a glance. She looked under her lashes at him with a little smile. As though he and she were conspirators. He felt a glow like a hot coal in his chest.

The rain beat relentlessly on and at about half-past six a brash wind started up. Because of the weather Alison's body was still not discovered on Monday night.

26

At three-thirty on Tuesday afternoon the rain stopped as suddenly as it had begun. The sun shone again. The birds came out of hiding and the roses gave forth once more their wonderful scent.

A small boy and his older sister, hand in hand, slithered down the sloping path near the railway bridge into the park.

The park was almost deserted. The grass was too wet to lie on. A young man ate a sandwich on a bench. He'd spread a supermarket carrier under him to keep him from the damp wood. Behind him, on the other side of the railings, trains clattered into Norwood Junction. Between trains it was quiet in the park, birdsong the prevalent sound.

The two children ran to the tiny coppice of pine trees and elder, the only cover on the smooth suburban triangle of green. They played for a time, ducking, stalking, hiding, pouncing. 'Hands in the air, Dummy, or you're dead!'

Janice, ten years old, crawling on her belly round the elder bush in spite of the wet ground, came across a shoe. It was a girl's shoe, size 37. She picked it up. Then she saw the foot to which it belonged.

The body was lying on its face, squeezed between the elder bush and the railings. It was very wet. Janice saw something black and crusty round its neck. She backed out of the bush on all fours. Her legs shook when she stood up. She took Patrick's hand. 'We'd better go home now, Pat.'

Her mother had told her they must never go alone to the park. Patrick, in the way of children, knew something was seriously wrong but didn't dare to ask what. They walked sedately down the path to the gate, passing the young man on the bench. They came out of the park, passed the comfortable houses, the gardens with gnomes and roses, the supermarket, the clock tower. They turned right into the High Street.

Janice saw two policemen come out of a building. They began to stroll towards her. She stopped. She wanted to run away. She wanted to hide. Standing still in the High

Street she turned her head this way, that way. Patrick looked up at her, perplexed. Then she ran full tilt at the tall policeman and threw herself sobbing against his legs.

Patrick stood amazed. Shocked. The policeman stooped down on his haunches to look at Janice. He held her arms above the elbow and talked to her. The other policeman came to Patrick and took his hand.

Several policemen went to the spot, not accompanied by the children. The area was cordoned off. It was ascertained that the body was that of a young blonde woman about five foot two, whose head was almost severed from the neck. It had been kept from discovery by the continuous rain. There was no handbag with driving licence or credit cards. No one had reported a girl missing. The body was put in a refrigerated compartment with a label reading, *Unidentified.*

27

George was afraid of his mother's ability to read his thoughts. Bubbles of anxiety kept rising into his throat. He was distracted from this worry by the presence of Kylie, however. She charmed his mother with little attentions and smiles. 'Those incredible meals you made for the boys. Brilliant, Mrs Fletcher, honestly.' 'I thought you only saw them on the telly, houses like this; I never dreamed I'd get to live in one.' 'Lovely furniture and things. You keep it so nice, Mrs Fletcher. It smells of furniture polish, you know what I mean?' Mrs Fletcher became almost flustered with so much flattery.

Whenever his mother's back was turned Kylie shot him little smiling looks of complicity and mischief: *We have a secret, you and I.* George was enchanted.

His mother didn't unbend enough to invite the girl to eat in the kitchen, however. So, at seven, she went upstairs to cook for herself. George could not follow her, had no way to make further contact. Not under his mother's eagle eye.

He made excuses to go upstairs several times: to look in on Kevin who still lay in bed round-eyed, sad and silent; to visit the bathroom; to fetch things from his bedroom. But Kylie was never on the landing or any-where to be seen or heard. She was there, in his own house, and it was more painful than if she lived a million miles away. George began to think about the flat in town.

Polly threw herself on her back on the bright coverlet. She covered her face with her hands. She laughed silently.

He put the second coat of paint on the new cupboard doors and sat back on his heels.

Chloe said, 'It's lovely, Jack.' She was astounded. She hadn't seen Jack so peaceful for years. He looked younger, even. Some terrible strain was gone from him. She didn't want to ask him what had brought about the change, for fear of bringing back the devil. She had a sneaking feeling that it was something to do with Polly not being in the house any more. But he'd loved Polly, hadn't he? The cogitation made her brain feel limp. She sighed.

Jack looked at her. 'You worried about Polly?' he said. 'She'll be all right, Chlo, I promise you.'

'Don't you miss her, Jack?'

'Nice just the two of us, Chlo.'

'Oh?' Much as she missed Polly, and in spite of her anxiety as to her daughter's whereabouts, Chloe's face began to gather a tentative joy. Was it Polly then who'd been the trouble between them all this time?

'The body of a girl was discovered this afternoon by two children in a play area near Norwood Junction...' It appeared as the first item on the London news at the end of the late bulletin.

John Bright's mother Lily called out, 'Oh, God, John, come and look at this!' But he was asleep. She wanted to wake him but didn't.

George, already in bed, lay thinking of Kylie.

Kylie/Polly lay thinking, in more practical terms, of George.

Mrs Fletcher, glad to be back in her own bed, snored.

For the first time for years Jack shared a spliff with Chloe. They sat facing each other cross-legged in the bare living room, just as they did in the days when they'd first met.

On Wednesday morning it was in all the papers and on the national news. South Norwood, a suburb the world was generally ignorant of, brimmed with news people and police.

A terrible noise woke George: his mother roaring about with the vacuum cleaner. He lurched upright to look at his clock. It was 7 a.m. Kylie wasn't in the bathroom. He hurtled through his morning ablutions, got dressed and hung about in the hall. He had to see her before she left for college. *Just to see her, that's all.* But his mother mustn't know. The vacuum cleaner stopped.

Suddenly the house was silent. George heard Kylie's little footsteps on the lino of the upper flight. He moved into the shadows. He heard her call out, 'Bye, Mrs Fletcher!' He came out of the shadows and showed himself. But there stood his mother, behind Kylie, on the stairs.

'Oh, George?' Kylie said. 'I'm ever so glad to see you. There's something I want to ask you about. I – you know – need your advice. I haven't got time now. Can I ask you tonight, would you mind?'

'Eighteen years old.' Lily Bright shook her head. 'That's what they said on the news.'

'On the bloody doorstep, Ma. No escape, is there? Even in South Norwood.' He went on reading while she looked at him. 'Oh, my God,' he said.

'What?'

'Won't be long.' Bright swept his jacket off the chair.

'Finish your coffee, John!'

He came back, gulped down half a cup of coffee then kissed the top of her head. 'See you, Ma.'

The house had always shaken when he went out.

Jack woke late, next to Chloe. The sun was shining again. He got out of bed and stretched. He had a shower. The water felt marvellous on his skin. He shook himself like a dog.

'Eating breakfast, Jack?' Chloe couldn't believe her eyes. White-faced but clean-shaven, and for the first morning in as many years as she could remember, he didn't have the shakes.

He put a hand under her hair at the back of her neck and kissed her mouth.

'Oh, Jack.'

'Rain's stopped. Wonder if there might be some racing today.' He felt optimistic enough to put some money on a horse. He went to the betting shop in the High Street. Chloe carried on to the supermarket for tobacco and food. He stopped off on the way back to buy a paper at the Indian corner shop. A group of men whispered earnestly in their own language, shaking their heads and sighing.

'What is the world coming to?' the newsagent said to Jack.

'Yeah!' Jack answered cheerfully. 'Still, the sun's shining,' he called out as he left.

The group of Indian men looked at each other mystified.

'Seen this?' Bright waved the newspaper at George. He shouted over the sound of the vacuum cleaner upstairs.

George read the account of the murder. His bewilderment was statuesque.

'No, you hadn't, had you?' Bright propelled George ahead of him into the kitchen and shut the door. He got his breath. 'I just wondered if you'd seen your little girl recently.'

'My? Girl?'

'Your little blonde lodger, George. Not surprising that she springs to mind, is it? Five two, slim, blonde, about eighteen years old?'

'Oh.' George's big hand trembled, his mouth went slack. 'Oh, John.'

'What's happened? Is she missing?' Bright was on his feet.

'No, no. I saw her. I saw her this morning. An hour ago. She was all right, she was fine. Oh, God.' George wiped his face. 'Oh, God.' He made a curious hissing sound through his teeth. 'Ss-ss-ss-ss.'

Bright relaxed. 'Ah well, never mind. I just thought – I always think– Well, never mind.' He looked shaken. 'Someone said I always think like a policeman,' he said. 'It's true. She was right. How's Kevin this morning?'

'Kevin? Kevin? He's – he's – the same. He's still got flu. He's still in bed. He's just the same.'

Jack looked at the mended kitchen and grunted with satisfaction. Those pine doors had been a good find. He opened the fridge. There were no provisions in the house since Polly had gone. Never mind, Chloe would bring fish and chips back or an Indian. He took a can of beer upstairs, opening it as he went. He took off his trainers and lay on his bed in his own room.

His was the tiny front room, box room really. It had never been decorated. He'd begun once, stripped the wallpaper revealing greyish pitted plaster. It stayed like that. He liked it. Lino on the floor. Original features and no mistake. He took a sip of the beer and put the can on the floor. He opened the paper to the racing page. The tail of something on the front page flicked at the edge of his mind. He turned back.

He sat bolt upright. He dropped the paper on to his knees. He stared at the window. He read the article again. He dropped the paper on to the floor. Picked it up. Looked at it. Looked away. He crushed it between his hands and dropped the crumpled ball. Then he went down on his knees to it and smoothed it out. He read. He put his head down on it. He got up and paced the four steps the room allowed. His two bony hands pressed hard each side of his head. He seemed to be trying to remember something. Or trying not to. He heard the key in the front door.

'Sounds like that Alison Hicks,' Mrs Fletcher said. She threw the paper down.

Bright looked at George. George slowly lifted his eyes to his mother. Their whites were yellowish, curdled-looking. He did not speak.

'Alison Hicks?' Bright said.

'Three doors down. Number twenty-nine. Her parents were on the same holiday as me. On the coach.'

'You know them well then?'

'On the same coach, I said! I hardly spoke to them. Not my type. Catholics. Common as muck but think they're a cut above.'

'They'd have reported her missing, wouldn't they?'

'Oh, they didn't come back with the rest of us. Oh, no.'

'What do you mean?'

'We got to Alicante, spent the night. Next day we were moving on. They weren't on the coach! The tour guide said they'd decided to stay on a bit. Make their own way back. The rest of us weren't good enough for them, I suppose.'

'When was this?'

'Oh.' She thought. 'About four days before the end. Five. Thursday it was. Yes, Thursday. Their seats were empty on the bus. We waited half an hour for them. Wasn't the first time they'd kept us waiting either. Then the hotel man came out and gave the guide a note. A note!'

'Pretty shocking,' Bright said.

She looked at him coldly. 'Bad behaviour's not amusing,' she said. She began to bang about, picking up cups and clonking them into the sink.

'Well off, are they, these Hickses?'

'No, I told you, he's an artist or something. They won the holiday in their church raffle. Kept telling everyone they couldn't have afforded it on their own. You'd think they were proud of being poor, to listen to them.' She plugged in the vacuum cleaner.

Bright moved to the door. 'Have you seen the girl – Alison, was it – since you came back?'

'How would I have seen her? I've only been back five minutes.'

'George?'

George took a long time to turn his face to Bright. 'I think she was in the garden on Sunday,' he said.

'In our garden?' She turned, clucking. 'She can't keep away from Kevin for some reason. Always coming over to help him plant his seeds.'

George felt a crazy desire to laugh. He was unravelling.

'And you haven't seen her since then?' Bright said.

George shook his head.

'Pity we can't ask Kevin.' Bright raised an eyebrow.

Only to get himself under control, George said, 'Have they called you in on it, John?'

Bright looked completely taken aback. 'Er – no! No, they haven't. I was just er...' He stopped and rubbed his head. 'Well, I said, you know? Always a copper.'

Mrs Fletcher turned on the vacuum cleaner. Bright had been given subtler hints in his time. 'Think it's time I went!' he yelled over the noise with a sideways look at George. 'Fancy a pint, George?' A certain neediness had come into his expression.

George looked at his mother. She determinedly did not look at him. He shook his head. 'Better not,' he said.

Bright tensed his mouth, nodded and turned to go.

'I think she works in the supermarket,' George said. A thumbnail scratched between his brows.

Bright couldn't hear over the roar of the machine. 'What?' he shouted.

'She works in the supermarket!' Mrs Fletcher yelled.

'They'd have reported her missing then!' Bright shouted back.

Chloe and Jack stared at each other in the hall. She looked like a child in a fairy tale who had been turned into a little old woman overnight. Jack was holding out two small shaking crumpled bits of paper.

'They were in my pockets all the time,' he said.

She took the pieces and tried to match them up. She could hardly see. But yes. It was Polly's writing, yes.

'I must have just forgotten I'd found it.'

His voice was a dry rattle in his throat. He had the shakes again.

'It's Polly,' she said. 'I know it is. I've had this feeling, one of my feelings. All the way back on the bus Sunday night, I knew. I just had this knowledge. That something awful had happened. I kept seeing–' She looked at the note again. 'I've got to go to the police station, Jack.'

'I'll go,' he said. 'You stay here. In case she – turns up. Or rings or– Just in case.' He had to get out on his own. Terrible pictures came and went in his head. He felt they'd been hiding in there in order to creep out and surprise him in their own good time.

'Can I have a word with Alison Hicks, love?'

'Oh, Alison's away this week! She took a bit of her holiday to get the place nice to welcome her mum and dad back. They come back Monday, right, Trace? Day before yes'day.'

John Bright went very still. 'A-ha?' he said. 'That right?'

'And then she was going up to her auntie in Birkenhead,' Tracey called. 'Not my idea of a holiday but you know Alison.'

'Oh, come on, she's fond of her auntie, Trace.'

Tracey rolled her eyes.

'Isn't it awful about this girl?' The woman clucked. 'We were saying this morning, that could be Alison, weren't we, Trace? But no, I mean. Her mum and dad would have been on to it, wouldn't they? If anything had happened to her, I mean.'

'Well, never mind.' Bright's face showed no concern. 'I'll catch her when she gets back. Thanks, girls.'

The wind had started up again. Sheets of newspaper and leaves swirled round John Bright's ankles. The steps of the police station were empty now, the news people scattered for lunch. He sprang lightly up the steps into the small lobby. A bony dark man with haunted eyes was being led away by a sergeant, a small piece of paper in each shaking hand.

When Jack saw the body he put one hand over his eyes and the other over his mouth. 'Yes,' he said, 'that's her. That's Polly.'

The doctor looked at the policeman by the door. The policeman opened the door, gave the thumbs-up sign to the desk sergeant in the lobby, then closed the door again and said to Jack, 'Are you sure now, sir? Take your time. There's no rush.'

Bright, in the lobby, showing the desk sergeant his warrant card, saw the thumbs-up sign. 'Definite ID?' he said.

The desk man looked over his shoulder to check there was no one about. 'Looks like it, yes, sir.'

'Name of Hicks by any chance?'

'Hicks?' The man looked puzzled. He checked the details Jack had given him. 'No. King. Polly King. Missing since last Friday night.'

'Thanks, mate.'

'You used to work here, didn't you, sir?'

'Long time ago now. When the HQ was on the High Street.'

'Bit different now, right?'

'A-ha. Bigger and better. And that's just the building.'

'Eh?'

'Sorry, mate, gotta go. Thanks for your help. 'Preciate it.'

He did not want to look at the dead face again. But the copper had hold of his arm. Jack turned back and did manage another brief glance. The shoulder-length blonde hair, the pretty features. He shut his eyes tight and lowered his head, breathing hard. Then he looked once more and could not move his gaze away. The inside of his head was a high-pitched scream. Was he really standing here looking at a body that ought to be Polly for Christ's sake but was actually another girl with her head almost severed from her neck? Or was he dreaming a bad dream, in which he would stand here for ever like this and would never wake up?

It was Polly. Surely? It had to be, didn't it? Had someone killed this other girl to make fun of him? To drive him completely out of his mind? Were the police trying to trap him here? Was Chloe in league with them? Was she trying to get him caught, or what? 'Just a minute,' he said.

'Well, sir?'

Jack raised his haunted face but said nothing.

'Is it her then, sir? You sure?'

Jack shook his head, as if it were a dead weight he could barely carry. 'No,' he said in his crackling dry whisper. 'No. That's not Polly.'

'Don't seem all that sure, sir. What was it made you think it might be her?'

'It's just that we really thought— And she's like Poll, you see. Just like her. But Polly's— But it's not her. I'm sure. It's not her.'

Out at the desk the phone rang. The desk sergeant picked it up and heard a wispy little voice. 'It's all right. She's back. My Polly. She's safe. She's okay. Is Jack still there? Will you tell him she's all right, please? This is her mum.'

The desk sergeant couldn't tell John Bright because John Bright had gone.

'Well, I didn't know, Mum, did I? I was in Croydon having a dancing class. I didn't

288

Quinton Library

Customer ID: **********3581

Items that you have checked out

Title: Every step you take [text(large print)]
ID: C8000000187269
Due: 19 January 2018

Total items: 1
Account balance: £0.00
22/12/2017 13:31
Checked out: 1
Overdue: 0
Hold requests: 0
Ready for collection: 0

Thank you for using the library.

know till lunchtime. They were talking about it in the caff.'

'You could have rung me, Poll.'

'I left you a note, didn't I?'

Chloe sighed. She put her hands over her mouth and said into them, 'I thought you'd been murdered.'

'Not me,' Polly said.

'You've got to tell me where you're staying. I've got to know where to find you.'

'No chance.'

'Polly, please.'

'If I tell you you'll tell Jack.'

'He's different now. He's better, you wouldn't believe.'

'You're right, I wouldn't.'

'I mean it, Poll.'

'He'd worm it out of you.'

Chloe couldn't argue with that. She looked hopeless. There was a silence while Polly floated round the room.

'What's it like, then? Where you are?' Chloe said in a squeezed little voice.

'It's brilliant. Great big house. They're really rich. He's a chief partner in this big firm. In the City. He's got a flat near there, as well as the house. They've got oil paintings and everything. My room's lovely. The woman – that's his mother – she really likes me.' She gave Chloe a look over her shoulder. 'So does he,' she said.

'Oh, Polly, be careful.'

'I'm going to do better for myself than you, Mum. I'm not going to live like this again.'

A shadow fell across the window.

'It's him. I'm going. I'll see you, Mum.' And she was down the passage, into the yard and out the back gate before Jack could fumble his way into the house.

'Alison,' Bright said. 'Kevin's little friend? It's not her. The stepfather just ID'd a Polly King from Brockhurst Road. Will you tell George, Mrs F? He looked a bit cut up this morning.'

She shot him a look of grim distaste. 'Gone back to bed,' she said.

'Tell him I'll see him around.'

She shut the door without bothering to respond. As he went down the path a cab drew up at number twenty-nine. A cheerful tanned couple piled out with shabby bulging bags. Bright watched them a moment then punched his right fist into his left palm and walked lightly away. He didn't know why he should feel so damn pleased, as though he had personally restored their daughter to them. After all, *someone's* daughter had got killed. It wasn't like he'd saved anyone's life.

The house had a deserted feel to it, Ros Hicks thought. She went to put the kettle on. Chris gathered up the slithering hillock of mail off the mat. Among the unsolicited junk was the card they'd sent to tell Alison their new arrival time.

'Ros?' he said.

They began to make telephone calls. His brother in Wandsworth, her sister in Birkenhead. The supermarket. Alison's ex-boyfriend. The mother of a girl Alison had been friends with at school.

'I'm sorry, I'm probably just being a hysterical father but – I've just heard about this – awful thing.' Chris Hicks looked as though the wind had blown him into the police station and was still holding him up by the hair. 'We've only just got back, you see. We'd never left her by herself before. But you know what they're like: I'm seventeen now, Dad, I can take care of myself. I'm sure she's okay really; it's just she's a reliable girl as a rule and she'd taken time off to make things nice for us, to be there, you see, when we got back and it's not like her to– Sorry, yes. Yattering on.'

'Now, sir. What was the name again?'

Thus at about four o'clock in the afternoon of Wednesday, the body was officially identified as that of Alison Hicks. Chris Hicks was kept at the station to answer questions. His alibi appeared to be perfect. While he was

291

questioned, however, it was being checked.

Two officers, one male, one female, went to number twenty-nine. They stayed with Ros Hicks until Chris was returned to her, then they departed. And the couple were left. Alone.

28

'I'm going now, George. Miss Adams – Kylie – says she'll keep an eye on Kevin. She'll bring you both your supper up. She seems an obliging enough girl.' Mrs Fletcher picked up the tray and strode to the door. 'I won't be late. Walter will bring me back. Make himself useful for once.' Walter was her sister's husband, an obliging man. 'After all, I'm going specially to show them my holiday snaps.'

George was in bed again, with flesh like melting butter. He knew it was fear that had brought about his relapse. He wondered if he was having a nervous breakdown, if this was how it began. If that was what had been happening to him all along. But then Kylie appeared at his door.

'I've brought you the paper, George. She's gone, your mum.' She came into the room, looking round her with a curious satisfaction, pleased that everything was as she recalled it, everything in its place, even George. She dropped the paper on to the bed. 'All right if I sit down?'

He could only nod, not speak. He knew his smile was fatuous. He didn't care. All troubles swept out of his mind by her mere presence. She seated herself on the bed, close to his feet. When he shifted them slightly to rest against her hip, she didn't move away.

'Isn't it awful about this murder, George?' Her voice was watery cool.

To wrench his eyes away from her he picked up the *Evening Standard*. 'The girl was five foot two,' he read out. 'Blonde with blue eyes.'

'Isn't that funny?' she said.

'What?'

'That your eyes are still the same colour when you're dead.'

'Why?'

'You'd think they wouldn't be any colour any more somehow, wouldn't you?'

'Well...' This was not an idea that had ever occurred to George.

'Well, anyway, I would.'

'Yes.' He went back to the paper. 'Small in build. Her clothes, short white cotton skirt, jeans jacket, black T-shirt, had possibly been bought locally. Anyone who may have seen the girl or thinks they may have known her should contact the police in strictest confidence...' George's voice faded away. He lifted his head and gazed at her like a mournful hound. 'It could be you, Kylie, it could be a description of you.'

'I'd never wear a black T-shirt with a white skirt,' she said.

A picture of Alison slid into his mind. Her vulnerable elbows. Her hands clenched in the pockets of her jeans jacket. The first time he followed her. Sweat slid down his face, he could feel it. It wasn't Alison. They'd said it wasn't. John Bright had said so. He closed his eyes.

'Here, George, let me.' Her cool little hand wiped his face with a tissue. 'That girl down the road wears things like that,' she said. She had seen Alison on Sunday in precisely those clothes.

'Oh, it's not her.' George spoke with unusual firmness.

'How do you know?'

'I was told. Someone identified the – body – this morning.'

'Who as?'

'Polly something, I believe. Polly King?'

The little hand stopped mopping. 'Who told you?'

'Oh, I – well – it's confidential, Kylie. A friend of mine in the police. He told me at lunchtime today.'

'Well, why doesn't the paper say that then?'

'Oh.'

'See?' Kylie seemed curiously angry. 'I know it's not Polly King.'

'How do you know?'

'Because I know her, that's why. She – she goes to the same classes as me. I saw her this morning if you want to know. So I know it's not her.'

'No, I'm sure...' George floundered in the face of her anger. He didn't know what he'd done wrong.

'So people shouldn't say things like that.'

'No.' George spluttered. 'But this friend of mine would have no reason to lie to me.'

'Well, he wasn't telling the truth, was he?'

We're quarrelling! George felt a mixture of pain and pleasure at the thought. Pain at the quarrel. Pleasure at the degree of intimacy such a quarrel implied. But his brain pulsated with too much new information. He sat up. 'Kylie,' he said.

'What?'

'Don't be upset.'

'I'm not.'

'Would you hand me my dressing gown?'

'Where are you going?'

'To phone my friend.'

'The policeman?'

'Yes.'

'What for?'

'Because you're right – there must have been a mistake. I'd better let him know, in case–' His words broke off. *He walks behind*

Alison. He stretches out a hand to touch her. She falls with an axe in her neck. He sat on the edge of the bed, not moving.

'Look' – Kylie helped him on with his dressing gown – 'I didn't mean– You don't have to phone him, do you, George?' She was standing between his thighs. 'George?' Her breasts were almost touching him. They were touching him. Her hands were touching the back of his neck. He was looking up into her fathomless eyes. 'George?'

'Ohh...' If he were to put his hands there, just at her waist, his fingers spread over her hips. Would she mind?

The phone rang.

Bright apologised for his mistake. 'I'm out of training, George. My mind's not working right one thing an' another. Not that that's any excuse. Don't know what came over me. Passing on information before it's been verified. Christ. Something about that little girl and Kevin. I don't know. Didn't want it to be her. Never used to get sentimental. What'll you tell Kevin, by the way?'

There was a silence.

'George?'

'Oh. Nothing.' George seemed to come back to life. 'Nothing yet. Not while he's still so sick.'

'I'm sorry, old mate. Couldn't be sorrier.' Bright sounded deeply upset. As though he had known Alison personally.

George put the phone down and stood with his back to the wall. He felt the world had stopped in mid-revolution and he was left revolving, all by himself.

29

'See you later, Ma.' Bright kissed the top of her head, ruffled her frizzy hair, did much the same to the Other George, grabbed his old leather jacket and left. His mother and the cat looked after him with much the same concerned expression. The front door banged. The house shook.

He was still getting into his jacket at the corner. He thought for a moment of going by way of Lisson Avenue to Oliver Gardens where the vast new police station stood. He winced and turned left, reached the High Street in two minutes, crossed over and carried on down to the tarted-up pub.

For all the pseudo leaded lights and tables with umbrellas the place was still a free house – at least you could get a decent pint there. And some old acquaintances of his hung out there too. He'd been avoiding them up to now, on his one visit with George Fletcher glad not to see anyone he knew.

She was there. Well-built, blonde, carefully made-up, attractive if you liked that kind of thing. John Bright was fond of her, had encouraged her ambition in the early days. She was a detective sergeant now, good going for a woman. He was the guy responsible for getting her into CID and out of uniform. She'd looked better in it, he thought. In plain clothes she didn't know what style to adopt. In emerald green tonight she looked like an air hostess.

'Hi, Jess,' he said. 'What'll you have?'

'John Bright! How's things? Visiting Ma?'

'Staying for a bit, a-ha.' He brought the drinks and put the *Evening Standard* on the table, front page up. 'What's the newest data on this?'

'Knew you had an ulterior motive. No such thing as a free gin and tonic. Cheers.'

'I got a good reason for asking.'

'I'm sure you have. Okay. It's proving hard to check the father's alibi. He can't even remember the names of half the places they stayed at in Spain after they left the tour coach, little flea-pit hotels and things.'

'He didn't do it, Jess.'

'No?'

'He'd have had to plan in advance. Come back on false documents on Sunday, go back to Spain or wherever, trust his wife not to tell which means she'd have to be in it with him. And why leave the poor kid out in the rain? He could have buried her in the garden.'

'Then we'd dig her up, wouldn't we, and know it was him?'

'A-ha. Good point.'

'So if it was planned and all, it was a pretty good plan.'

'Only you don't think it was planned, do you?'

'No, we don't.'

'So?'

'But we haven't got any other useful theories either, so we're following it up.'

'What about forensic? Any DNA?'

'She was out in the rain for nearly forty-eight hours, John!'

'Wouldn't have washed out semen if there was any there.'

'No sperm.'

'That widens the field. Any DNA at all?'

'Nothing except some human hairs. Not hers. Short. Dark. Straight. They've been checked. No match in the files.'

'So, no use calling in the usual suspects.'

'No.'

'No fibres under the fingernails, no struggle signs?'

'Nothing.'

'A bit hard to struggle with an axe in the back of your neck, right?'

'Too right. Yes. They think at least it was quick.'

'Had the usuals in anyway, in case they've heard anything?'

'Oh, yes. All the flashers and molesters. Not a pretty sight. They don't know a thing.'

'Natch. Might not be anyone local at all. Near a railway line. Close to the Junction. Not that far from Victoria, even, on the train.'

'Got to cast the net local first,' she said.

'Or question every guy who comes to spend the weekends in South Norwood with his ma.'

Her eyes stood still a second. So did his. In spite of the slight squint she could always tell what he was looking at. He wasn't looking at her now. Or at anything in the pub. He was looking at something that had just come into his head. He took a gulp of his Webster's.

'That's a point, John,' she said.

'It certainly is a point, Jess.' Now he was looking at her.

She took a good swallow of her gin and tonic, and ran her tongue over the perfectly made-up lips. She knew a significant thought had just occurred to him. She also knew it was no good trying to prise it out of him. But she trusted him to tell her when he was ready. She trusted him.

'Be careful, you've got to be careful, promise me.' Jack was shaking her by the shoulders.

'Me?' Chloe's teeth chattered. 'Nobody's

going to murder me!'

'You're small, you're blonde, you're just the same build.'

'But I'm not eighteen years old.'

'From the back you are!' He gripped her upper arms so hard she feared he might snap them off. He lowered his head and began to bray like an animal. Tears rolled out of him. He was shouting and moaning and wiping his face with his hand. 'They all look the same from behind!'

Seeing that body had upset him badly. She ought to have known. He didn't have the stomach for things like that. 'But you will get over it in time. You will. You will. Oh, Jack, you will!'

'It should have been Polly!' he screamed.

'Oh, Jack, don't. Don't torture yourself.'

'It should have been her. It was meant to be her.'

'You don't know that.'

'Oh, yes, I do.'

Chloe looked round helplessly. The tops of her arms were bruised from his holding her. 'I wish she was here now,' she said.

Jack laughed while tears still sprang out of his eyes.

'Jack, I'm scared.'

'So you should be. That's what I'm telling you. I'm telling you to be scared. Be scared. Be scared.'

'I just don't know what to do. Will you let

me call the doctor?' she said.

'Doctor? What for?'

'I think you need something to make you sleep.'

'Sleep!' he said. 'Sleep.' He laughed again. Chloe watched him, clutching her bruised arms.

30

The phone still hung from George's hand. 'It was her,' he said. 'The girl from down the road. It was Alison.'

'I thought it was.' Kylie gave a little nod. 'Soon as you read out about the clothes.'

George looked at her, appalled.

'Shall I help you back to bed?' she said.

He allowed himself to lean on her small body that looked as frail as a leaf but was as strong as steel rope. His hand brushed the top of her arm. Though for days, weeks, years, he would have given the earth for this contact with the smooth silk of her flesh, horror robbed him of his pleasure in her.

But he needed her support, his functions were suspended. He hoped he might be able to spend his life like this, incapable of action, of thought. If only he could get the jumbled impressions out of his head. She was about to help him into his bedroom, still entwined with him, when Mrs Fletcher came in at the front door.

Everyone stood still. His mother's jaw dropped. George watched this phenomenon with the sense of hysteria that had come upon him with what he thought of now as his breakdown. He couldn't remember before ever having seen the humorous side of things. Especially of things connected with his mother. He was probably smiling foolishly, he didn't know and didn't care. 'Hello, Mother,' he said.

'What do you think you're doing?' She was asking both of them.

Kylie replied. 'I'm helping George back to bed, Mrs Fletcher. He's not well.'

'He's still got the use of his legs, hasn't he?'

'Not really, no, actually. He got this terrible shock off the phone.'

'Shock? Off the phone?' She looked at it askance, as if it might give off sparks, or even explode.

Kylie gazed up at his face. 'Tell her, George.'

'It was Alison Hicks. The girl who was killed.' He spoke flatly. There was no way of breaking such news gently, any more than you could break a cup gently, a promise gently. A neck.

'Oh, I know that,' Mrs Fletcher said.

'Heard it on the news. They're back now, the Hickses.' She started to take her coat off. 'Go on then, get him back to bed, if that's what you're doing.'

'So how come you're so interested?' Jess Jones said. 'You're on leave, aren't you?'

'None of my business? That what you're saying? Not my manor?'

'I didn't mean that, John.'

'Sure?'

She smiled, blue lids lowered over green eyes. 'A little bird told me you were a bit – disenchanted with our chosen profession, thinking of getting out.'

'None of the little bird's business.'

'No.' She kept her eyes on him. Didn't smile. 'Nor mine either, that what you're telling me?'

He gave her a sideways look. 'I didn't say that.'

'I'm just wondering why you're so interested in this case. If you're really thinking of giving the police the heave-ho.'

'Yeah. Good question.' He looked at her dead straight now. 'Don't know why I'm interested, Jess. One of those feelings up the spine, hairs on the back of the neck. You know the feeling. And it's South Norwood! Weird, innit? Incongruous, right? The leafy suburb.'

'It's not leafy this side of the tracks.'

'No. My ma lives on the leafy side.'

'The right side.'

'Only by three hundred yards. What's this with the tracks anyway? You from this side then, are you, or what?'

'Yep. The wrong side. And how.'

'Yeah, I remember now.' He did remember her when she first arrived, scruffy kid, terrible hair, terrible teeth, all fixed now. 'Not that much difference any more, though, right, between that side and this side?'

'Don't you believe it.'

'When I was growing up our side was white and this side was Indian.'

'Well, haven't you noticed you hardly see a white face any more?'

'That's the gentrification of Brixton's done that. People got to move out somewhere. They've all moved here.'

'It's affected your mum's side as well.'

'Depends how far from the tracks you go. This Alison Hicks. Her street's still as it was when I was growing up.'

'See?' she said. 'Trying to change the subject but you come back to little Alison.'

He rubbed his face with a capable small square hand and sighed. 'Okay. I don't like young girls getting killed. Innocent kids who don't deserve it. Right?'

She saw that he couldn't go on, emotion choking him. She'd known him as cold as ice dealing with a case, his mind as tough as his wiry body. No holds barred. So this was new to her. And she didn't dare probe deeper for fear of his reaction. He'd been a great guvnor, she remembered. She wished they still had him around. She shouldn't say so, though, wouldn't be right, would it? Disloyal to her present boss. 'Wish we still had you around, John,' she said.

He stared into his empty glass, then at her. 'Still like being a copper then, Jess?'

'Sure I do. You taught me how.'

'Still glad you joined?'

'More than ever.'

'Why?'

'We're going to catch the bastard that killed Alison. That's why.'

'Did you know her then?' Kylie said.

'Not–' George swallowed. He was trying to pull himself together. 'Not really,' he said. 'No.'

'Kevin did,' she said.

George closed his eyes. He'd hoped in vain. 'Yes,' he said. 'They were friends.'

'Friends? Is that what you call it?' She gave a cool little laugh. 'It didn't look like that to me.'

'Oh?' His lips would barely move, his facial muscles as paralysed as his brain. 'What do you mean?'

'She took him into your shed with her,' Kylie went on. 'I don't think they were playing tiddlywinks in there, do you?'

The words sounded so odd, falling like clear drops of water from between her perfect, smiling lips. He could only look at her, not reply.

'They were in there on Sunday,' she said. 'For ages actually. Then she ran out. She looked upset.'

'Oh.'

'You know when I went to get Kevin in from the garden? He wasn't there. I don't think he came back that night.'

'Yes, he did.'

'I didn't want to worry you at the time.'

'He did come back.'

'He wasn't here in the middle of the night. I went down to look in his room and everywhere, when the storm started.'

'He was in the shed.'

'When did you find him there?'

'In the morning.'

'Oh, well, the morning,' she said.

George gazed at the beautiful blue eyes. She gazed back, head on one side, still with her little half smile. The cold water-drops of her words dripped into George's brain. He had to concentrate. 'Is that what you wanted to talk to me about?' he said.

'What?'

'This morning. You said you would want to talk to me about something.'

'Oh, no. Well, there hadn't been a murder

then, had there, George?'

'Then–? I'm so sorry, I don't understand.'

'No,' she said. 'I just said that because I wanted to be able to come in here and talk to you without your mum thinking it was funny. You know.' She came up close to him. He could smell her. Her clean, pure, baby-soap smell, citrus and rosemary. *Her hair...* 'Well, actually...' She stroked the back of his hand with one pink oval fingernail. 'There is something, George...'

'Yes?'

'Yes.' Her fine-veined eyelids lifted. *Her eyes...* 'The thing is, you see. You know I said I was a performance arts student? Well, it isn't quite true. Well, it's true, I am, I am studying singing and dance and that, but the thing is I can only do it part time. I have to do this awful job during the day to pay for it. I really want to do it full time and I should do really because I am good enough. My mum was a dancer but she got married and had me and then he ran off, so...' Polly shrugged. 'But she says I'm the one that should have been the performer, and I should be, George. But I just can't afford it, you see. Well, I just – you know – wanted to ask for your advice, that's all... You see?'

George did see. He saw clearly. He was reminded of the negotiations for the merger. He had the same feeling of defeat. Despair, really. *Ah,* he thought, *all you had to do was*

308

ask. There was no need to do it this way. Didn't she know he'd do anything, pay anything, without the threat thrown in?

There must have been something in the way he looked at her, because she backed away a little. 'Well! You don't have to look at me like that. I was only asking your advice, that's all. I wasn't asking for anything else.' She raised her chin in defiance. 'I wasn't!'

'No,' he said. 'I know you weren't.' He wanted to weep. For her? For himself? He didn't know. She wasn't as clever as she thought. Or as wicked, he suddenly realised. He was glad of that. The gladness filled his heart. He felt suddenly, meaninglessly, powerful, assured. He held out his hand. 'Kylie,' he said. His voice was gentle.

She came closer, a step or two.

'What would your lessons cost?'

'I don't know!' She sounded miserable. 'I don't know. I want a proper course at a proper place. I want a proper singing teacher, I don't know.'

'I would be glad to pay for your lessons.'

'I only wanted a loan. When I'm a professional, working, I can pay you back.'

'Very well. I'd be glad to do that. I think you'd be a good investment.'

She looked at him, lips parted. Not provocative. Perplexed. This was the first time he had seen her not in control. He liked the feeling this discovery gave him. In the midst of his crowding phantoms it was a bud of sanity. It might save him yet.

She started to say something. Then she ran out of the room.

31

'If only I could just get stoned.' But Chloe knew she had to keep her wits about her. She stood at the sink wondering how her life had become such a nightmare.

Jack had been out in the yard for hours. He had torn down the pile of wood. He had scrabbled through the bits, as though searching for something. The window was spotted with sawdust and scraps. Through this lacy foreground she watched as he threw everything out of the little lean-to that used to be the outside loo.

An old electric fire hit the back door, Polly's ancient pushchair flew close to but just missed the window. Chloe flinched. A roll of mildewed carpet slewed across the yard sending a swarm of wood chips whirling. *Oh, Jack, what are you doing now?* She went to the door but didn't dare open it for fear of being hit by one of the missiles.

He crawled backwards out of the lean-to and came into the kitchen muttering. 'It's been stolen. Someone's stolen it. Someone's hidden it. Why can't I find it? I used it the other day' He saw Chloe. 'You,' he said. 'Have you hidden it?'

'Hidden what, Jack?'

'Hidden what!' he mocked.

'What is it you've lost?'

'What is it you've lost! As if you didn't know.'

'But I don't know.'

'But don't worry. You won't stop me. Childish tricks.' He scrabbled in the broom cupboard, muttering under his breath. 'Stop me? Think they can stop me. Nothing can stop me. Justice has got to be done.'

John Bright ducked his head against the wind. *This is no business of mine, she's right. It's not my manor. I might not even be a copper any more this time next year. They'll catch the right bloke with or without me. I'm not bloody indispensable, I'm not even competent. What'm I trying to prove? That I can still hack it? Couldn't save what you loved most in the world but prove you can still do it for someone you don't give a toss about? Anyway I do give a toss. Poor little thing. Seventeen years old. Happy. Alive. Jesus. And there are people who still believe in a merciful God.* He lurched back as a sheet of newspaper flew at his face. He tore it off and crushed it into a ball. *Think you gotta take His place, that it? Rebirth of God as Detective*

Inspector Useless Pillock John Bright? He stopped, he sighed. He shied the screwed-up newspaper into a lidless dustbin on the corner of his mother's street. He turned and crossed the road to Lisson Avenue.

Mrs Fletcher's hand was clamped on Kevin's brow. His skin burned her palm like some substance not skin; hot sand perhaps. 'Have you been doing something you shouldn't have?' she said.

He made no sound, none of his silly noises, no smiles. Even sick, Kevin had always smiled. People had remarked on it. *Always happy, isn't he, Mrs Fletcher?* Well, he wasn't happy now.

'George!' She threw open his door. He had flu all right, as bad as Kevin, sweating like a great lump of lard. She didn't care. 'You just come here with me,' she said.

They stood at the door of Kevin's room. He lay curled round the hot water bottle, hugging it. His eyes stared. A shudder shook him and the eyes closed. Then the eyes opened again and stared. Then he shuddered again. Not a sound came out of him, however.

'Look at him,' she said. 'That's not just the flu.'

George could do nothing but shake his head.

'Oh, you've gone dumb as well now, have

you? Even when he's ill he makes his stupid noises, doesn't he? He laughs, doesn't he? Well, look at him now!'

'You must call the doctor.' George spoke very low.

'Doctor! Something's frightened him. Something happened here while I was away. You were never to be trusted, you great lummock, just like your father. What have you gone and let him do?'

Kevin shuddered again and squeezed his eyelids shut. She flamed across to the bed, grabbed him by the shoulders and shook him. His eyes opened sightless as a doll's. 'What is the matter with you?' she screamed.

'Mother! Stop that.' George had never used such a tone with her before. He was as astonished as she. She let Kevin go. She patted her hair. He fell back on the pillow. George drew the covers up over him. His eyes looked at George a moment, then away.

His mother stood in the doorway. 'I'll get to the bottom of this,' she said. Then she was gone.

George felt so tired he could barely stand. He sat on the bed and looked at Kevin. He put his big hand on Kevin's head. The heat startled him. 'Oh, Kev,' he whispered. 'Thank heaven you can't speak.' It was only then that he admitted the thoughts he had been trying to hide from himself. And it was at that moment the doorbell rang. And he

313

knew who it would be.

'George is sick!' Mrs Fletcher stood firm as a palace guard.

But old techniques die hard. Bright strode in without an invitation the way a policeman will, before the drugs can be flushed down the lavatory, the felon leap from the first floor back. He ran lightly up the stairs: 'Up here then, is he? Thanks, Mrs Fletcher, just a quick word.'

He wasn't quick enough for George, however. He was out of Kevin's room, on the landing with the door closed before Bright reached the top stair. He could simply have been coming from the bathroom.

'Hello, John.' He spoke easily. The sense of power experienced this morning with Kylie and just now with his mother had come back to him though he couldn't tell why. But he allowed Bright to lead him into his bedroom and shut the door.

'Look, George. How well did you know this little Alison Hicks?'

'Not well, John, how could I? I'm only here at weekends.'

'A lot can happen in a weekend.'

'I didn't know of her existence till a few weeks ago. She was planting seedlings in the garden with Kevin. I've never even spoken to her. Nodded in the street, that's all, taking Kevin for a walk one day. Why do you

314

want to know, John? I thought you said you weren't on the case.'

'How well did Kevin know her, George?'

They both knew this was the question he had come here to ask.

'Kevin?' George creased up his brow.

Bright spoke with extreme patience. 'Your little brother, Kevin, George, yes.'

'Well, I don't know. I don't think they – I mean, she was nice to him, you know, you could see that for yourself. She was kind to him. And he seemed fond of her.'

'Understatement of the year, George, from what I saw.'

'Well, you know what Kevin's like.'

'No, George, I don't. I hadn't seen Kevin for fifteen years until the other day. What *is* he like?'

'He's just the same, John. He hasn't changed.' George's eyes suddenly filled with tears. He was shocked.

'Unlike the rest of us. Yeah.' Bright didn't take his eyes off George, though his shoulders looked sadder. He put his hands in his pockets, jingled his keys. 'But he has changed though, hasn't he? He's a big grown-up lad now, pretty as they come. That little girl couldn't have missed that, could she? The thing is, George – what does Kevin do about little girls? Does he know where babies come from, George?'

'Are you insinuating that Kevin killed that

girl?' George stood up. He towered over Bright.

Bright didn't flinch. 'Do you have any idea where he was that night, George? That's the thing.'

'He was asleep in his bed.'

'Not when we found him in the morning. And when we found him in the morning – in the shed, not in the house – he was wet through.'

'He was in bed before the storm started. I know. I got up to go to the bathroom. I looked in on him.' He did not mention what Kylie had said. He knew that she would keep her mouth shut now. And he could not believe he was thinking like this.

'Why would you do that?'

'Do what?'

'Look in on him in the middle of the night.'

'He was in my charge. I was here to take care of him.' It was as though a hand crossed George's face, blotting out expression. 'While Mother was away,' he said.

'George, you said he hated storms. Why would he go out in one? Why would he go out anyway in the middle of the night?' Bright's hoarse grating nasal South London voice had gone very soft, become a catlike purr, as it could, disconcertingly, from time to time. 'See, it's a bit worrying, old mate. It's been worrying me.'

George walked away from Bright. He looked out of the window and saw a small blonde girl down there, going out at the gate. His heart turned over. He thought it was Alison. Then he saw it was Kylie, who had left the house without their hearing her. He watched her for a while walking away down the street. He thought about Kevin. He thought about Kylie's ingenuous attempt at blackmail. He thought about Marje and the turn his life had taken recently and how he felt a sense of loss so fathomless he would never reach the end of it till he reached the end of life itself. And watching Kylie disappear from his view, the empty street, he knew that without her the end of his life could come when it liked. His life was worthless without her. As it would be if anything happened to Kevin. Especially through fault of his. He stayed by the window in silence. John Bright stayed silent by the bedroom door.

Then George said wearily, 'I did it, John. I killed the girl.'

32

Chris and Ros Hicks sat on the sofa side by side. He put his arm round her but she moved away, so he clasped his hands between his knees. The stocky dark-haired policeman said they were waiting for the detective sergeant. A policewoman was roaming round the house.

They'd asked for photographs, so Alison's face was littered all over the coffee table. Her whole life seemed scattered there, in garish colour. The bell rang, the policewoman answered it and came in with a smart blonde woman. The woman was heavily made-up. She looked like an air hostess, so much so that when the stocky policeman introduced her as Detective Sergeant Jones, Chris thought it was a joke.

The woman asked who among the neighbours knew Alison. He said Mrs Fletcher at thirty-five, a few people at the church, anyone who went to the supermarket. 'She had a word for everyone,' he said. 'People knew her by name.'

Ros supplied the names of a couple of school-friends. 'But she doesn't see much of them these days. They've moved on.'

'Boyfriends?' Jess Jones asked.

Ros did not reply. Chris looked at her but she wouldn't look at him. He said, 'She was sort of a one-boy girl. She fell in love very young, about fourteen, with a boy at school. He was a couple of years older than her. We were worried. Not that he wasn't a nice boy but they were just so young. It went on for – well – till she finished school. She–' He stopped talking and stared hard, his eyes open very wide and his throat moving. Then he said, 'She wasn't all that bright, you see, Allie. Not in an academic way. The boy stayed on to do A levels with a view to college of some kind. She expected them to go on as before, I think, but...' He lifted his shoulders and opened his hands. 'The boy quickly made it clear it was over for him. It took her some time to realise what had happened. It hadn't been a happy few months for her.'

Ros made a frightening noise beside him like a distant animal roar.

Jess Jones said to the policeman, 'Nick, go and make a cup of tea?' She framed her next question with care. 'Was he – replaced – this boy? Recently? At all? In Alison's affections?'

Chris Hicks shook his head. Ros Hicks nodded.

'Who?' Chris said, turning to her, astonished.

'Kevin Fletcher.' She spoke so angrily it

was more an expletive than a reply.

'No!' he said. 'Kevin's a nice lad but – no, darling, that's not true.'

Ros said to Jess, 'Men don't see what's under their nose. That's why I didn't want to go away. He insisted I needed a holiday. I didn't need a holiday, I needed to be here.'

'A nice lad but what?' Jess said to Chris.

Chris said, 'Well–'

Ros said, 'He's not the full shilling.'

'He still goes to the special school,' Chris said. 'On Selhurst Road. He's twenty-four but illiterate, can't even speak. Brain damage at birth, I believe. Born soon after the father's death. The mother was in a bad way, I expect. We babysit, as it were, sometimes. Mrs Fletcher leaves him here now and then if she has to go out. Not often; she's a conscientious woman. Overprotective, some would say. Kevin liked being here, we thought. Alison was fond of him, yes, very. She'd play with him like he was a big puppy dog but–'

'Over the walls.' Ros spoke still in this constrained roar. 'She'd go over the walls to be with him in his garden. She thought we didn't know.'

Chris said, 'Well, she helped him with his gardening. He likes gardening. He's good at it.'

'She'd go in the shed with him.'

'Well, it's a potting shed, Ros.'

'For ages.'

He was beginning to be convinced. 'You never said.'

'I didn't want to overreact. I might have been imagining– Now look.'

'Look what?'

'Who else could it have been?'

'Darling, you mustn't say these things.'

'Why not? Why shouldn't I? Who will if I won't?' She stared ahead at nothing.

Chris looked helplessly at the smart policewoman. 'I don't know what to say.'

'Can you give me a description of Kevin?'

'Oh, hell, I don't think you should–'

'Don't worry, Mr Hicks.' Jess's voice was soothing. 'We'll be following up all the people you've mentioned. There won't be any prejudice on our part, I promise you.'

Chris must have looked more sceptical than he meant to, because she repeated the bit about prejudice and Ros said, 'He's small, with dark hair, extremely good-looking.'

'Dark hair?' Jess said.

Then the tea came.

'I have to say, I don't believe Kevin would harm a fly,' Chris said.

Ros Hicks made the frightening noise again.

Several policewomen stood at the clock tower with clipboards. They questioned people who came out of the supermarket. There was a stand like a newspaper hoarding with a poster on it of Alison Hicks's face.

Polly blazed with resentment. *Just because she was stupid enough to have got herself killed.* She felt impatient with all of them. The girl wasn't worth all this fuss. It was the living needed fussing over, not the silly dead. The dead were out of it. They didn't have their way to make. George needn't have looked at her like that just because she wanted to make her way in the world. A policeman looked at her closely now as she passed, but she wasn't questioned. She wondered what she would say if they asked her, *Did you know this girl?* Polly smiled bitterly.

She went down the slope to the mouth of the tunnel. One of the strip-lights was broken so it was darker than usual. The wind howled down there, sucked in through the tunnel's black throat. The roof dripped because of the rain, dank dark drops down the graffiti-scrawled brick. There were people behind her, voices as well as footsteps. She was glad of the voices, they made a friendly sound.

She didn't see Jack until she was sitting on the train. He stood in the shadow of a doorway on the station platform and stared at her, though whether he could see her she wasn't sure. His eyes were bloodshot. He needed a shave. That was nothing new, but he looked terrible, as though someone had reached a hand inside of him and pulled everything out. Like the stag in the morning room at Lisson Avenue.

She felt scared but she didn't show it. She ran her eyes over the surface of him as though he were part of the buildings, not a human being, let alone someone she knew. She was terrified he would get on the train. But she didn't dare to check as it pulled out for fear of meeting his eyes again.

There was no sign of him at Croydon. She made sure before setting off for her class. But she held her keys like a dagger in her right hand, ready for him.

Bright said, 'Don't say that to anyone else, George. Promise me.'

'Why not?'

'Because it's not true.'

'I was obsessed with her. I followed her in the street. I hung round the supermarket. I climbed over the garden walls at night to watch her undress, I watched – I even watched–' He stopped.

'What? You watched what?'

George sighed. 'You can't stop me confessing,' he said.

'They won't believe you, George.'

'Why shouldn't they? Why should I confess to something I haven't done?'

'They'll think you're protecting Kevin,' Bright said.

'I've told you–'

'It'll draw attention to Kevin. You saying you did it.'

George heard again Kylie's icy declaration that Kevin had been out all night. He thought of his own cruelty to Kevin. If Kevin had been driven to one of his uncontrollable tantrums and done something terrible, it was George's fault and his alone. 'Whatever happened,' he said, 'I tell you I'm to blame.'

'Oh, for Christsake, George!' Bright shot out of the door and across the landing before George could stop him. He pushed Kevin's door open. 'Kev,' he said. 'Listen, mate.' He hunched close to the bed, on a level with Kevin's frightened eyes. 'You know the night of the storm? Brm, brm, thunder, lightning?' He jagged his hands in the air. 'Big lights in the sky? Rain, rain, wet like a dog? You were out, Kev, remember that? Out at night, on your own?'

Kevin made no response. His eyes followed Bright's movements. But he didn't seem to hear the words.

'Stop it,' George said. 'You've no right to do this.'

'Better me than some, George, believe me. Kev. Look at me. Storm, loud, night, rain, outside. In the park. Alison. Did you see Alison? Was Alison out in the rain too? Was Alison in the park?'

'I'll report you,' George said.

'Did you see Alison, Kev? Lovely little Alison out in the rain? Brm, brm! Alison in the thunder in the park?'

Suddenly Kevin's arms were beating the air. Bright put up his hands to protect his head. George blundered to the bed to restrain his thrashing brother. Noises came out of Kevin, spit sprayed through his clenched teeth. He bucked like a donkey, he brayed like one.

It took both men minutes to quiet him. Then he lay as before, as though the fit had never happened, curled on his side, eyes wide. That was how he was when Mrs Fletcher appeared in the doorway. 'What's this? What's going on here? Oh, it's you. I might have known.' She gave John Bright a look of contempt. 'Kevin's ill. You shouldn't be up here disturbing him. Get out of his room. Both of you. Come on!' Just as she had when they were fourteen, she stood to one side waiting to be obeyed.

Bright opened his mouth to say something. His eyes had a strange look, sorrowful, ashamed. Then he nodded. 'A-ha,' he said. 'Okay.' He led the way out.

George hesitated.

'Go on, you too.' She shooed him away as if he were a pigeon. 'You're as bad as him,' she said. She stayed in the room, shutting the door in his face.

Bright took George's arm. He hurried him

along the landing. He spoke under his breath urgently. 'Kevin saw something, George. He saw something that's scared him to death.'

'I told you, he's frightened of storms.'

'This is more than the storm, you know it is. You've got to get it out of him.'

'He can't speak!'

'I've got to go.' Bright started down the stairs two at a time.

'I've told you what happened,' George shouted in a whisper after him.

'For the time being, if anyone questions you, just keep your bloody mouth shut, George!'

Jack sat shaking at the kitchen table, eyes like hellfire, skin like raw dough.

Chloe was scared. He'd never been as bad as this. But having to see the body of the girl was enough to unnerve anyone, let alone someone with a nervous system like Jack's. She kept her distance, well out of arm's reach, to say, 'Please let me get a doctor, Jack?'

Unaware of her, apparently, he didn't reply.

She suddenly ached with hunger. How long was it since they had eaten anything? 'I'll make one of my salads, shall I?' she said. 'You like those.' She came to life and started to bustle about with her fragile bruised little arms.

Chloe's salads were a melange of anything not completely rotten that she could find in the fridge. Today she found two carrots too limp to peel, half a cauliflower that she had to cut the black bits off, two lumps of three-day-old cooked potato, an apple, a green pepper with one good side. Three not quite mouldy olives she washed under the tap just in case.

Although she hadn't smoked any dope for a whole day, she was so used to an altered state of consciousness that she moved at a sub-aqueous pace. The selecting and chopping took the time of a three course meal. Neither she nor Jack was aware of this. Jack continued to sit, shaken with feverish convulsions that arrived, attacked, and left him, sweating and cold. Where his hands touched the table they left dark stains.

Chloe tasted, added a little shake of Herbes de Provence from a supermarket jar, a little more lemon juice, a drop of olive oil. The mixture looked quite pretty in the only green bowl that Jack had not smashed. She groped in the cupboard where the bread was kept. There was a loaf. She tried to squeeze it. 'It's a little bit hard,' she murmured, 'but I can cut off the crusts.' At the back of the cupboard she spotted a tin of tuna, three years old. She added it to her salad. 'You've got to have protein,' she said.

As she folded the tuna in with a bent fork,

she felt a longing for Polly, so strong it nearly struck her to the floor. She put the fist with the fork in it against her chest and pressed it there till she got her breath back. 'Here's some food, Jack. The bread's a bit chewy but it tastes all right.' She placed her offerings in front of him. He might as well have been blind, deaf. 'Are you missing Polly, Jack?' She couldn't stop asking this because it was the only subject in her mind. Her little faded eyes filled with tears which she wiped away with the back of her hand.

Jack's lips opened like glued things pulled apart. His side teeth showed. *Like a dog's in a snarl,* she thought. As with a dog, she was wary of getting too close, of moving suddenly, of touch. 'Jack,' she whispered, 'Jack. You should eat.'

The snarl faded. She broke off a small piece of bread and approached his mouth with it. It went in. Then a small forkful of her salad. He began to chew, a painful process, like something he'd forgotten how to do.

With the hand not feeding Jack, Chloe continued to brush away the tears. She forgot to feed herself until Jack had had enough and knocked her hand away. She forked some pretty bits into her mouth. It tasted nice. She remembered times when she used to cook. Polly coming home from school. The days before everything went wrong. She stared into space beyond Jack. 'She'd just be coming back now,' she said.

Jack made a growling noise in his throat.

Her eyes focused on him. 'Polly,' she said. 'From Croydon, I mean. She'd just be getting back about now.'

Jack's chair scraped the floor and banged the wall behind him. He tore his jacket off its back and it fell over. He kicked it and swore and then he was gone.

Chloe put her little hands over her eyes. All the colourful bits fell off the tines of her fork.

Bright knew the procedure. He had a good idea where Jess would be. He passed number twenty-nine with a yearning look. He'd never been orthodox but knew he couldn't barge in there. He thought of putting a note through the letter box. But what would it say? *My oldest mate has confessed to the murder; don't believe him. His dumb brother knows something; don't arrest him?* He admired Jess. She was bright. But she wasn't original. She might be tempted to go for the fast solution. It would put her in good with the boss. He knew who her boss was now. Egerton. Christ. Egerton had started at South Norwood the same time as he. Both eighteen they were. Twenty years and Egerton had never moved. He was thick to start with and promotion wouldn't have made him cleverer; it didn't usually. Giving people power didn't normally make them better human beings. Pleasing Egerton would not necessarily mean getting to the truth of a case. What it would mean was finding an easy culprit and making an early arrest. And if the dark hairs found on Alison's body turned out to be Kevin's. As they only too easily might, considering their relationship…?

As he loped past the clock tower he glimpsed a man out of the corner of his eye. A tall bony dark thing, he hovered in a doorway, shoulders up against the wind. Bright had seen him before but he couldn't remember where. This nagged him as he turned along the High Street to go back to his ma's. He was just outside the Wimpy Bar when a clear vision came to him: the police station lobby, that dark bony man stepping like a crow behind the constable, going in to identify the body. The man who'd identified it at first as his stepdaughter. Bright turned and retraced his steps, punching a number into his mobile phone.

'Just a social call,' he lied to the desk sergeant. 'I know Jess is busy, but if she could give me a bell? Soon as she can?'

'Sure, John. Can I tell her what it's about?'

'No. She'll know. By the way, that bloke – the guy who made the false ID of the body? Any follow-through on that?'

'Yeah. The girl's mother rang up. The girl had come home safe. She'd moved out, see. Left a note as it happens. We asked the guy to show us the note. He did, no problem. All above board, seems like. Then Alison's dad turned up just after. So. We eliminated this guy from enquiries.'

'A-ha.' Bright nodded absently a few times. 'Yeah. Well, there you go. Tell Jess call me, okay?'

33

'I'd just like to ask you a few questions. We're talking to everyone in the area who knew Alison. Would you mind if my sergeant and I come in for a moment? We won't keep you long.'

Mrs Fletcher stared, bereft of speech, drying her hands on her apron. She stood back to let them in and after a hesitation she opened the door to the morning room. At the sight of the stag in the gloom Jess and Donakis swapped a sideways glance. Mrs Fletcher opened the velour curtains. A narrow shaft of light made its way in. 'I keep them closed to protect the furniture,' she said.

The furniture looked substantial enough

to protect itself, Jess thought.

'I was away when it happened,' Mrs Fletcher announced. *My presence would have prevented all these goings-on,* she implied.

Jess had a cold moment, wondering if that was true. 'But your sons were here, I believe.'

The letter box mouth slammed shut.

'I wonder if we could have a word with them? They might have seen Alison while you were away, might have noticed something that could help us. Would you mind? Are they in at the moment?'

'They're sick. They've both got flu. Caught it while I was away. Anyway, Kevin's – he's retarded. He won't be any use to you. He can't speak.'

'Ah now, Kevin's the one who was such friends with Alison, is that right? Perhaps we could just pop up and see him a minute. Could we, do you think, Mrs Fletcher?'

'I told you, he can't speak.' She was actually barring the door, her back hard against it, her arms spread.

There was a push against it from outside. She shuffled forward with the door as it opened, as though she were stuck to it with adhesive.

A large man stood in the doorway, heavy-faced, skin and eyes yellowish, hastily clothed, shirt half out of his trousers. 'Are you the police?' he said.

'I'm Detective Sergeant Jones. This is

Detective Constable Donakis.'

'I killed the girl,' he said. 'I killed Alison.' He held out his hand to be shaken. 'I'm George Fletcher.'

Jess and Donakis found themselves shaking hands with him.

'I'm sorry, Mother,' he said.

The man was still there, hunched like a raven on a rock. He fingered things outside the hardware shop but not as though he intended to buy. The owner came out with his assistant to take the zinc buckets and brooms back inside. It was closing time. The antiques woman was carrying in the last box of books. Bright's Raven had the look of a vagrant, nowhere to lay his head. Suddenly Bright found himself at the man's side. 'Hey, Frank,' he said to the hardware man.

'How's tricks, John?'

'Not so bad. Lousy change in the weather.' He turned to the Raven. 'Right, mate?' he said.

The Raven slowly swivelled round to face him. But he didn't reply.

'Summer's over, right?' Bright spoke clearly as to a deaf man.

But again the man did not speak.

'You okay, mate?' Bright said.

All at once the quiet square was full of people. Two trains, one up, one down, had vomited their cargo from the tunnel. The man's head jerked away from Bright. His hellfire eyes searched the crowd. Bright's slight squint led people to believe he could look in two places at once. This was almost true. Not because of the squint, however, but because of his policeman's soul. Jude said he was always and everywhere a cop. Even Millie Hale, his first and only other great love, had said once that policemen had eyes like mouths: 'gobble, gobble, everywhere they look.' Both these observations were true, he admitted it, and both applied to him.

He raked the moving crowd, following the Raven's gaze, though the man was unaware of this. Suddenly the bony body jerked back like a bow that has just let the arrow fly. You could almost hear the twang.

A-ha. I see. The small blonde girl gliding like an angel. She'd stand out in any crowd but Bright had seen her before. The man had ceased to be the bow; he'd become the arrow. He shot away from Bright's side in the direction of the girl.

The crowd split at the supermarket, one stream flowing left towards the park, the other flowing straight on. It split again at the clock. Some went left up to Selhurst Road, some right, down the High Street. Seven or eight crossed the High Street to make their way up Oliver Gardens past the police station. The girl was among them. The man stalked her, twenty yards behind. Light-footed, Bright strolled after him. The tail. It wasn't till the girl turned the corner into Lisson Avenue that he knew for certain who she was.

The Raven stopped so suddenly he nearly tripped Bright up. Bright needn't have worried. The man was conscious of nothing but the girl. They both watched her turn in to number thirty-five. The Raven waited till the girl was safe inside. Then he walked past, checking the number of the house, noting that it had a side entrance, before striding on. Bright left more distance but kept his quarry's heels in sight, in spite of Jude's condemnation, the old clutch of excitement in his guts and in his throat.

Polly had started to go up the stairs before she saw the figure standing there. A shadowy statue next to the newel post. 'Oh!' she said.

Mrs Fletcher's apron wrapped her hands tight as a muff. She stared but said not a word.

'Mrs Fletcher?' Polly said.

The statue nodded. Polly went closer and explored her face. Was she going to give Polly notice to leave? What had George told her? Polly knew she was capable of dealing with both of them, mother and son. She had to find out how to play it, that was all. But now she was closer to the woman she could see that this was nothing to do with herself at all. 'Are you all right, Mrs Fletcher?' she said.

Mrs Fletcher let out a sort of gasp, as though she'd been holding her breath.

'Mrs Fletcher, what is it? Can I do anything?' Polly was the picture of concern. She reached out to touch the apron which muffled the hands. Mrs Fletcher swallowed. Her mouth opened and closed again and again but no sound emerged.

'Can I get you a glass of water or something?' Polly tried.

Mrs Fletcher swallowed once more. Her head shook, and then she spoke. Her words were thick as though her tongue had swollen to fill her mouth. 'They've taken George,' she said.

Bright stood on the corner of Brockhurst Road studying the window of the Indian shop. He watched Jack let himself into a house maybe a quarter of the way down. Some minutes later he strolled past the house. It was number sixteen. At the next corner he slipped down the side street and found himself in an alley between the backs of the houses. Each high wall had a doorway into a small shabby yard. He padded down the alley, counting the yards to number sixteen, then tried the door. It was not locked or even bolted. He opened it cautiously and saw the wreckage in the yard.

34

'So tell us again, Mr Fletcher. What time did you go out?'

George sighed. 'I told you. I waited until my brother was sleeping–'

'Yes, what time was it again he went to bed?'

'His usual time, as I said, about ten. Possibly earlier. I told you I had flu and therefore–'

'Yes, the flu. You had a temperature, you said.'

'Yes.'

'So why would you go out?'

'I have explained–'

'Yes, you were obsessed with Alison. But it was pouring with rain, Mr Fletcher, thunder and lightning. And you had flu.'

Undaunted, George sat in dignified silence.

'It seems your brother – Kevin, isn't it? – was pretty fond of Alison too...'

He felt very tired. He perfectly understood where their questioning was leading. But if he went on doggedly insisting that he was the culprit, what could they do?

There was a knock. George shifted his

bulk on the small chair, thankful for the interruption. A constable in uniform stuck his head round the door. 'Phone, guv – ma'am, I mean. For you.'

The air hostess detective sighed and stood up. 'Sorry about this, Mr Fletcher. I won't be long, I hope.' She went out.

George and the stocky detective with the Greek name sat in silence. This bleak room in the police station reminded him of school. He felt just the same as when he used to be up before the headmaster, for some misdemeanour generally associated with John Bright. Perhaps he felt like that because in this bad behaviour, too, Bright seemed obscurely involved.

Polly was dumbstruck for the first time in her life. It was obvious that George had confessed to save Kevin. It was obvious he believed Kevin to be in danger because of what she had told him – about Kevin being out that night. It was her fault. She had to think. She could save George easily – just say she'd looked into his room during the night. Because he was ill. She could say the same about Kevin. That would get the whole family off the hook. They'd owe everything to her then.

But in order to do that she'd have to go to the police. She'd have to give her real name. All her lies would come out. Once George

338

and his mother knew she had lied to them they'd not want any more to do with her. All her hopes would be dashed. Her dreams of fame and riches began to race away.

The kitchen door banged open. Kevin stood there in creased pyjamas, damp and flushed, hugging the cold hot water bottle to his chest. When he saw Polly he backed away terrified. She pursued him. She stood in the doorway and looked at Mrs Fletcher. The woman sat like a loose collection of bones. Nothing held her together any more.

'Kev,' Polly said softly. 'It's all right, Kev. No one's going to hurt you. Come on now. Come and sit down. Look, come and sit by your mum, come on now. I'll put some water in your bottle, shall I? Warm it up for you?' She put out her hand to the bottle but he backed off again. 'Mrs Fletcher,' she said, 'Kevin's here. He wants you.' She spoke loudly into the woman's face. Slowly the face came up. God, she's ugly, Polly thought.

Mrs Fletcher spoke, again slow and thick as though her mouth were full of tongue. 'Him back to bed,' she said.

Kevin seemed arrested by this utterance and by the altered appearance of his mother. He began to sidle slowly into the room, keeping the table between himself and Polly. He pulled a chair closer to his mother and sat on it. He put a hand on his mother's hands in the tight-rolled apron. He gazed up anxiously into his mother's face.

Polly turned to the window. She couldn't go out and leave them. Not in this state. What was she to do? There were bars on the outside of the window. She was as much in prison as George. *Mum,* she said to herself. For the first time in her conscious life she felt need of another human being.

'Jess? The guy who made the wrong ID. What was his name?'

It took her some time to catch on. 'Oh, him? He was eliminated from the enquiry John. His stepdaughter was missing. He was in a state. He made an understandable mistake.'

'He made the mistake because the girls look alike.'

'That's right.'

'What if he made another understandable mistake? What if Alison was a mistake? What if it was his stepdaughter who was meant to get the chop?' He waited for this to sink in.

'That's far-fetched, John.'

'Jess, I've seen him following the other girl.'

'What?'

'He knows where she lives. I watched him stalk her there. Tell me his name, Jess.'

'John, you are strictly out of order here.'

'When wasn't I?'

She leafed through the file notes, the phone stuck between her shoulder and her ear. 'Okay. Here it is. He's called Jack King. He lives at–'

'–Sixteen Brockhurst Road, yeah. And the girl?'

'Polly. Polly King.'

Something scratched at his memory. He'd heard this name before. Where? When? Didn't matter now. He'd think about that later. 'She's in danger, Jess.'

'John, you don't know that. The guy's her stepfather, he's worried about her, he wants to know where she is, that she's okay.'

'So why stalk her? Why not go straight up and speak to her?'

'Could be lots of reasons. Say she left home because she doesn't get on with him, or–' Jess stopped. She sighed. They both knew the implications.

'You've got to put some extra strength on this,' he said. 'Or sure as hell there'll be another death.'

'John, you know Egerton. We've got to play this by the book. George Fletcher confessed. He handed himself to us on a plate.'

'George didn't do it.'

'He didn't do it but his brother did – that's the theory round here. We've got to keep George till he tells us that.'

'He'll never tell you that. He'd never tell

you that even if it was true. I know George. I've known him since I was five years old. He's slow but he's stubborn. Meanwhile this lunatic from Brockhurst Road is roaming the streets after his stepdaughter, possibly carrying his axe, and now he knows where she lives.'

'Oh. Yes. Where was that? Where she lives?'

Bright gave a groan, or maybe a laugh, she couldn't tell. 'Thirty-five Lisson Avenue.' He paused, listening to Jess's silence at the end of the line. 'A-ha, that's right,' he said. 'George's house.'

Jack burst into the kitchen and picked her up. He hugged her so hard her breath squeezed out in a little cry. He turned in a slow circle, clasping her against him. She didn't know what it meant but she lifted her little bruised arms round his neck and hugged him back. He put her down, looked round, saw the remains of the salad, picked up the bowl and began to shovel the bits into his mouth with the wooden salad spoon. He threw back his head and laughed, then went on shovelling.

Chloe said timidly, 'Shall I cut some more bread, Jack?'

He grinned at her. She took that for yes and went to the draining board where she had left the end of the loaf. She looked puzzled. She searched about, lifting things and putting them down. 'I'm sure I left it here,' she said. She looked around the room, even under the table. 'God, the state I'm in, p'raps I put it in the garbage by mistake.'

Jack, still shovelling like a starving man, gave a sort of grunt.

Chloe, stooping under the sink, searching through the garbage bucket, said, 'That's funny. The bread knife. I can't find it, Jack.'

As she said it, she knew it wasn't funny at all. Though behind her Jack was laughing quietly to himself.

'The name Polly King mean anything to you, George?' Donakis asked.

George looked puzzled then shook his head. 'No.'

'What's the name of the girl who lives with you?'

George mumbled and blushed.

Donakis had never seen a man as big and dignified as George blush before. He was intrigued. 'Sorry, George, what was that again?'

'Kylie Adams,' George said, more clearly.

'Sure of that?'

'Of course I'm sure.'

'What was her former address?'

'I'm afraid I don't know.'

'Didn't you take up references?'

He spoke with dignity. 'It was my mother who was responsible for letting the room. I

343

left that sort of thing to her.' Nevertheless, George had a troubled look.

'I believe she looks like Alison,' Donakis said. 'Spitt'n' image we're told. That so?'

George mumbled again, dignity fraying.

'What's that, George, sorry?'

'Mm, they're quite alike, yes. Superficially.'

'Alison was pretty, small and slim, with blonde shoulder-length hair, about eighteen years old.'

George cleared his throat and raised his eyebrows, making it clear the subject was beneath him.

'Not making a collection, are you, George, by any chance?'

'I'm sorry, what?'

'Polly King is one as well.'

'Who? What? Is one what?'

'A pretty little eighteen-year-old blonde.'

'I don't know who this Polly King is.'

'Looked to me like you did know. When I first mentioned the name.'

'Yes, I – I mean no, I thought for a moment that I'd heard the name before but I can't recall how– Oh yes. Of course.'

'Yeah?'

'Yes. It has come back to me. She's the girl they thought it was, isn't she? Before they knew it was Alison.'

Donakis said nothing. He waited.

George thought for almost a minute. Then

he said slowly, 'Kylie knows her. They go to the same college. A college for the performing arts. Kylie would be able to give you the information you need.' George's eyes were pitiful to behold. 'The college is in Croydon. I don't know the address. She's not – missing too – is she? This Polly King.'

'Well, George, that's something we don't know. Yet. That's something you might know more about than us. Let's go back to the beginning, shall we?'

'I think I should be able to have my lawyer here, surely?'

'But you haven't been charged with anything yet. You came here of your own accord. We're not accusing you of anything.'

'No, but I confessed. Doesn't that give me the right to a lawyer?'

'We haven't cautioned you. You normally get your lawyer after you've been cautioned. However, I'll look into it. Hold on a minute.' Donakis got to his feet. He went outside and conferred with the air hostess policewoman. George could see them through the glass but he couldn't hear what they said. They turned and looked at him. He looked away. He closed his eyes.

Polly heard the bell ring. She ran to the morning room window. The stag followed her with its terrified rolling eyes. She peeped round the curtain. She saw a small man in a

345

leather jacket standing on the step. It was that horrible policeman, she was sure, George's friend, the frightening one, the one with eyes like flick-knives. He mustn't find her here or question her. In panic, she dropped down on all fours and scurried like a crab out of the room. She had to get out of the house before he came in. She ran to the back door.

'We have no reason whatever to barge into this man's house, this Jack – King,' DCI Egerton said. 'There is no excuse for issuing a warrant. The victim looked like his daughter–'

'Stepdaughter.' Jess was trying to control herself.

'–his stepdaughter, who was missing. It was a perfectly reasonable mistake to make.'

'He followed a girl who is possibly Polly King – his stepdaughter – to George's house! Sir. Like he was stalking her.' Jess hoped he wouldn't ask where she got that information. If he knew John Bright was involved she'd get no concession out of Egerton ever, he would become tight as Fort Knox. And she didn't like to lie.

Egerton said patiently, 'We have a confession, sergeant. In record time.'

'With respect, sir, George Fletcher didn't do it.'

'We don't know that. He knows something he is not telling us, right?'

'Yes, but–'

'What if we let him go, and he kills this girl you say is lodging with him? You'd look pretty silly, don't you think? And not nearly as silly as I would look.'

'Sir, please. I need a warrant to enter the Kings' house in Brockhurst Road.'

'I'm sorry, sergeant. The police are in enough trouble at the present moment in time for using, shall we say, unorthodox methods. No excuse would be found for this.'

'Sir, we need photographs. Of this Polly King. And of her stepfather, Jack. Just so's we can keep up low-level surveillance if nothing more.'

'Sergeant Jones, I'm a busy man. We are living under an acute imminent threat of terrorist attack. The whole capital is in a state of alert on the back of the incident in Madrid. The whole of Europe is. Two hundred people were killed there. This is just one girl. Yes, yes, I know this murder is priority, but it is not the only pressing problem on my hands. Please just get on with your job and allow me to get on with mine. We will review this situation later.'

'Yes, sir,' she said, through gritted teeth.

Bright had his whole hand pressed on the bell. For the first time in his life he actually wanted to see Mrs Fletcher; why wouldn't she come to the door? 'The garden,' he said. 'Shit.' He ran round the side of the house.

He could see no one in the garden. Or in the surrounding gardens. But through the kitchen window he saw the shadowy figures at the table. He barged in and got the gist of things with one glance: neither of these people could help him. 'Sorry, Mrs Fletcher' – he spoke on the run – 'I'll be right back.'

No one in the other ground-floor rooms. No one anywhere on the first floor. In the gaily coloured attic room he tore back the curtain that covered the alcove. Polly's Kylie gear swung from side to side. Bright searched the drawers. He saw nothing but a few pathetic cosmetics and clothes. Little piles of cheap underwear scrupulously neat. In a deep drawer below the divan he found an empty tote bag. He scrabbled inside it. Right down in the corner of the pocket he felt something. He pulled out a creased old snapshot. It showed Polly, a small older woman who closely resembled her, and a man, arms round each other's shoulders, on a beach. That was the Raven all right. And that was the girl.

'Mrs Fletcher.' He spoke loud and clear, looking her close in the face. 'Your lodger here. Is her name Polly King? The girl staying on your top floor. Polly. Is that her name?'

The woman stared. Not at him but

348

through him. 'Polly King, Mrs Fletcher. Is that the name of the girl who– Oh hell.'

Bright went down on his haunches to look into her eyes. 'Mrs Fletcher–'

'Ky – lie,' she said thickly. Very slow.

'Kylie?'

'Kylie Adams.'

'Not Polly?' He was nonplussed. 'Not Polly King? You sure?'

Kevin reached out to him. From old habit, Bright put an arm round his shoulders. Poor Kev in all this. Kevin clung to Bright's leather jacket. He spluttered. He nodded his head furiously up and down. 'Ghoghee, Ghoghee,' he said.

Mrs Fletcher stood. She tried to speak but something happened to her face. She clutched the back of a chair. The chair fell and she fell with it. Bright knelt and picked up her wrist then took out his phone.

'Ambulance. Get an ambulance over here.'

Polly, crouched in the front garden of number twenty-nine, raised her head and peeped above the sill. She saw Alison's parents sitting on the sofa, two police people standing up. Why had she picked this garden? Squeezed into a dark corner between an acrid-smelling shrub and the bay window, she didn't dare move. The door of George's house opened and someone came out. It was the awful policeman with the eyes.

He came down the path. He was coming to get her. She lost sight of him behind the bushes. Then he was standing outside George's gate looking up and down the street.

Polly watched the ambulance arrive. She saw someone carried out to the ambulance under a red blanket. She couldn't see who it was, but she could guess.

She was glad now it was getting dark, though she had to admit she was frightened and didn't know what to do. The heat would depart as dark arrived. It was already getting colder. *I can't stay here all night.* If only that awful policeman would leave. Then she could go back into the house.

She watched the ambulance drive off. The frightening policeman went back in. But he didn't shut the front door, she could see the light from the hall shining on the path. He came out again almost right away. He came down the path into the street. He had a torch. He waved it over the garden wall of number thirty-three. He was coming down this way. Polly gasped.

She began to crawl under the window on her stomach. Out of the bushes, on the path, she'd be visible for a minute, but she had to take the risk – her only chance was the gardens at the back. On all fours she scurried into the open past the front door then fled down by the side of the house.

Mum. For the first time for as long as she could remember she felt almost ill with the desire to be at home.

Bright heard soft footsteps behind him and turned, ready for anything. Kevin was coming out of the gate in his bare feet, trying to tie the belt round his dressing gown.

'Go back in, Kev. Please. There's a good lad.'

Kevin vehemently shook his head.

Bright groaned. He turned off the torch and took Kevin back into the house. He shut the door. 'What in hell am I gonna do with you, Kev?'

35

Jack almost danced along the street, smiling to himself. He kicked a can. The noise made a kind of music. The music kept him company. He kept a hand in his right pocket round the handle of the knife. Like a sunburst in his head the code broke. *Knife.* Of course. That was why they'd taken the axe away: because this time it had to be a knife. And it was Chloe who had given him the knife. That was a sign also. Chloe was in on it. He was doing it for Chloe too.

A few times he laughed. He looked round to see if they were following but no, they'd never allow themselves to be seen. Anyway he didn't care. It didn't matter what happened to him. He was only the instrument.

The fact was Polly had tricked him into taking an innocent life. She was the source of the evil. If she were allowed to remain alive, more and more girls would die. She would make sure of it. He knew only too well how she could convince a man of anything. He wondered how many other men had killed because of her. None. No. He was the chosen one. The only instrument.

When he ordered his scotch the barman winked at him. You see? He'd never done that before. That showed the man could read his thoughts. The wink meant, You're doing it for all of us, Jack.

When he paid for the drink, Jack winked back. The man looked surprised, even offended, as though denying he'd winked in the first place. Jack laughed. And nodded. The man had to pretend. After all, the whole world wasn't in on it. Only some. The few who knew. He couldn't be the only one.

He looked around the bar to see if he could tell. There were bound to be signs. Look. Yes. The guy cutting lemons behind the bar. Now look. The man had stopped slicing. His hand leaned on the chopping board but the blade of the knife stood straight up. He was giving Jack a look over his shoulder. It was another signal. A signal of confirmation. Jack raised his glass and winked. He laughed and shook his head.

There were so many signs. They were all around you, if you only knew where to look. He knew now. He would be given signs every step of the way. He didn't have to worry. For instance those two guys who'd just come in. They were leaning over the bar talking to the barman in a confidential whisper. They were plain-clothes policemen, you could always tell, and they were asking the barman about him. The barman's index finger lifted. This was his next sign. The sign that it was time to go. He drained the scotch.

He knew how to disappear. That was his code name: The Shadowman. He could become a shadow at will. As he climbed out of the Gents window into the yard, he knew he hadn't been seen. Nor would he be seen until his task was done.

He had to stay around until they'd searched the yard. But in a place where they wouldn't find him. It wouldn't be difficult. Lads who became policemen were not geniuses. They were thicker than most criminals, and most criminals were thick. He wasn't a criminal, he was an avenger, and he wasn't thick. He pulled himself up on to the low roof of the extension in which the lavatories were housed.

He lay flat as a shadow along the join between the flat roof and the back wall of the pub. It wasn't long before the two policemen came creeping out. They shone their torches into dark corners. One of them was even bright enough to sweep his up to the roof. The beam stopped short of the long flat black shadow which was Jack. And naturally the copper didn't have the nous to climb up there and find him. The torch beams died and the policemen went back inside the pub. He'd lie here for a bit, safe now, and work out the rest of his plan.

It was no use going to the house in Lisson Avenue, the house where Polly was living, not till after bedtime. He wanted everyone in the neighbourhood asleep. Then he'd go in and get her. He mustn't kill her in that house, of course, he knew that. It was important to give a sign. It had to be Seen that She was the One who was Meant to have been Killed. That She was the One Responsible for the Wrong Death. So she had to be killed in the same place as the other one, the wrong one. He knew the place was locked at nine each night. He knew there'd been a policeman on each gate for days. But he knew another way in and she knew it too, better than he. He'd heard her talk about it to Chloe. He just had to get her there.

'I didn't know what else to do with him, Ma.'

'Ach, he'll be fine with me, won't you, Kevin?' Lily held out her hand.

But Kevin did not come to her. He stood in the corner near the phone where John was, too fearful to come farther into the room. His eyes were not a pleasure to behold.

'He's had a bad fright, John. What's a frightened him?'

'Oh, Ma, how long have you got?'

'Okay, I'll ask no questions. Kevin, my wee love, come to Lily. You remember your Lily, don't you, Kevin? You're my clever wee man. You said my name, remember?'

But he did not come any nearer. He clung to John's sleeve. John dialled a number and as he did so he took a snapshot out of his pocket. Kevin began to back away. His breathing became desperate. He shook. He turned round and round looking for a way out of the room. He was blind with terror. His eyes rolled. Only Bright could have heard the panic beneath Lily's calm voice: 'Now, Kevin, it's all right. Lily's here. Lily won't let them hurt you. They can't get in here. John won't let them in.'

John took a careful step closer. Kevin continued to back away. Lily caught his arm. He went down on his knees by the side of her chair. The wheels got in his way, or he'd have choked her in his embrace. He gabbled in his incomprehensible language, his head pressed into her stomach.

'I can't tell what he's saying, Ma.'

'It's that photo, John. It was when he saw that.'

John showed her the picture.

She said, 'It's that girl, isn't it? She passes here sometimes. I pointed her out to you once.'

'She's lodging at George's place.'

'No!'

'A-ha. Unlikely to be her he's terrified of, though.'

'Hm.'

'And I can probably rule out the little hippy woman too.'

'Her mother,' Lily said. 'The girl looks like her.'

'She doesn't look like him.'

Lily gave a shiver. 'That man would frighten anyone, John.'

'Not the way he frightens Kevin.'

'Ah, don't be frightened, Kevin.' She stroked his head.

'But where could he have seen the bloke, Ma? And when?'

Lily looked up at him. She said nothing. She waited for him. Between his eyes and hers a theory began to hover. He put the snapshot slowly back into his pocket. 'Detective Sergeant Jess Jones, please,' he said.

'It's gone now,' Lily said. 'Gone now, Kevin, the nasty thing. Nasty picture. Can't

356

hurt you now. John is telling the police. They won't let it hurt you. Sh, now, shsh.'

'Jess, I've got a snapshot of the girl who's staying with George. I'll bring it round, get George to ID it, right? Right.'

At the sound of George's name Kevin's face lit up. 'Ghoghe!' he said. He ran at Bright. 'Ghoghe? Ghoghe?' He clung to his arm and wouldn't let go.

'Yes, Kev. I'm going to get George. I'll bring him back here.'

'Yes, you stay here with me, Kevin. We'll look at the nice book.'

'Yes, Kev, you stay with Lily–'

It was no use. There was no shaking Kevin off. He began to throw his body back and forth. Strangled cries came through his clenched teeth. His arms flailed around sweeping three framed photos off the bookcase. And it was clear this was only the start. Bright and Lily exchanged a hopeless look.

'Is this the girl who is lodging at your house?' Jess said.

George looked at the photograph. He closed his eyes a moment. 'Yes,' he said.

'What's her name, Mr Fletcher?'

'Kylie Adams,' he said.

'Do you know who the other people are?' George shook his head. 'No.'

'And you're sure this girl is Kylie Adams?' George sighed. 'Yes. I'm sure.'

Jess took the picture back. She looked at Donakis. She left the room. Donakis and George sat wearily looking at each other again.

'Where did you get the picture?' George said.

She went into the little waiting room where Bright paced the floor and the poor idiot paced behind him, still hugging his cold hot water bottle. In other circumstances she might have laughed.

'Well?' Bright said.

'He says she's Kylie Adams.'

'What does the song and dance school say?'

'Closed for the day. We phoned the principal, got her answering machine. Someone from Croydon nick's been dispatched to her house to wait for her.'

'And George definitely doesn't know this Polly King?'

Kevin's head began to jerk up and down. 'Ghoghee, Ghoghee!'

Bright rolled his eyes. 'This is what it's like.'

'What's he saying?'

'I don't know, I think it's an attempt at George. Yes, Kev, yeah, okay, okay, you'll see George soon. I promise you. Just as soon as a connection is established between the prime suspect and this girl.' He raised his eyebrows at Jess.

She said, 'Egerton won't let me have a search warrant for sixteen Brockhurst Road.'

Bright looked at her and she looked at him. He moved between her and Kevin, blocking Kevin's view. He held out his hand. She put the photograph face down into his palm. He said, 'Can someone take care of miladdo here?'

36

He wondered where he was. He seemed to be on a roof somewhere. Was that the yard of the pub down there? He wasn't sure. Was this really a roof he was lying on or was it just a trick, a mirage? How could he tell? Panic filled his throat like bile. His watch. Now that was real. Nobody could mess with the time. If he could see the time, he was awake, he was here. If the time was real, everything else was real. He looked at his watch. Luminous in the dark. His little lighthouse. The watch said ten fifty-five.

He was okay. This gravel cutting into his face, the cold bricks at his back, the pub yard down there, they were all real. He had to go for her at eleven o'clock, that was the plan. The pubs would close then and there would be many people, many men, out on the streets. This would make him hard to find. Just keep his eyes on the time, he'd be all right. His teeth chattered.

He didn't know why he was scared. He was carrying out the task, wasn't he? He was doing the right thing? A sudden terrifying noise made him cringe into a foetal knot. The noise nearly split his head. It was in his head. They had come to destroy him before it was time. The time must have lied to him. NO! Just as his head blew apart he knew.

It was only an aeroplane. He could see its lights. It was flying low, specially over him. This was the final sign. This put him in the picture. The noise passed over and faded slowly away. And as the pieces of his skull reconstituted themselves he knew everything: if he failed, then he would be held responsible for the other death. He would be destroyed himself.

His chest was full of fog. He fought for breath. But it was okay. It would be okay. He wouldn't fail. He looked at the watch again. It was time. He heard loud voices. The pub was letting out. He prepared himself to drop off the roof and mingle with the crowd. Only it wasn't to be so simple. He was to be tested again. All the terrace lights suddenly came on. And the lights in the yard below him.

The policemen were still there. They

watched all the people as they came out of the pub. He faded back into his shadow in the right angle between the back wall and the roof. Outstretched on his front he inched along to the other edge. To this side, the side away from the yard, there was just some rough ground, then a wall, then rougher ground bordering the railway. Would they have police over there? He had no way of knowing. This was part of the test. He would be expected to take every risk. Okay.

He jumped down, ten feet or more, into the rough grass. He missed a broken bottle by inches. Thistles spiked his face. He loped low and swift to the wall. There were pieces of glass embedded in its top. He threw his sweater up to cover the jagged edge. He got cut just the same but it wasn't too bad, it could have been worse.

He jumped again, off the wall, into the rough ground by the railway track. He began to clamber up the slope on his stomach. A train was leaving the Junction, he heard it. Not so many, this time of night. He looked at his watch. Ten past eleven. Real railway, real train. The train roared above him, spilling light over him, and head-shattering noise. Then it was gone. The rails hummed. He had to get over the rails. He would be protected until the task was done.

'Polly, Polly, I've got you!'

Polly struggled out of the enveloping arms. 'Leave it out.'

'You're safe!'

'Course I'm safe. Nothing can happen to me.'

'But Poll, he's gone out and he's got the bread knife. I didn't know what to do. I think he's gone after you, Poll. I think I've got to call the police to him. He's got to be locked up.'

Polly shivered. 'You can't call the police.'

'Why? He's really dangerous. I really think he is.'

'If you call the police I'm leaving again.'

'No!'

'I mean it, Mum.'

'*Why*, Poll?'

'I've got to, that's all.'

'Where will you go?'

'Back where – back where I live. Oh, Mum.' The self-sufficient Polly sat at the table and covered her face with her hands.

'What is it, Poll?' Chloe sat down opposite.

'Jack's the least of my worries,' Polly said.

'You'd better tell me, hadn't you?'

Polly took her hands away. 'I told all sorts of lies – at the place where I'm living. I gave them my wrong name – I didn't tell them I worked at the school – I didn't want Jack to come looking for me. I wanted to be a different person, Mum. I wanted a different life. And then George, I mean, the man there. You know. He was – like – well, he liked me. You know. And I thought– Oh, I don't know. And then I told lies about – something else, and now George has told the police he killed that girl and they've taken him in and his mother's ill – she's gone to hospital under a red blanket – does that mean there's a lot of blood? – and then this policeman turned up – he's an awful man, his eyes go right through you. So I ran. I didn't know where else to go. And if you get the police they'll find out all about me and I'll be turned out of there and–'

'No, Poll, no! You haven't done anything really wrong. And anyway you can come back here!'

'I don't want to come back here! I want to get away from here!' She saw the look on her mother's face. 'I've got to get away from Jack,' she said.

'But if I call the police they'll section him. So he'll be gone then anyway.'

'They'll only let him out again. They let him out before.'

'But he doesn't mean *you* any harm, Poll. He thinks the world of you.'

'Oh, *Mum!*' Polly screamed in exasperation. 'You're so thick!'

'What do you mean?' Chloe's little voice had almost disappeared.

'Nothing. I didn't mean anything. Only don't call the police. They don't know who I am there, the people where I live. I can make it all right again with them. If you tell the police they'll know everything. They'll know it's all my fault.'

'What did you mean, I'm thick?' Chloe leapt out of her chair as the knocker banged on the door. She and Polly stared at each other paralysed.

Polly moved first. She fell on all fours and scuttled into the living room. She crouched under the window in the dark and looked through the old lace curtain. *Oh God.* It was him. The man with the eyes. Even here he'd followed her.

'Don't go, Poll. Don't!'

But Polly was out of the back door, too panicked even to answer her.

Just as he reached safety on the other side of the rails, a train thundered past. He rolled down the rough grass, laughing loud, the sound of his laughter covered by the noise of the train. His fall was stopped by the footing of another wall. Over the wall he could see a garden and a little house, the end of a terrace of small houses like those in Brockhurst Road, only a little bit posher this side of the tracks. Gardens with flowers. He could smell them. *You could faint from that smell. Christ.*

For a moment he breathed it in. For a moment he had no mission. He didn't have to kill her. It was all crazy. You could just lean here in the dark, drinking in this wonderful scent in the dark, then go home and go to bed and sleep. Sleep. Imagine that. Then the plane came again, down, down, down, to split his head. 'It's okay,' he said, crouching, clutching his head, 'It's okay, I'll do it. I will.' The plane went away again then, satisfied.

The flowers exuding the scent hung ghostly pale along the top of the wall. He hauled himself up to them. They were roses. Their branches twined and intertwined, like his thoughts. He fought his way through them. Their thorns were worse than the jagged glass, worse than his thoughts. He was scratched and torn. The branches clutched at him, caught him, wouldn't let him go. Even when he landed in the flower bed below, they clung to him, embedded in his clothes, his flesh. He wrenched himself out of their clutches. It was the nearest he had been to panic. He had to get out of there no matter who was after him or what awaited him. He felt his way along the side wall, the claws still tearing at his clothes. He found a wooden door with a latch and a bolt. It wasn't locked. It was easy. It opened on to a narrow alley that led up to the street. There was no one waiting on the other side.

The front of the house was in darkness. Perhaps there was no one in. But through the grubby stained glass panels he thought he could see a faint distant glow. He was just about to go up and around and into the back alley again when the door opened. It was the little hippy woman from the photograph. Her whole body trembled.

He showed her his ID. He said, 'I'm a police officer, love. Can I come in and have a word?' He was already over the threshold. 'It's okay,' he said. 'I'm not going to hurt you. Just a few questions, that's all. Like where's Jack.'

She backed away in terror down the hall. 'He's out.'

'I need to talk to him.'

He followed her down the passageway. He felt a draught coming from that direction. He squeezed past her. The kitchen light was on. The back door was still swinging on its hinges. He went out into the yard. The yard door too swung back and forth. He ran to the end of the alley between the yards. No sign of anyone. He speeded back to the house where the woman still stood in the hallway shivering. She put her little hands over her face and rocked back and forth, wailing. Her fragile little arms were bruised all over.

He went into the living room and picked

up an Indian bedspread that was draped over a couch. He came back into the hall and wrapped it round her. She took her hands from her face and looked at him astonished.

'What's your name, love?' he said.

'Chloe,' she whispered.

'I'm not going to hurt him, Chloe. But I've got to stop him hurting your daughter.'

She let out a loud cry. 'Oh, he's after her, I'm sure he is. Now she's out too. I think he's got the bread knife, you see. That's the thing. He's going to kill her, I'm sure he is.'

'When did he go out?'

'A – an hour or – more, I – don't know–'

'And your daughter?'

The woman wailed.

'When did your daughter leave, Chloe?'

'Now, just – now, she – ran out when you came, she–'

'Okay, calm down.' He'd already punched the numbers and was asking for Jess. He took out the photograph and showed it to the shivering woman. He said, 'Is that him? Is that Jack King?'

She nodded but her mouth was paralysed.

'And who's the girl?'

'That's my daughter. That's Polly,' she said.

37

It was a miracle there was no one about. He could see groups of people talking down by the traffic lights on the High Street. People came out of the pub but they didn't want to go home. He knew that feeling. He realised he was under a lamp and slid out of its aura. In a patch of comparative darkness he crossed the road. He knew that people would be kept from seeing him. But he must not tempt fate. He had to do everything right. He must keep away from the people and embrace the dark.

He turned the corner into Lisson Avenue. The number was easy to remember. Number thirty-five. The house was in darkness when he passed. *Good.* He slipped up the path and round the side like a black cat. The back door was locked and there were bars on the kitchen window. Was she in there or not? He needed a sign. But he must not stay there. He must not be seen before he had finished his task. He slipped away into the darkness, a shadow among shadows. The dark embracing the dark.

Chloe wrapped the bedspread tighter round

herself, but she couldn't stop shivering.

Bright said, 'You're sure that's Polly King?'

'I'm her mother, aren't I?'

'This is not Kylie Adams?'

'Kylie? Adams?'

'She's a student with Polly.'

'Student?'

'Polly's studying singing and dancing at this college in Croydon, right?'

'Oh!' The woman's face cleared. 'Poll goes to classes there. Three evenings a week and Saturday mornings. But she's not a student. She's got a job.'

'Where does she work?'

'She's a helper at the special school on Selhurst Road.'

Kevin's school. He said, 'It's not a residential school, is it? I mean there wouldn't be anyone there at this time of night?'

'No.'

'Is there anywhere you can think of she might go? Friends? Relations?'

'No, no—' Chloe's eyes were becoming wild again.

He sighed. 'Okay, okay. Now tell me about Jack. He got any previous?'

'He was up for GBH. It was ten years ago. They pleaded balance of mind disturbed. They put him in Rampton. They got him on medication and everything and he really seemed all right. He came out a year and a half ago. He was okay for a bit. Then every-thing went bad again. But really bad, I can't tell you. They think they're all right so they stop taking their medication, you see. I don't know why but I think he's got some crazy idea in his head about Polly. He's going to kill her, I know he is.'

He heard footsteps on the path. Going into the hallway he worked on the information Chloe had given him. If Jack had previous for GBH his DNA would be on record. They'd checked and found no match. That meant the dark hairs found on Alison's body were not Jack's. *Jesus.* That made it more imperative to find the bloke. He opened the door. A young WPC stood there. 'What's your name, love?'

'Lucy.'

'Lucy's going to take care of you now,' he said. 'This is Chloe, constable. She's in a bit of a state. Make her a good strong cup of tea, there's a good girl.' As he went out of the door he said, 'Find out anything you can about Jack King.'

Egerton with ill-disguised sheepishness stood in the doorway of the CID room. He was saying, 'To have moved before this would have been premature.'

'Yes, sir. Right, sir.' Jess strode away nearly at a run. Her team were throwing on jackets, picking up cigarettes, wallets, pocket

370

recorders. She had a quick word with one then another, and dashed on. On the downstairs corridor she picked up Nick Donakis. She was halfway out of the building before she remembered. 'Oh my God,' she said. 'Tell the custody sergeant to let George go.'

He inched up to look over the wall of one of the Lisson Avenue gardens. He saw figures darker than the dark. They flitted about in the garden of number thirty-five, the house where Polly now lived. They knew everything then. Even where he would go next.

But they were one step behind him. And his hearing was more acute than theirs: he could hear their thoughts. His eyesight was sharper too: they couldn't see him in the dark, but he could see them. And at this moment they did not know where he was. And they did not see what he could see.

Bright watched George shamble out to the desk. He looked wrecked. He said in a bewildered way, 'They're letting me go. But I did do it, you know. I am responsible.'

'Give it a heave, George. Come on, pick up your stuff.'

On the desk was a pathetic little pile of possessions: wallet, change, watch, keys. George signed for them and stowed them about his person. He stood swaying on his feet. 'The detective constable with the Greek name,' he said. 'He told me they're after another man. That this man is after a girl called Polly King. Kylie knows this girl. Kylie may be in danger too.'

'There's no such girl as Kylie, George. It was an invented name. It's Polly King who's been living with you.'

George's face was a massive landscape. All Bright could do was wait while the cloud shadows moved across it, one idea chasing out another in slow progression. At last George spoke. He said only, as though to himself, 'Her name is Polly then?'

'Did you know she works at Kevin's school?'

At this moment a blurred shape threw itself upon George uttering cries of joy.

'Bit of a handful, isn't he?' the desk sergeant said.

Out in the street George just stood. *It's dark. How extraordinary. Cool air on my face. This is how freedom feels.* Kevin clung to his arm. Kevin looked happier than he had for some time, though the haunted look had not left his eyes.

Bright needed to get them off his hands so that he could join the hunt. He wished he could leave them to their own devices but it was clear he could not, not yet. He said, 'Your mother's in hospital, George.'

'Mother?' George spoke as though from

372

far off.

'They think it's a slight stroke.'

'Mother?'

'We'd better get you home. It's way past Kevin's bedtime.'

George nodded slowly and began to move. 'Mother,' he murmured. The wind cut through his crumpled shirt. Walking, he lifted his feet high in an attempt to control his legs. 'A stroke?' he said.

Polly was crouched next to a terrible smell. Trust that stupid girl's family to keep a pile of garbage at the end of their garden. What did they think the bin men were for? You paid your council tax for them to take this stuff away. If it wasn't for that stupid girl, Alison, she could be in George's house now, sleeping in her lovely room. George would be there instead of down the nick and George's mother would be there instead of in hospital or dead or whatever she was. *Oh, God.* She just had to get in to get her things, that's all. Her Kylie things especially, she couldn't leave without those. But while the police were milling about she couldn't budge.

There were torches moving now, dancing like insects in the dark in George's garden. Soon they'd be coming over here. Now the people in number thirty-three came outside. Their horrible little dog started yapping.

She could hear a policeman asking them to keep the dog quiet.

'Oh, right!' the man said in a dramatic whisper. The pair of them started racing round their garden trying to get the stupid animal indoors, calling it in exaggerated whispers, while the thing jumped and yapped, thinking they were playing a game. In different circumstances she might have laughed. 'Stupid,' she whispered.

And a hand came over her mouth.

It was the leather jacket policeman with the eyes. She knew it was him but he was behind her so she couldn't see. She bucked and heaved but one hand covered most of her face while his other arm gripped right round her chest, keeping her arms pinned. On her knees she was helpless. She struggled to get to her feet so that she could kick. She was raging with anger. He didn't have to do this to her to keep her quiet, did he? She managed to turn her head and saw his face. It wasn't the policeman. It was Jack.

The policewoman, Lucy, said, 'Don't worry, love, we won't let anything happen to her.'

Another one said, 'Any idea what happened to the axe?'

A policeman in jeans found the scraps and ashes in the grate in Jack's room.

Another asked her, 'Have you got anything

of his? Something he wears a lot?'

Chloe pulled out of the basket a dirty old black T-shirt of Jack's, soft with wearing. She bunched it in her two small hands. As she handed it over she realised what they wanted it for. 'You're not putting the dogs on him?'

'Don't worry, they won't hurt him, love.' The policewoman gave the grubby handful of cloth to the guy at the door. They both wore latex gloves. They exchanged a glance. 'Nobody'll harm him, will they, Scottie?'

The guy at the door winked with the eye away from Chloe. 'No. Don't worry, love. He'll be safe with us.' He went out with the soft T-shirt. The policewoman shut the door on him.

Chloe was still searching through the laundry basket. Tears ran out of her eyes. 'There's nothing of Polly's here!' she said. 'She took everything with her when she went.'

38

'Fancy me finding you here,' he whispered. 'I was going to wait in your garden shed but I saw your watchers there. I was frightened I wouldn't be able to do it tonight. And it's got to be tonight, you see. I've got a knife, Poll. Knife.' He looked into her eyes with meaning as though the word knife was of significance. He smiled a conspiratorial smile, sharing a secret with her. 'Knife,' he said. 'Do you see, Poll? And don't worry, Chloe wants me to do it. She gave me the knife. Look. It's the bread knife from home. I always kept it nice and sharp, didn't I? She liked me to. It's as though we must have always known. Don't think you can get away, Poll. I've got to do it. I've got no choice, you see.'

The mayhem had died down in the garden next door but one. The torches had gone. The quiet was as suffocating as his hand on her face. She thought her jaw might break. They were lying in this terrible heap of garbage, it was horrible. Even through the stifling gag of his hand she could smell it. There were loads of police about. But were they looking for Jack? Whoever they were looking for they'd find him, wouldn't they? And her? Surely they'd find her? They were only a few gardens away, weren't they? She just had to go along with him and hope.

He laughed quietly all the time. She wished he'd stop. He inched his way backwards on to the wall, lifting her with him, one hand over her mouth, the other over her breasts, her waist, her crotch, wherever he could get a hold. It reminded her of when

376

she was a kid and couldn't fight him off. He swung her round and down the other side. The point of the knife was sometimes in her back, sometimes sticking up an inch from her face. It was no use struggling now. There was only one wall to go before they ran out of gardens and reached the street. If he lost his grip on her she might have a chance to run. But it would be better to wait. There were lights in the street. There'd be other people maybe. Police even. They were bound to catch him, weren't they, before he could do anything really bad? Anyway, he was only Jack. Nothing really to be frightened of. She'd always been able to control him, whatever her mother said. They crossed the garden, he crouching, dragging her, behind some bean plants growing up poles.

The last wall. Jack slowly raised his head to peer over it. There was no one in the street. But down by the clock tower there were always people about. And this was Oliver Gardens where the big new police station was. If they went down this way they'd have to pass it. So they'd stay in the leafy avenues a while. He pulled a long black scarf out of his pocket. He said, 'Here. Tie this over your shining hair.'

She tried to grab the scarf but he held on to it. He placed it quite gently over her hair, then he suddenly brought the other end round across her mouth. He pulled it tight, forcing her mouth open, hurting the corners of her lips. The scarf dragged hard across her tongue, nearly choking her. He wound it back round her neck where he tied it like the tourniquet she'd been taught in first aid at Kevin's school. It squeezed her throat, and the woolly stuff filled her mouth.

Opposite the Wimpy Bar George stopped walking. Kevin looked up at him. So did Bright. George said as though he had just woken from a sleep, 'Did you say my mother has had a stroke?'

'A slight stroke, George. They think.'

'And she's in hospital?'

'Yeah, but she's going to be all right.'

'Then we must go there now.'

'George, there's nothing you can do.'

'She'll be worried. I must set her mind at rest.' A spasm shook his face. 'On some points at least.'

'It's midnight, mate.'

'That does not alter anything.'

Bright sighed. 'Okay. We'll walk up to the clock tower and get you a cab.'

The tall man and the small woman with a black scarf round her head strolled casually, not fast, not slow. His arm was clasped protectively round her shoulders. The couple who passed them at the far end of Lisson

378

Avenue looked politely away as he drew her into a close embrace in a dark gateway. They recalled their days as young lovers. A group of five teenage boys they encountered later barely noticed them. None of them saw that he was holding a knife under the scarf, its blade across her throat.

They turned left and made their way down to the main road, away from the lights and the life of the High Street, up in the direction of the dark church and the school. Cars passed in a steady flow. But there was nobody walking in the street.

He held her arm with a grip like a lobster's claw. With the same hand he pulled at the knot he had tied at the back of her neck. With the other he held the blade of the knife. It started to penetrate her skin, she could feel it.

He stopped her at the zebra crossing opposite the school. 'You know the secret way into the park from the school, don't you, Poll?'

She shook her head.

'Oh, yes, you do. I heard you tell Chloe how you used to skive off out there when you should have been working. You see, Poll. I remember everything. It was a sign, you see. You know the secret way and you're going to show it me.'

She tried to turn her head to see if there was anyone at all to notice her. He yanked

379

her back and the blade shifted against her throat. She thought for a moment of trying to run but the world of people was too far away, he'd never let her get that far. The acrid wet wool of the scarf was almost choking her, but she thought she might be able to shout.

He dropped the claw-like grip. His arm came around her breasts and his long bony hand gently covered her mouth again. 'Ah no,' he said. 'There'll be no one to hear you now.'

As soon as George stood still again Kevin put both his arms round the large body and leaned on him. George had never tolerated Kevin's displays of affection in the street but he allowed this. The kids hanging round the clock tower laughed. Kevin laughed back, flapping his arms. But George remained oblivious. From time to time he shook his head, muttering a few words.

They stood for a few minutes but no cab came. Bright had spotted a couple of young coppers in camouflage among the crowd. He was ashamed of his embarrassment, which was extreme. He wished he could leave these two social misfits to themselves but he felt responsible. 'Come on,' he said, 'we'll try up the main road.'

Passing the Church of the Holy Innocents George said, 'Kylie. Polly. Polly – King?'

'They've got the dogs out after him, George. She'll be all right, I promise you.' Bright wished he believed his own words.

They were passing the school drive now. Kevin was in front walking backwards. This was the best way to keep George in his sights.

'Polly,' George said.

'Ghoghee, Ghoghee!'

George looked at Kevin a moment as if reminded of something. Kevin flapped his hands in the direction of the school.

Bright said, 'She works there, George.'

'Here? At Kevin's school?'

'A-ha. I told you.'

'Ghoghee, Ghoghee! Ghoogh, ghoogh!'

'Looks like Kevin's trying to tell you the same thing.'

'He's tried to tell me all along, John. I wasn't listening.'

Then Kevin stopped his wild flapping and gurgling, so suddenly that Bright and George almost fell over him. The fear came back into his eyes. He began to make gibbering noises of unmistakable terror. Bright cautiously tried to take hold of his arm. He ran out into the road. But only George ran out to catch him. Bright stopped still.

He saw what Kevin had seen. He saw two dark figures disappear into the shadow of the side wall of the school.

Jack stood transfixed a moment. That creature flapping its arms in the road. He had seen it before. And it had seen him. Exactly the way it was seeing him now. It stopped its weird cavorting, then it moved in that strange way and made those strange noises, more animal than human. 'Ah!' Jack lowered his head.

He had started to shake. This frightened her more than his previous unnatural calm. He shook. But his hand gripped even tighter and he pressed the point of the knife into the side of her neck. His eyes were living things that might ignite, might liquefy like lava. 'Why?' he said in his throat. 'Why are you mocking me like this?'

Polly said nothing, just watched him. He wasn't looking at or addressing her. She couldn't turn her head to see what he had seen. She didn't even know if it was something real.

'That creature saw me. It saw me. But it's not a human thing. It can't speak. It's there to mock me. That's what they've sent it for. It's a test. Well, I tell you, Poll...' He held the knife in front of her face. 'The Knife will not be mocked.'

The back of the school was deep in darkness. He sensed bushes, and guessed there would be a thick shrubbery to keep the village idiots out of the park. And the village vandals out of the school. His torch showed him he was right. Thick high bushes and not a sign of the man and the girl. They had to be here. Unless they'd got inside the building. What if Polly had a key?

He heard a thumping and panting behind him. He turned to enjoin silence then realised it was too late for that. And what was the point now anyway? George was pounding up the drive as hard as his big flat feet and his big flabby body would allow. He dragged his brother by the hand. Kevin was pulling the other way, holding him back, gibbering. George turned, grasped Kevin by the arms and hissed some words, into his face. A moment of stillness then Kevin pulled away from George's hand. His face was alight now with a stew of exhilaration and fear. Then he hared ahead straight into the bushes. Bright went in after him and heard George crashing behind.

Kevin knew the way as well as Polly. Going into the park through the hedge and a broken railing was frowned on by the senior staff. Rescue parties were constantly being sent to gather the few pupils with intelligence enough to remember the way. It was hard for Kevin to keep the silence George had enjoined on him. But they couldn't stop him. They needed him to show them the way.

The dark in the bushes was thick as wool,

enveloping them. The man might be immediately in front of them or well ahead, they couldn't see. Nor could they hold Kevin back, just follow blindly where he led. Branches clawed them. They fell over stones, roots. They picked themselves up. But nothing could stop Kevin. Bright whispered, 'What did you say to him, George?'

George whispered, 'Save Alison.'

'Jesus.' These brothers had more in common than they knew. Bright's mind while he crunched and crashed through this terrible undergrowth went into overdrive. *Save Alison* had transformed Kevin from a state of craven terror to this raging heroism. Kevin had recognised the picture of Jack King. The picture had reduced him to abject gibbering. Kevin was out in the storm the night Alison was killed. Ever since that night he had been ill with fear. He saw this man kill Alison. No one could ever prove it. And Kevin's evidence would be no use to anyone anyway. In fact the physical evidence might be all against him. But Bright was as certain as if he had seen it himself.

Then Kevin disappeared into a high hedge six or eight feet thick. Branches with small leaves flicked across their eyes, their mouths. If they lost Kevin now he was in bad trouble. If the lad had seen this bastard kill Alison he wouldn't have a chance. Then a hand grabbed Bright's sleeve and Kevin's face loomed close. He had come back for them.

Again he disappeared and the hedge closed behind him. Bright squeezed through the gap. It was harder for George. Bright wasn't sure his great bulk would make it, but he couldn't stay to help, Kevin was off over the grass like a hare. Bright had to catch him. He couldn't afford the death of another friend. Once in a lifetime was more than enough. Never, never again.

'Kevin! Wait!' He had to risk the whisper. The wind in the high trees would cover it. And anyway Bright could hear George behind him now, blundering like an elephant. He groaned and ran on. Kevin wouldn't stop. He was making for the far corner the police had taped off. The place where Alison's body had been found. Oh, yes, he'd seen her murder all right.

39

Now that he had got her to the place, he breathed easier. The gates were locked and guarded. They had even made a little enclosure for him, of blue and white striped shiny tape. 'Look, Poll, they've made a special place for us. See.' He lifted out one of the metal rods that carried the tape. He held it ceremoniously as he would a door for a lady to enter a room. 'Go in, Poll. Go.'

She wouldn't go. She didn't understand.

So he went first, holding tight to her. 'Come in,' he said. 'Don't be afraid. There's nothing to be afraid of now.'

Strangely she almost wasn't afraid. Life had gone into slow motion. *If I go in there it's over. If he closes the tape, nobody else will be able to get in. Just me and Jack.* She went in and he replaced the tape across the opening like closing a door.

Stupid! Suddenly she was too angry to be afraid. That she had got herself into the same stupid mess as that silly Alison. That she was going to end up a mess of blood and death before she'd even become a proper singer, let alone become famous or rich. She was furious. She was wild.

'Kneel down, Poll.'

'I won't. The grass is wet.' The words were all choked up in the tight wet woollen mess of the scarf.

'Kneel down.' He pushed hard on her shoulders. She knelt. He knelt facing her.

'Do you know where I'm going to put the knife?' he said.

She glared at him but her mouth was trembling.

'Do you, Poll?'

She would not speak. Or imagine either. For fear of transmitting the pictures from her mind to his.

'You see,' he said. 'The other girl. The wrong girl. She was running away from me. She shouldn't have done that, Poll. I couldn't see her face, you see. That was why she was felled like an animal. I thought she was you. So you have to atone, you see, Poll. You have to atone for her death. Your death must be a ceremony so that everyone will understand. So they'll understand what you did.' He leant forward and whispered in her ear, *'Else you'll betray more men.'*

She held on to his sweater. She whispered, 'Jack, I'll let you do it, I will. What I wouldn't let you do. I'll let you do it now, Jack. It was only because of Mum I wouldn't let you. I wanted it really. I wanted you. I still do, Jack. I do.'

He threw her off. She wriggled on the ground trying to pull away from him. 'You're a whore, you're a whore!' He banged her head on the ground, he shook her like a sack of bones. She kicked out wildly with her feet. She must have got him in the crotch because he yelled out and one of his hands let go of her. She rolled away and tried to get to her knees and knew she'd done the wrong thing because she saw the knife shine up past her face and she could feel that his arm was tensed and that he was going to strike.

It wasn't till he cried out that they located him. And a train roared by and it illuminated in fitful shivering light the man with his arm raised and the little body heaving beneath his other hand. Bright was fast and light on his feet but he wasn't in love with Alison. Kevin got there first.

Like a flying bat, he swooped on to the man's back and hung on squealing. The man screamed, bucking to try and heave him off. He flung him away, then saw who he was and screamed louder. 'No, not you, no, not you!' Over and over. He ran. Kevin ran after him. George ran after Kevin. Bright ran in a wider circle to cut the man off.

Suddenly the man stopped running and turned. He came at Kevin with the knife. Kevin didn't stop. He didn't seem to see the knife. But George did. As the man's hand shot out George lunged at Kevin and knocked him to the ground. And the knife went into George.

The blade was going into George for the third time when Bright hurled himself on to the Raven's back and gripped his bony wrist. The girl was racing over to them. Bright shouted, 'Get help, Polly King!'

When she reached the gates the police were just coming in. And more emerged from the hedge with their nice friendly Labrador dogs in front and their unfriendly slavering Alsatians behind. Polly, the heroine, turned back and flew along ahead of them, leading the way, pulling the scarf off her shining hair.

Kevin was trying to beat the face of the Raven to pulp. Bright was trying to hold Kevin off while keeping his grip on the man. He did not manage both. Jack pulled himself out of Bright's grasp to pursue Polly and ran into the first policeman and his dog.

Kevin was whimpering over George when the second policeman arrived. There was a lot of blood. Bright was almost whimpering with him. 'Oh, no, not George,' he said. 'Oh, no, not George.' Over and over again.

Jess handed him a hip flask. 'We've got an ambulance at the gates,' she said.

It took four men to hold Jack, with the dogs straining in a circle round their feet. Then he suddenly became still. He stood tall. He smiled. 'You needn't think it's over,' he said, in a hoarse grating raven croak.

'It is for you, mate.'

Jack laughed. 'You know nothing.'

'Come on, let's get Superman where he belongs.'

'In the shower if you ask me. How'd he get to smell like that?'

'It is the smell of evil, my friend,' Jack said. 'You should recognise it.'

'Oh, yeah, that's what it is! Just slipped my mind a moment there.'

Jack turned round to look at Polly. She stood wrapped in a blanket by the gate. 'She smells of it,' he said. 'She always has, she always will. She will do to other men what she did to me. Until I'm allowed to carry out my mission. You'll all be sorry in the end that you prevented me carrying out my task.'

'Oh, yeah?'

'Let's go.' Jack swung in the direction of the gates. The group strode off. Jack, taller than the others, set the pace. The others scurried round him, even the dogs.

John Bright handed back the flask. 'What made you think of here?' he said.

'We didn't think, the dogs did. Shaming, isn't it.'

'Took them long enough.'

'They were diverted by a hysterical Yorkshire terrier and then a compost heap. Made by Alison Hicks's father, ironic if you like. What made you?'

'Not me,' he said. 'Mastermind over there.' He indicated Kevin who was stroking George's head and whispering to him.

The ambulance men approached Kevin and tried to ease him away from George. Bright went over to Kevin and took hold of his arm. 'Let them help him, Kev. Come on. We can go with him. I won't let them take him away. We'll go too. They're going to make him better. Come on now, Kev.' Kevin kept one hand on George. The paramedics had to work round him. Bright and he walked either side of the stretcher across the park to the avenue of trees. Kevin held on to George's hand. There was a lot of blood, apparently coming from the stomach and chest, and George's face looked white, thinner, and old.

As the stretcher was carried through the gates, George floated back for a moment from wherever he was. He opened his eyes and saw Kylie. *Polly.* He believed he had died and come to heaven. Everyone had a personal heaven awaiting them and she was his. He closed his eyes again and they carried him into the ambulance. They had to let Kevin come too; he wouldn't let go. Polly went off the other way to the police station with the police.

Jess and Bright stood watching the procession dwindle. 'What would we have done without you, John?' she said.

'Had another dead girl on your hands. Where the fuck were you?'

'Egerton–'

'Egerton my arse. If you can't deal with the Egertons of this world, don't be a copper.'

'You try being a woman doing this job.'

'There are no excuses.'

'You're giving it up, why should you care?'

'What kind of a mess do you think you'd all be in now here if I hadn't been around?'

'I did my best in the circumstances.'

'Your best? You had the whole great juggernaut of the Metropolitan police behind you. I did this with the massive assistance of one emotional cripple and one mental retard. What kind of copper ever has to work like that? And I still got here ahead of you!' He stopped shouting as suddenly as he had begun. He rubbed a hand over his face. The hand trembled.

'Welcome back, John.'

He hadn't done much. A girl had died. He suspected the wrong girl had died. He hadn't saved her. Two parents sat in their empty house blaming themselves and grieving. But the police had witnessed Jack's state. They wouldn't have got there in time but for him. Those dark hairs on Alison were Kevin's and a half-decent lawyer could make a meal out of that when Jack came to trial. Not that Jack was denying anything, he'd plead guilty while the balance of his mind was disturbed. And how. So Kevin was saved too. He just hoped to hell that the knife hadn't finished George. As those crazies in France had finished Jude and the promise of happiness with her.

'Maybe,' he said. 'Maybe. There's stuff to see to yet.'

40

He smelled the roses before she came in the door. His sense of smell, like all his senses, was sharper these days, since he had come round from his surgery. Warren was still talking to him but he did not hear. He simply waited for the sight of her.

'Get out of that terrible office, George. Buy yourself out or whatever you have to do. Work from home. Just do actors. I can bring you more people, mate. Take it easy. Make it the way you want it for a change, eh?'

She carried the bunch of pale roses. They were garden roses, the floppy kind with thorns. Their smell resembled honey and white wine. She was dressed to match them, in some very pale short silky thing, and her hair shone.

Warren stood up. His eyebrows rose almost to his hairline and he looked in astonishment from her to George and back again. She seemed not to notice him. She said, 'Oh, hi, George!' as though surprised to see him there.

'Hello.' He paused and coughed. 'Polly.'

She almost blushed when he said her real name like that. 'You look awful,' she said.

She seemed quite shocked at his appearance. The great bandages and the intravenous drip. She looked out of the side of her eyes at Warren. 'I don't like the smell of hospitals. Do you?'

'Er, not a lot. I can think of more attractive smells.' Warren indicated the roses. 'So can you apparently.'

She smiled and put the flowers daintily under her nose.

Warren grinned at George and shook his head. 'Well, George, I'd better be going.' The big man pulled his overcoat from the back of the chair and hung it round his shoulders. Polly watched him. Her eyes widened suddenly and a faint pink crept into her cheeks.

'Ciao,' he said to Polly. He winked at George over his shoulder: 'Be seeing you, mate. Think about what I said,' and softly closed the door.

'He's on the telly.' Polly's head turned slowly back to George.

'Yes, he is.'

'I saw him in that James Bond.'

'Yes, that was his last film.'

'How do you know him, George?' Her voice was filled with awe.

'He's a client of mine. I look after his tax.'

'Have you got other – you know – famous people? Clients?'

He smiled, as best he could. 'One or two, yes.'

'Oh,' she breathed. She gazed a moment, so absorbed in her thoughts that George could see she was for once unaware of the effect she made, standing there in her pale flower of a dress, holding the soft pale flowers loosely at her waist. 'Oh,' she said, in a different tone. She came back to her surroundings. 'I should put these in water really.'

She looked around then pulled the chair to a cupboard and stepped up on to it to reach for a grubby glass vase on the top. So light and graceful were her movements, it seemed that she was more lifted from above than propelled from below. And her beautiful legs were visible right up to the delicious shadow at the top of her thighs, hidden in the folds of her tiny skirt.

Ah. He loved to watch her do these things, so consciously unconscious of the effect she made. She was a truly old-fashioned girl, he discovered, a coquette, in a way that other girls nowadays simply were not.

She floated down from her perch. She filled the vase at the tap and pushed the roses into it. She brought it to his bedside and gave him a little smile. She said, 'I can't sit on your bed here, George.'

'Ha. No.'

'I went to see your mum.'

'Did you!'

'She's not so bad. She speaks a bit funny but she's okay apart from that. She knew who I was. Kevin's at your auntie's.'

'Oh, Polly, it's so good of you.'

She smiled. 'Are you getting better then?'

'I'll have to take it easy for a while. One of the lungs was punctured quite badly, they tell me.'

'You saved my life, George.'

'Er, no. It was Kevin who did that, actually.'

'Well' – her head gave a little shake – 'you saved his so it's the same thing.'

George needed to scratch between his eyebrows but couldn't move his arm. He gave a little cough instead.

Polly arranged herself on the chair. She crossed her thighs and sloped her legs slightly sideways. She delicately lifted and let fall the petals of her skirt. She clasped her hands on her lovely knees. She said, 'George, I'm sorry about all the trouble I caused.'

George would have laughed if he could have done it without pain. 'That's all right,' he said. 'Polly.'

She tossed her head again at his teasing tone. 'Oh, don't, George.'

Though utterly charmed, he felt he ought to open her eyes to the seriousness of the matter. He said, 'But you told a lot of lies, you know.'

She bent her head in a shamefaced way and looked at her hands. She nodded. 'I know.'

'You must promise not to lie to me again,' he said.

'Oh, I won't, George. I never will. I've learned my lesson, honestly I have.'

George knew she would lie and lie and lie again to get the things she wanted. It was her nature. For him, it was even part of her charm. Her lies were the silly, transparent, gossamer veil she wrapped her beauty in. He emerged from his fond reverie, and recalled his purpose. He said with great seriousness, 'Alison died, remember.'

'That wasn't just *my* fault, though, was it, George?' She looked at him very straight.

A spasm of pain crossed his face as he remembered. His conduct towards Kevin, the probable reason that Alison was out in the streets that night.

Polly watched him for a moment then came close to the bed. Her cool little hand touched his. 'Don't be upset,' she whispered. And when he didn't respond, 'Are you all right, George?'

'Yes,' he said sadly, 'I'm all right.'

Her pearly fingernail traced a circle on the back of his hand. She said in a tiny voice, 'Can I ask you something?'

'Ask,' he said. His voice was thick with love.

'When you come out, can I come and see you sometimes? I could help with your mother. And things.'

'I'm going to engage a full-time professional carer for Mother now. But of course. Of course you may. Oh, yes!' He felt full of power and possibilities. *And things,* she had said, help with your mother *and things...*

'Oh. Right. Okay.' The fingernail traced another excruciatingly pleasurable circle on his hand. 'And you did say one day – you did promise really, didn't you, George? – to show me your flat in town.'

This time, George knew well what was in store for him. He welcomed it with arms open wide. All of it. 'So I did,' he said.

The publishers hope that this book has given you enjoyable reading. Large Print Books are especially designed to be as easy to see and hold as possible. If you wish a complete list of our books please ask at your local library or write directly to:

Magna Large Print Books
Magna House, Long Preston,
Skipton, North Yorkshire.
BD23 4ND

This Large Print Book, for people
who cannot read normal print,
is published under the auspices of

THE ULVERSCROFT FOUNDATION